wired man
and other
Freaks
of nature

wired man

and other

Freaks

of Nature

SASHI KAUFMAN

carolrhoda LAB
MINNEAPOLIS

Carolrhoda Lab™ is a trademark of Lerner Publishing Group, Inc.

Carolrhoda Lab™
An imprint of Carolrhoda Books
A division of Lerner Publishing Group, Inc.
241 First Avenue North
Minneapolis, MN 55401 USA

For reading levels and more information, look up this title at www.lernerbooks.com.

Cover and interior images: © WIN-Initiative/Getty Image (woman); © Ken Jacobsen/
Illustration Works/Getty Images (ear cover); © Karin Smeds/Folio Images/Getty Images
(man); © iStockphoto.com/magurova (lines); © iStockphoto.com/ilbusca (ear interior).

Main body text set in Janson Text LT Std 10.5/15.
Typeface provided by Linotype AG.

Library of Congress Cataloging-in-Publication Data

Kaufman, Sashi.
    Wired man and other freaks of nature / Sashi Kaufman.
       pages cm
    Summary: "Ben has to wear hearing aids, but being inseparable from the super-
popular Tyler allows him to think of himself as normal. But Tyler blows him off senior
year and Ben needs to rethink who he is—and who Tyler is" —Provided by publisher.
    ISBN 978-1-4677-8563-1 (lb : alk. paper) — ISBN 978-1-4677-9564-7 (eb pdf)
    [1. Interpersonal relations—Fiction. 2. Identity—Fiction. 3. Hearing impaired—Fiction.
4. People with disabilities—Fiction. 5. High schools—Fiction. 6. Schools—Fiction.] I. Title.
PZ7.K16467Wir 2016
[Fic]—dc23   2015017912

Manufactured in the United States of America
1-37918-19187-2/25/2016

FOR TaRa,

FOR FRiENDSHiP,

WiTH LoVe.

FALL

CHAPTER 1

Ben stared out the sliding glass doors into the backyard. The music inside was loud and was pumping through the speaker out into the night. Some kids were waiting for a turn at the keg. A few girls were standing in a tight little knot talking the way girls always seemed to. But Ben didn't really care about what was going on outside. Staring out meant he could also see the reflection of what was behind him, and it was an easy way to keep an eye on Tyler, who was laughing and slapping the table with an open palm. The guys playing cards with him, Asshole or B.S. or some other game that was little more than a fun way to all get drunk at the same time, weren't soccer guys. He knew them the way you knew kids you'd gone to school with since kindergarten: first names and random stats. He didn't realize Tyler was friends with them. But Tyler was like that. He knew everyone.

Ben took out his phone and shuffled through a few apps to look like he was doing more than just checking the time. Probably nobody noticed, but he did a lot of things to seem normal when probably no one noticed. It was only ten thirty and he was ready to leave, except his curfew wasn't until midnight and he knew Tyler wouldn't want to go. Sometimes it sucked having a best friend who knew everything about you, including the fact that you could probably break curfew with a simple phone call to let your parents know where you were. Ben's eyes flicked back to the reflection of Tyler again. His nose twitched slightly as Tyler gave some goon a fist-bump. He was definitely wasted if he was fist-bumping at ten thirty. This was a party, so why wasn't he having a good time? He was bored. He glanced at Tyler, who was wiping beer foam from his chin. And annoyed.

It didn't used to be a regular occurrence for Tyler to drink like this. Of course, they *did* have things to celebrate. That morning their soccer team had clinched a spot in the playoffs with a two-one win over Danvers. So it was expected that the team might relax their pact to lay off drinking during the season. But lately Tyler didn't seem to care who saw him drinking, and he was treating tonight like his own personal last supper— a liquid diet version. But now wasn't the time to tell Tyler to slow down, not in front of everybody. He would say something some other time when it was just the two of them. He looked at his phone again: 10:34.

In his reflection-view, one of the other guys was whispering something into Tyler's ear. Whatever it was, it made Tyler crack up and knock his beer all over the card game, causing everyone to groan loudly and make a pathetic effort to mop up the spill with their T-shirts. It was the kind of thing that Ben would never do. He always went out of his way not to call attention to himself, but it was the kind of thing that Tyler got away with all the time. Tyler stopped trying to pretend to clean up. He just hunkered down with the other guys and listened to the rest of whatever had been so funny and so fascinating in the first place.

Probably it had to do with a girl. Ben never read lips in social situations. Too weird to look like you were staring at someone else's mouth—especially another guy's. But he was pretty good at picking up the gist of a conversation from body language. Shoulders up, face leaning forward, and quick movements usually had to do with something school-related. But hunched over, elbows resting on knees, legs spread, and arms moving slowly, almost languidly—probably a girl. No one ever leaned forward to talk about sports.

Ben looked toward the kitchen. Maybe he'd kill some time in there. He swished around the last quarter of warm beer in his plastic cup and thought about going outside to get a refill. But then the conversation behind him got louder. A few guys burst into loud laughter and the table got smacked a few more times.

"No way, Nuson!" one of the guys was saying to Tyler. His name was Albert or Alfred or some other unfortunate grandfather inheritance. Everyone just called him Al. His hair was shaved high and tight for the football team.

"SON!" another guy hollered and gave Tyler a high five. It was Tyler's old nickname from when he was a boy.

"Now, seriously, both of them?" Al was leaning forward, licking his lips and waiting for clarifying details. Now Ben knew what they were talking about. The twins: Alexis and Alicia Sheehan. It was one of Tyler's infamous conquests from the beginning of the school year. Ben thought everyone had heard about it by now, but apparently this kid hadn't.

The story was that Tyler had hooked up with one of the twins at a party. Then he'd left the room to take a piss, at which point he had run into the other twin in the hallway, gotten confused, and hooked up with her too. It wasn't until Monday, when they both confronted him, that he realized what he had done. But the most bizarre part of the story, at least as far as Ben was concerned, was that both girls were still friendly with Tyler and acted like it was some funny escapade that they had all been a part of. Maybe it was less embarrassing that way, or maybe, and more likely, it was just the power of Tyler—something Ben had come to accept, like the weather or the changing seasons.

Thinking about the twins made Ben think about what else had been different about Tyler lately—the hooking up with girls had become more frequent, more random. It seemed almost desperate to Ben, ever since that weird rumor about Tyler and Lindsay Walker. But how could he say anything, even if Tyler was his best friend? How gay would that be? Hey, why are you hooking up so much? His stomach turned at the thought of it. What if Tyler turned the question back on him? Why don't you *ever* hook up?

Besides, Tyler had explained everything to a bunch of them in the locker room the Monday after. Lindsay was drunk and sloppy, he told them. She wanted it but he didn't have a glove, and there was no way he was going there without protection. She got pissed off, and he was stoned and for some reason got the giggles. Then she got even madder and made up that bullshit story about him crying when she went down on him.

And it had all made sense, pretty much. Everyone on the team seemed to accept the story, and Brandon Rosetti tried to get Tyler to give details about Lindsay's legendary giant tits. But Ben, even though he wasn't sure what Lindsay had said was true, knew for certain that what Tyler had told them was not.

There was a lull in the conversation. Ben glanced over his shoulder and saw all the guys staring out the window at the girls in the backyard. The twins were right there in the center,

4

clutching their keg cups like life preservers and flipping their hair as if they knew the boys were looking at them. Then Ben saw Julie Snow come into the living room through the swinging door. She was a senior with curly brown hair that was now pulled back in a ponytail. She assessed the guys leering out the window at the younger girls. "Gross," she said. "You guys have no class."

"It's only because classy girls like you won't even talk to us," Tyler said winningly.

"Yeah," Julie agreed as she walked toward the kitchen. "Sorry that I'm not interested in letting your drunk ass slobber all over the side of my face while you try and stick my hand down your pants. Guess that makes me a romantic."

Tyler was undeterred. "You'll never know until you try it."

"I'll take my chances," she said and sashayed past them. Ben smirked. Julie was part of a small group of senior girls who seemed permanently unimpressed and even annoyed by high school. Being a senior girl had to be a little different from being a senior guy. His older sister Shannan and her friends complained bitterly during their senior year about the maturity of guys their age. But Shannan didn't really party anyway, and she was as charmed by Tyler as everyone else. Julie really was the only girl he knew who talked to Tyler like that; she was pretty much the only *person* who talked to Tyler like that.

"Which one is which?" one of the guys was asking Tyler.

"Dude, don't ask him, clearly he can't tell the difference!"

Tyler grinned, unashamed. The girls outside seemed to notice they were being talked about and were staring in at the living room while chatting more intensely.

"What are they saying?" Tyler said loudly to the room. No one responded.

"Hey, Wireman," he called out again. "Stick your head against the glass and turn up the volume so you can hear if they're talking about me."

Time froze while the words bore into Ben's skull. His body knew first and sent an immediate surge of bile up the back of his throat. Hot pangs of anger climbed up out of his collar and raked his neck. He caught Tyler's eyes. Tyler looked away. *Good, he knows what he said.* Everyone else looked at the floor.

"Sure," Ben said easily. His voice seemed to come from somewhere outside his body. He leaned his head against the glass. He didn't let the glass touch his ears or his hearing aids hidden beneath his shaggy haircut. The hell if he was going to give anyone a full show just to prove a point. He acted for a second like he was listening intently. "Nope, nothing," he said. And then, "Oh wait. I can hear them." He paused, drawing out the anticipation. Making sure he had everyone's attention. "Something about a tiny, hairless . . . uh, wait, not sure I got that last part. Oh yeah, tiny, hairless Asian dick. Yup, they're talking about you all right."

The room erupted in laughter.

"Wireman, that was clutch!"

"Freaking hilarious!" someone else called out. Al looked like he was going to need someone to deliver a couple chest thumps to get him breathing again. Ben heard them all but was watching only Tyler. Anyone else would have seen some good-natured embarrassment and then laughter, enjoyment even at being the butt of a good joke. But Ben saw more. He saw the slight twitch around Tyler's eyes, almost a blink. Ben knew he'd made his point.

He collected a few high fives from the guys at the table and walked into the kitchen. He thought seriously about walking out to the street and calling a cab, but pride got the best of him. He wasn't going to skulk out of there like some loser. He tilted a few bottles of booze that were sitting on the counter, trying to guess which ones might contain something drinkable. He settled on a lemon-flavored vodka, pouring himself a measure of it and mixing it with some half-flat Sprite he found in the refrigerator. *Whose house is this anyway?* He studied the family photo stuck to the fridge door with a Domino's Pizza magnet.

Then the kid's name came to him: Josh. He was a freshman who played on their JV team. Everyone was talking about how he was the future of the varsity program. Ben looked around. The kid's house was going to get trashed tonight. He hoped his parents were far away and not coming home until late on Sunday.

"What are you making, bartender?" Julie Snow said, coming into the kitchen. She was wearing jeans and a hooded softball sweatshirt cut open around the neck. She looked like she was someone's older sister hanging out at the party to keep an eye on the better furniture.

"Nothing good," he said, glancing down at his cup.

Julie shrugged and handed him her empty cup. "Make it a double. The party can't get much lamer."

Ben poured what was left of the lemon-flavored vodka into her cup and added some of the flat soda. As an afterthought he went back to the fridge for a splash of orange juice. Julie smirked. "Getting fancy?"

"Nothing but the best," he said.

They took a quiet drink together. The kitchen was wrecked. An open jar of salsa sat on the counter with two drowning tortilla chips poking out. There was a pizza box on the round kitchen table, its only occupant a greasy piece of wax paper with a few blobs of cheese and a single green pepper stuck to it. Popcorn and some pretzel sticks were scattered around the feet of the four kitchen chairs. In the corner there was a small pantry, and sticking out of the pantry Ben could see a pair of sneakers and pair of brown UGG boots. He could hear the low murmur of conversation but couldn't make out any words.

"I'm so done with this," Julie said.

Ben gave a noncommittal shrug.

"You can't tell me you're not ready to move on," she insisted.

"And leave all this behind?" He gestured grandly at the food scraps and half-empty keg cups littering the kitchen. He took a slow sip from his cup. He was trying to be ironic, but her question bothered him. To even make it through the door of a party like this one would have been unthinkable as a freshman, maybe even as a sophomore. And now, midway through their senior year, when they were at the top of the social food chain, they were supposed to act like it was all suddenly beneath them?

He shook his head and pretended he'd actually been listening to Julie talk about the colleges she was applying to. It was a conversation that everyone seemed to be having lately and not one that he especially liked. He dreaded the thought of so many new things being thrown at him at once. He nodded and made eye contact occasionally as she talked. The sound of her voice was calming, smoothing out the flashes of anger that coursed through him every time he thought about Tyler.

"So?" Julie said.

He'd missed the question. "So what?"

"So, where are you applying?"

"Oh." That question. "Um, I don't really know yet."

Julie stared at him quizzically. "Ben, you know the deadline for early decision is like the end of next month?"

"Yeah. I mean no. I didn't know that. But yeah. I don't really know where I want to apply yet. So I guess it won't be an early decision." He tried to make it sound like a big joke.

Julie laughed, but she seemed surprised. Impressed even? "Okay, Ben," she said. "Badass Ben. Didn't really know you had it in you."

Was she flirting? Before he could consider the question, Tyler staggered into the kitchen. He smiled winningly at Julie, who rolled her eyes, and then hesitantly at Ben.

"Gotta take a piss," he said and pointed in the direction of the bathroom.

"Charming," Julie said.

"What do you see in him?" she asked when Tyler left the room.

"What do you mean? It's not like we're dating."

"Might as well be. You're always together."

"Whatever," Ben said. He felt prickly, even defensive about his relationship with Tyler. Two girls could be tight and no one made a big deal about it. So what if he and Tyler were always together? Why did it have to be a big deal?

"Don't get annoyed," Julie said. "Why can't guys talk about their relationships without getting paranoid that they're being called gay?"

"I don't even know how to answer that."

"It just seems like you've got a lot more going on. I mean, Tyler's just Tyler. We all know what he is. But you're different."

Ben felt that hot feeling creeping up his shirtsleeves. The angry fingers starting to tighten around his neck. He didn't want to know who Julie thought he was. Or who she thought Tyler was. Everyone loved Tyler. That's just the way it was.

Why did she act like they didn't? And why did she think *he* was so interesting? Was she just messing with him?

Tyler was standing in the door. His fly was down, but since Ben was still pissed off about the hearing aid comment, he decided against telling him. Tyler looked at Julie and then raised his eyebrows at Ben. Ben could hear the question as if it had been spoken. *"Is this going on?"* Ben shook his head slightly. "Hey," Tyler said. "Justin Greenwood's going to smoke us out. You want to come? You too, Julie," he added generously.

Ben shook his head. "No. I want to get out of here." He wanted Julie to hear how forcefully he said it. Just so she'd know he was more than Tyler's entourage.

"All right," Tyler said. But he looked uncertain. "How about we toke up—just a bit, you know, to top the night off—and then go home?"

Ben could argue, but what was the point? Tyler would get his way in the end. "Whatever," he said. Julie declined to join them, and he followed Tyler out of the room without meeting her eyes. He knew what he looked like to her. But it wasn't really like that with him and Tyler. They didn't have to discuss every decision they made like girls did. They just knew each other well enough that most of the time they could decide stuff without even talking about it.

He stood outside in the bushes with a group of guys and Molly Hamermesh, who seemed to appear any time a bowl was being passed around. He took the smallest hit possible without looking like a complete weenie and then stepped back from the circle. It was good weed, not the stuff that most people had that burned your throat and left a thick feeling in your mouth, like sucking on trash can lids. Afterward, he and Tyler walked out to the car without saying much.

When they got to Tyler's dad's old Saab, they both walked toward the driver's side. "Come on, man. Give me the keys," Ben said.

Tyler looked at him straight-faced. "I'm an excellent driver," he said. Ben rolled his eyes. "Uh oh," Tyler continued. "Fifteen minutes to Wapner. I'm an excellent driver. Kmart, gotta be Kmart."

Ben held out his hand for the keys and tried not to crack up. "I *am* an excellent driver," Tyler said again, but he dropped the keys in Ben's hand without an argument. "But you know I love it when you chauffeur me around."

When they got in the car, Tyler put his feet up on the dash and then down again. He fiddled with the radio, trying to find something he could sing along to. Pot always made Tyler hyper. At the bottom of the hill Ben turned left on to Beacon Street, which would take them over to Lower Falls where he lived. Tyler could text his mom—she was always up late—and crash on Ben's floor. They hadn't gotten very far when Tyler said, "Oh man, wait. Stop at Store 24."

Ben sighed. "There's food at my house."

"Mmm, but are there Cheetos?"

Ben crossed the double yellow line and flipped a U-turn in the middle of Beacon Street. "YES!" Tyler shouted. "Excellent decision! Excellent choice!"

"Just Cheetos," Ben cautioned. "Then we're going home."

They sat in the parking lot of Store 24 with a family-sized bag of Cheetos between them. "This is disgusting," Ben said as he tossed a couple of cheddar-coated cheese sticks into his mouth. "We're definitely going to get some kind of cancer from this." But they were so good. Each crunch set off a cheese Olympics in his mouth and prompted him to grab another handful. He leaned forward and took a big slurp of the blue raspberry slushie set between his knees. The ice at the bottom gave a hollow death rattle as it flew up the straw.

"All right," Tyler said, suddenly getting serious. "Who's this?" He was holding a Cheeto, his fingers grasping the skinny end. It had a bulbous top with two large bumps.

Ben cocked his head to the side. "Mrs. Oliphant," he said decidedly, thinking of their heavyset World Studies teacher.

Tyler nodded appreciatively. "Yup, yes, I see it. I was going to say Gabby Trudeau, but I think it could go either way."

"She'll *be* Mrs. Oliphant in a few years anyway," Ben said as he crunched a few more Cheetos. "How about this one?" He held up a long, skinny one. He was thinking of their soccer coach, Jack Sersich, but Tyler didn't come up with it.

"I don't know," he said. "Tom?"

"Which one?"

"The one who runs track. The skinny one."

Ben just shrugged and popped the thing in his mouth. They were usually completely in sync. Tyler pawed through the bag. "Oh wait," he said suddenly. "This is perfect." He flicked on the dashboard light and held up the Cheeto specimen so Ben could get a good look. It *was* perfect. Ben knew exactly who it was too. "On three," he said. "One, two, three."

"Julie Snow!" they both shouted out. Maybe it was the pot or the tension breaking from earlier in the night, but they both laughed so hard that Tyler started to blow slushie out his nose and Ben had to get out and take a leak behind the car so he didn't piss himself.

"Here," Tyler said all seriously when Ben got back in the car, holding out the Julie Snow Cheeto. "I want you to have this."

"Thank you," Ben said, crunching down hard on the bubbly top half that was Julie's trademark ponytail.

"I think she likes you."

"Nah," Ben said. "She was just bored."

"Nope. I definitely think she likes you, man. She was at the very least seriously considering letting you, what did she say, slobber all over the side of her face?"

"While I shove her hand down my pants," Ben finished.

Tyler shook his head. "That's just wrong," he said. "Completely unfair characterization of my moves." Ben nodded but didn't say anything. By senior year everyone just assumed you knew what they were talking about when they talked about hooking up. "I mean, I would at least squeeze her tits before I shoved her hand down my pants," Tyler continued.

"And she thought you weren't very romantic," Ben said.

Tyler grabbed his chest and threw his head back like he'd been shot. He held the pose for a few seconds and then let his hand fall down at his side. He sat there staring up at the sky through the sunroof. "I'm sorry," he said quietly. "It was a total dick move. I don't know what I was thinking."

"It's okay," Ben said. He just wanted Tyler to stop before he said anything else about hearing aids or deaf kid jokes—anything else that would bring the content of his comment back into the foreground. He knew that Tyler understood that "it's okay" did not mean that what he had said was okay, but rather that he was forgiven. He opened up the bag again and shook it around until he found what he was looking for. He held it up: a small stunted cheese curl indicating that they had reached the bottom of the bag and the end of the game. Tyler nodded. Ben leaned forward and started the car.

"Time to go home," he said.

CHAPTER 2

In the morning, Tyler was gone. He never actually slept over. He just lay on the floor next to Ben's bed until his buzz wore off, and then sometime before dawn he crept out quietly.

So the noise the next morning definitely wasn't Tyler. It sounded like someone emptying the dishwasher while making sure to bang each individual glass plate into the other. Ben rolled over and tried to ignore the strip of bright light streaming in through the crack in his dark green curtains and the foul taste in his mouth, a mix of lemon vodka, Sprite, and Cheeto crumbs. "Hey!" he yelled out, knowing his voice wouldn't carry out of the bedroom. "I'm only partially deaf, you know."

It was a joke he'd never make out in the world. He barely felt comfortable saying it when he knew no one could hear. Supposedly when you lost a sense, your other senses became enhanced to compensate for it. Ben hadn't noticed any improvements in his vision, but sometimes the thoughts in his head were so loud he wanted to scream to block them out. And they weren't even his thoughts. They were his, of course, but they came from the not-so-subtle comments of the kids in his class and the people around him. They were always staring, wondering what else was wrong with him.

His mom could tell when it was really bothering hi. heard her talk to Dr. Usarian, the hearing specialist, abou. he was *adjusting*—a word that always seemed to be emphasi. whenever anyone was talking about him. For the first six years of his life he'd been normal, and then in first grade, when he'd failed the hearing screening, he had been cast out of the main-stream and made different by the plastic pieces he now had to wear in his ears. Supposedly it was easier for kids who'd always had to wear them, but he'd never gotten completely used to it. In first grade, kids don't try and hide the fact that they're star-ing, but it was more in a wondering kind of way. It was much worse in middle school. The looks turned into whispers, and he built the walls higher and thicker—the sum total of which was a tiny protected island with entrance granted to his family and Tyler, and really that was it.

The only place he truly felt normal was at home. He was sure that the way he joked with his parents, the way they accepted and loved him, worried about him and annoyed him, was normal. Leaving for college wouldn't just mean leaving his carefully structured social life; it would mean leaving them too. He was trying very hard not to think about what Julie had said or about the pile of college application materials sitting on his desk. What about the roommate he would be assigned for next year? Was *hearing impaired* something you had to list on one of those forms you filled out to be matched? What would his future roommate think? Worse, what if they matched him with some other partially functional loser?

He pulled the pillow up over his head, hoping to muffle the thoughts and go back to sleep. Too gross: it smelled like Cheeto cheese and head sweat.

There was a loud, purposeful rapping on the door.

"Come on, Mom," he yelled in the general direction of the hallway, but he was already clawing the nightstand for his hearing aids, not liking to be caught without them any more than he actually liked wearing them.

The slick plastic fit snuggly in and around his ears. Instantly the sound of chirping birds outside his window came into focus. There was a tiny bit of relief, like finally scraping the bottom of the pool with your toes when you've been swimming in the deep end. He shook his head once to let his hair fall back into place and then let his head flop back on the pillow. Mom had opened the door and was standing in the doorway, pretending to find some cracked paint on the trim interesting.

"What is it? What do you want?"

"Honey, do you know what time it is?"

"I don't know. Ten? Eleven?"

"It's after noon, Ben," she said reproachfully.

He picked up his phone. "By like ten minutes," he said, ignoring her glare. "I was getting up anyway."

"Don't you have homework to do?"

"Not really."

"Well, then maybe you and I can take a look at some of those college applications. Did you know that the early decision deadline is coming up?"

"Sort of."

Mom stared down at him. His sister Shannan had made it pretty easy for them. She applied to three schools and got into all three. She probably had the applications done the summer after junior year. She was in the engineering program at the U of Maine in Orono, something their parents seemed both puzzled and proud about. His father was co-owner of a printing and graphic design business, and his mom was a social worker helping old people get meals on wheels and stuff like that. More arts and words people than numbers people. It was one of those lines they spouted when talking about Shannan to other people. Even if they didn't fully get it, they were proud of her. That was good. They should have at least one kid to brag about.

"Well," his mother started, "I just think that . . ."

"Fine." Ben rolled over and stuffed his face into the pillow. "We can talk about it. But I need to take a shower first."

"Okay, great!" his mom said happily. Then she sniffed the room. "Ben, are you hung-over?"

"No!" he shouted into the pillow. "Shower!" he shouted again.

"Okay," she said. "Well, I'll be downstairs. Just come down when you're ready." There was a pause. "Ben, was Tyler here?"

"Uh huh."

"I wish he wouldn't do that. Leave in the middle of the night, I mean."

"What's the big deal?"

"I just don't like the idea of him driving home so late."

"Better than driving drunk."

"I thought you said you weren't drinking."

Ben gave a loud exasperated sigh. "Tyler, Mom, not me." It sounded like a lame excuse, but it was true. He drank, but never enough to lose control.

"All right," she sighed. There was another pause before she left the room. Like there was more she wanted to say about Tyler. Or was she going to make it about him? Ben didn't lift his head off the pillow. He could talk about pretty much anything with his parents, but this topic felt off-limits. Maybe because they would ask questions about Tyler that he couldn't answer himself.

CHAPTER 3

There were only a few minutes until homeroom, and the main hallway was packed with people. Even with all the background noise, Ben could tell he was being followed, and he had a pretty good idea who it was. Abby Simmons was the absolute, unqualified bane of his existence. Her title was Hearing Impaired Integrator or some other crap thing like that. She was worse than a teacher who just tried to pretend he was like everyone else. The whole point of Abby Simmons was to make him stick out—that was her frickin' job.

"Ben!" Oh shit, she was shouting. He'd have to stop now or risk creating an even bigger scene. He turned around, scanning the hall for an alcove or open classroom he could duck into to avoid being seen with her. No such luck. He was stuck in the hallway, where the kids flowing by stared at him openly.

"Hi!" she said brightly when he finally met her gaze. Her hands flew up to start signing, and then, just as quickly, she dropped them.

In their first meeting, he'd made it very clear that he didn't know ASL and didn't have any interest in learning. "I know you don't need it," she had told him, "but it's a lot of fun. And it can be a good way to get involved with the *community*." Ben had cringed. He found it really hard to understand what was fun about sign language or, for that matter, why you would want to isolate yourself from normal people so you could hang out with a bunch of weirdos who were talking with their hands.

Midway through third grade, their elementary school had gotten an upgrade on textbooks. He hated them. They featured a series of diverse characters with weird names and, in some cases, physical disabilities. Suzy and Elizabeth were replaced by Raga and Hassan and their friend Jamyle who rode around in a wheelchair, accompanying his friends on all sorts of canned fictional adventures. It became a thing among the kids to ask about Jamyle and how he was able to participate in the various adventures to the science museum and the rope swing. Their teacher, a young woman whose name Ben had forgotten, took their interest to be genuine instead of trying to get her off topic, and spent what felt like hours talking to the class in uncomfortable terms about the normalcy of people with disabilities. Ben had never felt less normal in his life.

Abby was smiling brightly at him. Had she asked him a question? It was loud in the hallway, but he would rather have died than ask her to repeat herself. "Okay, I guess," he said, hoping she had asked him how he was doing.

But he wasn't that lucky. "Really?" she exclaimed. "That's great!" Shit, what had he just agreed to? "I'll call you down tomorrow when he gets here." Ben's mind whirled, but he couldn't bring himself to ask her what she was talking about so he could come up with a reasonable excuse, and he couldn't simply refuse now without knowing what he was refusing. As much as he couldn't stand her, she was hard to just plain hate. She seemed to truly want some kind of relationship with him, and the patheticness of this made her annoying as all hell but not hateable. She beamed at him, showing her horsey teeth. Her hair, pulled back into a half ponytail, was a little greasy at the roots.

"I gotta go," he said and gestured down the hallway at some unknown destination. Anywhere but here was preferable.

"Oh, sure," she said, "get to class on time." She smiled like she wanted him to acknowledge that she was some kind of cool teacher because she wanted the kids to call her by her first name and would never *really* tell him to get to class on time. "You know," she added, "we're still meeting on Wednesday afternoons if you're ever interested in checking it out. It's a really fun group."

"No," he said. She seemed momentarily taken aback by the sharpness of his tone. "I mean, I'm busy, with soccer and other things."

"Oh right," she said. "That's so exciting! The State Championship."

"Well, it's just the playoffs right now. We have to win three more games to get to States."

"Sure, States," she agreed, happily.

Ben started to turn away, unable to think of any less awkward way to end the conversation. He pointed down the hall, and she just smiled again and kept nodding her head. He had a sudden vision of her as a high school student, greasy hair and all, and realized that it probably hadn't been that different for her than it was now. He couldn't imagine coming back to spend your life in a place where you had been so socially unsuccessful. It was a bit like watching a video game character get stuck in a corner, bouncing back and forth between two hard surfaces.

The annoying interaction with Abby Simmons stayed with him for most of first and second periods, but by the end of the day he'd managed to let it go. After school the mood in the locker room was somber. "Jerk Sausage knows about the party on Saturday night," Tyler whispered to him as he changed for practice. That meant they'd be running today, more than usual. Coach was a fitness fanatic. The rumor was he got up at four thirty every morning to work out before school, ran at practice with the team, and then ran on his own after school. He ate almost no carbs—something called a paleo diet he was always trying to talk to his players about. He was the winningest high school coach in the Eastern Massachusetts League, and there was always talk that this would be his last season before moving up to a college team. And he was gay. Easton was a liberal enough town to accept an openly gay soccer coach, as long as he was winning.

"On the field, gentlemen!" Coach's voice boomed in the locker room and was punctuated by two quick fists to a locker door. Clearly Coach knew what had gone on the night before. Their warm-up run was twice as long as usual, and the normal relaxed feel of their drills was missing. And instead of letting Ben, who played goalie, go off with the other defenders and let them take shots on him, he kept everyone together and kept them moving through a particularly brutal drill that he called the Eliminator. If you missed a pass, you had to run sprints and up-downs until the next person missed and you could go back in. It was kind of twisted in that the only way to get out of your mistake was to hope for someone else to screw up.

In the middle of one of the drills, one of the underclassmen sent a sloppy pass to Tyler, who missed the ball. Coach blew his whistle and pointed at Tyler, an indication that *he* should run for the mistake. Tyler threw up his hands in frustration and then booted the ball over the goal into the parking lot. Coach blew his whistle again; this time it flew from his mouth with the force of air. He waved his clipboard at Tyler and jabbed in the air toward the ball rolling slowly between parked cars. "Everyone take a lap, full sprint, while Nuson goes and gets that ball." They hesitated. A couple guys groaned. Coach blew his whistle again, and they all began to run for the far side of the field. Ben watched Tyler jog to retrieve the ball. He didn't seem to care that he was pissing off Coach *and* making the team run more.

In the second half of practice Coach seemed to loosen up a bit after the offense successfully executed a number of complicated set plays. He even let them scrimmage for the last twenty minutes. But Ben was still on edge, watching Tyler for any other flares of anger. Then, as everyone else was running for the locker room, Coach called his name and beckoned him over with the back of his clipboard.

The sun was already setting behind the high school, and half the field was cast in a long shadow. He could feel the sweat cooling on his back as he jogged back over to where Coach stood. He came to a standstill and rocked back and forth toes to heels, something he often did in goal to keep himself moving and warm.

"I know about the party last weekend," Coach said. "Josh Miller's father called me. Apparently their house was a mess afterwards. He was pretty pissed when I got on the phone with him, but I managed to calm him down."

"Josh is a freshman," Ben said.

"There were a lot of kids there Saturday night," Coach said. "I don't believe for a second that all of them were freshmen." Ben said nothing. "And Mr. Miller said he managed to get it out of Josh that it was some of our guys on the varsity team who convinced Josh to have a party."

Ben fought the urge to roll his eyes to keep his face impassive. *Josh was such a tool! How lame did you have to be to blame your screwup on a whole team?* Coach continued, "But he wouldn't give names. Frankly, I think Mr. Miller was glad. Not about the party but the fact that he couldn't give me any names. He's a big supporter of our program. He doesn't want to see anyone get benched or worse because of this." Ben started to bounce up and down lightly. He could feel the hair on his legs lifting up in protest at the brisk November breeze that was blowing across the field.

"Ben, I'm telling you this because you're a senior and I know you're levelheaded. I expect you to be a leader on this team." Ben looked down so Coach couldn't see the skepticism on his face. Why wasn't he having this little chat with one of the other guys? Brandon maybe, or Tyler? "I talked to Tyler too, but lately it seems like he doesn't hear a thing I say. I'll bench him if I have to, but I sure as hell don't want to. Is something going on with him? I mean at home?"

Ben shook his head. Tyler had been blowing Coach off lately, little things that Ben had hoped Coach wouldn't notice, like cutting short the last half of a run or slacking off on some of the drills. "I don't think so," he said without lying. He was pretty sure whatever was making Tyler act differently lately didn't have anything to do with his family.

"Well, you let me know if there's anything you think I should know."

"Yeah, awright."

"All right then," Coach said. He seemed satisfied with their chat. "You ready for Wednesday?" he asked. He kicked the ball up with his toe and drove it at Ben's shoulder. Ben quickly brought his fists up and punched it away. "Good man," Coach said. "Now run that ball down and go clean up." Ben started to jog after the ball, which had skittered its way down the side of the field and stopped in some tall grass. "Ben," Coach called after him, "where's the team dinner tomorrow night?"

"Uh, I think it's at the Rosettis'."

Coach grimaced. Brandon Rosetti's mom made incredible lasagna, but she always served it with a side of her tits in your face. She really liked Coach and was oblivious that for a number of reasons he would never reciprocate her interest or attention.

By the time he got to the locker room, there were only a few guys still packing up. Someone had written on Coach's whiteboard "Coach Sausage" with a picture of the aforementioned meat product looking suspiciously phallic surrounded by its bun. Ben studied the handwriting. The block letters could have been anyone, but Ben had a feeling. He took his arm and brushed it across the board so the drawing became obscured and only the word "Coach" was left. He looked around to see if anyone had seen him doing it, but the corner where Tyler usually stashed his soccer bag was empty.

CHAPTER 4

On Wednesday Tyler was late. Ben tugged on the collar of his collared shirt, a requirement for team dinners. Before every big game he trotted out the same slightly small dark blue polo with the little red horse over his chest. Then he threw his soccer jacket over it. He stared out into the driveway, willing the lights of the Saab to appear. He texted Tyler again, but there was no response. Being rude and being late were Coach's two least favorite attributes in his players. Playing sloppy was the third, but at this rate he and Tyler were going to be riding the bench anyway.

It would kill Coach to bench them. Ben knew he was a solid goalie. He put up good stats last year, good enough to get some interest from Division Three schools looking to round out their roster with a backup goalie. But Tyler was the real talent. Tyler had a fluidity to his play and an incredible sense of the field, knowing where to be and where to pass before his opponents—and often his own team—did. There were a lot of schools interested in Tyler, but the only place Tyler talked about applying to was BU, where his father was a professor. As a faculty brat, he was pretty much guaranteed a spot and a full ride. He actually seemed less interested in the school itself than in the path of least resistance. Ben was glad they both seemed to harbor the same ambivalence about life after high school. It made him feel more normal.

Sometimes soccer coaches called Tyler's house while Ben was there, and he watched as Tyler put them off with loose commitments to visit the school or come to a game. "You want to go?" he'd ask Ben. And if Ben said yes, sometimes they'd take a ride and watch whatever team was playing, enjoying some hot dogs and chips courtesy of the school. But if Ben was busy or simply didn't feel like watching a game, Tyler would never go on his own. Ben didn't really get it—some of the other schools that had shown interest in Tyler were pretty nice, with lots of brick and ivy and green courtyards. After a visit to Amherst College to watch them take on their archrival, Williams, Ben even pushed him on it a little. The Amherst campus was really nice, and every girl they met was incredibly hot. On the car ride home, Ben asked him if he was going to apply. "Probably not" was Tyler's response. "I'd rather be somewhere where I can exceed expectations, not fall short. Even if I screw everything else up, with soccer at BU, they can't kick me out unless I'm failing."

Ben secretly imagined that Tyler couldn't really envision a future of which he, Ben, was not a part. This had certainly occurred to him. He had gone so far as to check out the acceptance stats for BU and figured he had a decent shot at getting in on his academic merit. But something had stopped him from mentioning the possibility to Tyler: he needed Tyler to ask him first. Not in any big marriage proposal way, but some sign that would indicate that a future in which the two of them were together was all right with him.

But by the time the lights of the Saab turned into Ben's driveway at twenty past seven, he was fuming—and imagining a future without Tyler because he was going to strangle him with his bare hands. They still had to drive ten minutes to Brandon's house, but Ben waited until eight minutes passed in complete silence before he spoke.

"What the hell, Tyler? Coach is going to kill us!"

Tyler looked over at him, and Ben realized that what he had mistaken for a tense silence had just been inattentiveness on Tyler's part. He looked confused. "We're not that late," he said lamely.

"We're half an hour late," Ben corrected.

Tyler made a face that was somewhere between amused and impressed with himself. "We're fine."

"No, we're not fine. We're late and you're going to take the blame for it, because I'm sure as shit not getting benched because you can't show up to a team dinner on time."

"He's not going to bench us," Tyler said, but he sounded less sure.

"That's not what he was saying on Monday."

"He said something to you too? About Josh Miller?"

"Yeah, that, and other things."

"Other things like what?" Tyler drummed his fingers on the steering wheel.

"He wanted to know if something was wrong with you. He asked if something was going on at home. He thought you seemed off. You know, different." The last part was not anything Coach had said, but Ben added it on because it seemed like as good a way as any to voice his own concerns.

"So what did you tell him?"

"Not much," Ben said. *Because I don't know, because you are acting weird but you won't tell me anything*, he thought. He took a deep breath and said, "Is this about what happened with Lindsay?"

Tyler looked startled. "I told you. She freaked out, I laughed at her, she got pissed and made up that whole bullshit story." He was so casual. It was easier to believe him this time. "I told you that already."

"No," Ben said, "you told the team."

"Yeah, and you were there," Tyler said, starting to sound annoyed.

"Yeah, right, whatever." How could he not see the difference? Ben fell silent. He had gambled and been shut out. Whatever was going on with Tyler, he couldn't or wouldn't share.

"Anyway, Coach needs to mind his own business," Tyler said sharply.

"What's your problem?" Ben asked, pissed and a little bruised. "The guy's worried about you."

"Maybe he has his own reasons," Tyler said. They were turning down Brandon's street.

"Like what?"

"Like trying to get into my pants," Tyler said as he parked near the house. He pulled the key from the ignition, and the dome light came on. Ben noticed the dark circles under Tyler's eyes.

"You're not serious. Give me a break. Coach is about as interested in you as he is in Mrs. Rosetti. Besides, he has a—" Ben stumbled a bit with the term. "—boyfriend or whatever. That guy in the suit who comes to all our games."

"Haven't seen him in a couple weeks though, have you?"

"I don't know," Ben said. "I don't really pay attention to which of his friends come to our games. What makes you think he's interested in you as a replacement anyway?"

Tyler shrugged. "Why's he care so much about how I'm doing? I'm just saying."

"Because he's our coach, numbnuts! Remember when Mike's dad drove into that telephone pole? Coach drove Mike to the hospital. He helped his mom figure out their health insurance and shit. That's just stuff he does. You should be careful what you're saying," Ben said. "Shit like that could get Coach in a lot of trouble if it's not true." He wanted Tyler to take it back, shake his head, and start laughing, something so they would both know how ridiculous the accusations were.

Instead Tyler opened the door. When he reached back for his jacket, Ben saw that his hand was shaking. But then he said, "You're right. I'm being a dick. Forget about it, okay?"

Ben nodded. "All right, but you're making excuses to Coach—and make them good. And stop being such an asshole to him."

"No more asshole," Tyler said, stepping out of the car. "Are you still pissed at me for being late?"

"Yes." He didn't want to let Tyler off the hook so easily.

"Okay, but I'm going to make you love me again."

"Homo," Ben muttered.

"Fag," Tyler retorted.

But the exchange didn't feel as light as it should have. It seemed that, without meaning to, he *had* let Tyler off the hook anyway.

Inside the Rossettis' house, most of the guys were on their second helping of lasagna, sitting around the living room and den, balancing paper plates on their knees while a few parents milled around in the background. They were able to slip in and grab a plate of food before anyone noticed they'd been missing. By the time Coach found them, they were eating and looking like they'd been there the whole time.

Coach eyed their full plates suspiciously. "Running late?"

"My fault, Coach. Left it on empty and had to stop for gas," Tyler said.

Coach grunted, but he didn't chew them out like Ben thought he would. After dessert, a sheet cake decorated with soccer balls and topped with vanilla ice cream, Coach thanked Mrs. Rosetti and gave them a little pep talk about the game. This was mostly for the benefit of the parents who were there. The real talk would come tomorrow in the locker room. So Ben only half listened as Coach talked about the importance of focusing on the game and not giving in to the temptation to start thinking about a bid for the state title. The other team was Chelmsford. They had beaten them twice in regular season play, but both games had been tough one-goal wins with one going into overtime.

Secretly Ben loved overtime. All the pressure was on him to be perfect. It filled him with a psychotic feeling, the adrenaline pumping through him, threatening to burst his blood vessels. Everything he did in practice was turned up to a mind-splitting level. Ben tuned back into the conversation just as Coach was done with his little speech and everyone was finishing up their food, talking about the game.

"Dude, we're all going to Mohawk it if we make it to States!" Anthony Kapstein said loudly. "Bzzzzz." He made the noise of the clippers as he drew his hand up the side of his head. Ben stiffened.

"My dad's got clippers," Kapstein added.

"One game at a time," Chris O'Toole cautioned. Chris played midfield as cautiously as he did everything else. Ben rolled his eyes, even though the Mohawk thing presented its own set of problems for him.

Ben looked around the living room for Tyler. Tyler would

get what Ben was feeling. But Tyler was gone. He took his plate into the kitchen and stuffed it in the oversized trash bag hanging by yellow plastic handles on the back of the basement door. As the food slid down into the bag, Ben noticed a light coming through the crack under the door. He twisted the handle, and the door creaked as he opened it.

"Oh shit," he heard someone say as he looked down the basement stairs.

"Jesus, Wireman, you scared the shit out of us," Tyler said from the bottom of the stairs. "Come down, and shut it behind you."

Tyler and two other seniors were gathered around Brandon Rosetti, who was holding a bottle of what looked like some pretty expensive liquor.

"My dad's eighteen-year-old scotch," Brandon said. "Want a snort? It's like what the Scottish lords used to do before they went into battle." Ben shrugged in a way that could be taken as yes or no. Brandon poured a half inch of the golden concoction into a clear plastic cup. He held it up to the light before passing it to Ben.

"To victory," he said. "To States," he added more daringly. It was clear he'd already had more than a few snorts—they all had.

"States," everyone echoed as they tipped back their cups. It didn't burn like some other hard alcohol Ben had tried. It warmed his throat all the way down to his belly. He was doubtful about the historical accuracy of Brandon's comment, but he could imagine having a few of these before heading into battle. He felt bolder just walking up Mrs. Rosetti's basement steps with the other guys. And when Mrs. Rosetti rubbed his shoulders with her long red nails as he thanked her for dinner, he stared right down the front of her shirt. He didn't even try and pretend he was looking anywhere else.

But as he and Tyler walked down the Rosettis' front walk, the alcohol thing started to gnaw at him. It wasn't just Tyler drinking, he tried to reassure himself as they got into the car. Drinking with some other guys in the basement wasn't like drinking alone or one of those other "warning signs" they talked about in health class.

"We're still in season, you know," he said.

"Yeah, so? I didn't see you turn down a drink."

"One drink," Ben said.

Tyler stiffened. His shoulders pulled up toward his ears. "It's no big deal," he said. "You're just worried about the game. Dude, did you see O'Toole? I thought he was going to take notes while Coach was talking tonight."

"Yeah," Ben said. One syllable and he was letting Tyler turn the conversation away again. Why? He wanted badly for things to be okay between them.

They pulled up to a light, and Tyler said, "Goalies are different."

"What?"

"You wear different shirts and gloves. You use your hands. It wouldn't matter if you didn't shave your head like everyone else. No one would care," he added.

"Uh huh," Ben said, because he had to say something. He felt warm. His hands and feet and belly felt warm. It could have been the scotch. Or that Tyler got it.

CHAPTER 5

Growing his hair out had been Tyler's idea. They were a couple of weeks into middle school, and it was brutal. Hundreds of new kids to stare and point and whisper about Ben and the plastic pieces attached to his head. New kids in his class to roll their eyes when he was assigned to work in their group.

Lunch was the worst. Supposedly there were adults responsible for monitoring lunchtime, but it never seemed like it. For twenty minutes every day, the cafeteria belonged to a hundred or so adolescents and the gray-haired ladies in hairnets tucked safely behind the Plexiglas divider. It was so loud, not like in elementary school where you ate in your classroom and the lunch monitor kept you in for recess if things got too noisy. The lunchroom was a constant din of crashing trays, screamed conversation, and whispered gossip. For Ben it blended together into a wall of white noise, a sea of sound where he could never get his head above water. The staring, which was minimized around teachers, was in full force. There was even pointing, and in the din he was left to imagine that everyone who was whispering was talking about him. Tyler seemed oblivious to all of it. He happily ate his cardboard crust pizza as though they were sitting at a table with all the popular kids instead of crammed beside the quiet boys and a few members of the Lego Robotics club. For a few weeks Ben stopped eating entirely during lunch. Starving by the time he got off the bus, he would stuff his sandwich into his mouth while walking up the driveway to avoid questions from his parents.

"You should grow your hair out if it bothers you when people stare," Tyler said casually one Saturday in the middle of a particularly gruesome Call of Duty battle.

"What do you mean?" Ben was picturing one of those terrible ponytails his dad's friend Barry-the-Massage-Therapist had.

Tyler obliterated two of his best guys and then said, "You know, like a skater haircut, shaggy."

"I'm not a skater," Ben said.

"Pretty sure no one's going to check on that. Everyone had them in California."

The long hair felt like protective gear—like a helmet of normalcy he could hide under. It wasn't the first or the last time Ben felt rescued by Tyler.

Their friendship began in fourth grade when Tyler was the new kid and the only nonwhite kid in their small suburban town twenty miles west of Boston. His mom was from the Philippines, but when he first got to Easton a lot of kids asked him if he liked Chinese food. It got meaner from there, with whispers of "ching-chong" in the halls and when the teacher's back was turned. Ben wished in the history of their friendship that he had been the one to stand up for Tyler with some grand gesture like beating up one of the kids who picked on him, or at the very least explaining that no one in Tyler's family was from China. Maybe then their friendship would feel more like one of equals. But really, it had been the other way around. Tyler, who never seemed bothered by what kids said about him, was the one who reached out to him.

It was a windy, cold day in late November, but they went out for gym class anyway. Ben remembered running the required lap around the baseball field, hanging in the middle of a pack of boys, which is where he always ran. There were a few girls who sprinted ahead, but most of them jogged in the back so they could chat. And there were always a few walkers—kids too out of shape to make it all the way around the outfield. Ben's strategy was simply to run with the pack and never get noticed for falling behind, or called out for being first.

Whenever they played kickball, Mr. Colpitts let whichever boy and girl finished the lap first be captains. So the run around the field had a decidedly more competitive edge on those days.

Tyler was the new kid, coming in midyear, but even so, once he learned about this opportunity he never missed a chance to be captain. Not once. He was kickball captain every single time in the second half of fourth grade and midway through fifth grade, until Mr. Colpitts moved to the middle school and his replacement believed in giving everyone a turn to be captain. Ben remembered how Colpitts had reacted to Tyler's unflagging determination to win the position. Impressed and then annoyed—"Give other kids a chance sometimes"—and finally, resigned admiration. To his credit, Colpitts never changed the rules.

On that particular windy day, Tyler picked Ben first. And on every subsequent kickball day, he picked Ben first. By the fourth time that Ben was invited to Tyler's house, he learned not to be intimidated by the huge white columns or the shiny stone countertops in the kitchen and in every bathroom. So he asked him the question that had been bugging him: "Why do you always pick me first?"

Tyler shrugged. "Because you're good," he answered simply. Ben decided that this answer covered the other question that had been bouncing around in his brain. *Why are you friends with me?* Tyler thought he was good, either a good person or good at kickball, maybe both. Those were the terms of the friendship according to Tyler. It had been enough to get Ben through middle school and to give him confidence to go out for high school soccer. His friendship with Tyler and his family was the binary star system around which the planet Ben revolved.

The day of the playoff game against Chelmsford was as windy and cold as that day when Tyler plucked him out of fourth grade obscurity. Ben checked the batteries on his hearing aids and threw in a new set for the game. The idea of having to stop play to make a switch was as horrifying as missing an easy goal. He put on his jersey and his soccer jacket along with a pair of khaki pants—required by Coach for home and away games. He looked in the mirror at his hair, which had never once in the past six years been shorter than his earlobes. He couldn't do a Mohawk. Tyler was right; goalies were different. That would have to be enough for the team. Being a senior, even a gimpy half-deaf senior, he didn't think anyone would give him too much shit about it. He blinked several times at his reflection; another one of his long eyelashes had bent in and was driving him crazy. He rubbed at it and blinked a few more times, hoping it would come away on the pad of his fingertip. It did. He glanced over his shoulder, making sure no one was around. He thought for a moment, then made his wish and blew the eyelash off into oblivion. *Don't let me blow the game.*

It was the only moment of fear or doubt he would allow himself before the game. Goalies had to be brash and egotistical, not nervous and insecure. But these weren't the traits that made Ben a good goalie. His obsession with perfection, with the perfect art of projected normalcy, was what made him a good keeper. Keen observation, attention to detail, and the expectation of perfect performance. These things might make him a paranoid lunatic in life, but it meant a ball rarely slipped by him on the field. He was completely, 100 percent invested in maintaining that perfection.

He shouldered his backpack, lifted the strap of his soccer bag over his shoulder, and went downstairs to grab a snack and his water bottle out of the fridge. There was probably time to come home after school ended and before the game if he wanted to, but he didn't want to. Better to stay where the energy would be most intense and he could get pumped up for the game. His dad came into the kitchen. He was carrying a section of the paper, and Ben heard the telltale sound of the toilet running.

"Can I give you a lift this morning?" his dad offered.

"Nah, I'll ride my bike."

"Okay. I won't ask you if you're nervous."

Ben grinned. "Great, 'cause that would be really annoying."

"Wouldn't it though?" his dad agreed. "We'll be there," he added. "I hope you have a lot of fun out there, Benzer. Really enjoy it."

"Okay, Dad, I'll try." He smiled and shook his head as he walked out the door. His dad was the master of the noncompetitive pep talk. The one season in elementary school that he coached Ben's team, he provoked the ire of all the parents by playing each child for exactly the same number of minutes, regardless of ability.

Ben got on his bike and pedaled out of the driveway, shifting his weight around on the seat to balance his various bags.

There were no big hills on the mile-long ride to school. He turned right at the end of his street. Park Street was a long, sloping ride past the municipal golf course. He let his hands play loosely on the handlebars, sitting upright to get the bright cold breeze full in the face.

He could feel the wind numbing the tops of his ears. He loved the sound of it, whistling and hollow as it flowed like a river past his ears, lifting the back of his hair. It was an equalizer. On his bike, moving swiftly toward school, he was like everyone else.

Learning was a lost cause that day. He managed to focus in English class, because they were watching a movie version of *Romeo and Juliet*. Calculus seemed particularly impenetrable, as did the many causes and effects of World War I. So he was relieved, even a little excited, when the teacher's phone rang during AP Bio and he was called out of Mr. Nichols's thrilling explanation of the structural differences between vascular and nonvascular plants.

It didn't bother him to be called to the office. He knew he wasn't in trouble. Maybe he had left something at home and his dad had dropped it off. He checked his phone, but there were no messages. He walked into the office, blithely unaware of what might be waiting for him, and walked right into Abby Simmons.

She was beaming at him and standing with a few other people he didn't recognize. He ignored her super-grin and walked up to the counter to find out if there was a message. Suddenly Abby was at his elbow. "I had you paged, Ben," she said cheerily. "I'm sorry. I have a copy of your schedule, but it must not be current. We went to the gym but, of course, you weren't there."

"I had to change it," Ben murmured, "to fit in the lab for bio." He studied the people with Abby. There was a kid, maybe eighth or ninth grade. He wore hearing aids, and standing on either side of him were two anxious-looking adults. Slowly Ben's mind began to put the pieces together.

"So, this is Shane," Abby said. The kid stuck his hand out and gave Ben a limp, cold handshake. In addition to hearing aids, he wore wire-rimmed glasses over his big, unblinking, watery blue eyes. "I thought you could take him on a tour while I go over some things with his parents about our program here."

Suddenly Ben remembered their conversation earlier that week in the hall. A cold sweat broke out on his lower back, and his knees felt like a loose connection between the two parts of his legs. This must be what he had agreed to.

"Um, yeah," Ben said, stalling for time and looking help-lessly around the office. "That's why I came down. But I can't miss class right now. We're having a test."

Abby's sunny demeanor clouded over. "But Mr. Nichols said he was lecturing."

Ben shook his head. "Yeah, on Friday. The test is on Friday, but we're reviewing so I really can't miss it." He ventured a glance up at the kid and his parents. "Um, sorry," he said. The parents looked like they might even be relieved—as though the lack of a tour might mean their kid would never have to start high school. "I'm sure Kitty Hudson would do it," he suggested to Abby, ignoring the painful look of disappointment on her face. He turned and walked out of the office without waiting for her to respond.

CHAPTER 6

He told himself it wasn't a big deal. But for the rest of Bio, and the rest of the day, his head was hot and buzzing. He told himself it was the game and the pressure he was feeling, but that wasn't true. All he could think about was Shane. Sad little Shane. Was the kid even a hundred pounds? And those giant ears—worthless ears. Those glasses and those big scared eyes. In his nightmares he was Shane. Wasn't that how everyone saw him? Thinking about the parents was almost worse. How could he not think of his own parents? Of all the crap they'd had to go through, all the extra meetings, all the times they'd had to work so hard to get him involved and included. He swallowed hard on the acid tide rising in the back of his throat.

That was one advantage to going to college, he supposed. They wouldn't be around to see him fail. He stood up. What class was he in anyway? He glanced up at the board. French. The day was practically over. He threw his backpack over one shoulder and mumbled something incomprehensible at Madame St. Clair. Foreign language teachers never knew what time it was anyway. She looked mildly confused at his exit, but she didn't stop him.

He walked slowly down to the gym but paused at the entrance to the locker room. Coach would be the only one in there, and he really didn't feel like a heart-to-heart with anyone right now. Running alongside the locker room was a small hallway, an equipment room, and a door that led outside. He walked past the locker room quietly. The hallway and equipment room were empty, and he kept walking until he pushed through to the outside into kind of a brick alcove. He'd never been here before, though he knew the stoners who hung out there regularly called it the Bridge. On three sides of him were the walls of the school, and in front of him was a paved path that led out to the athletic fields. There was a huge piece of machinery—clearly some part of the heating system—and on either side of it, the brick walls of the school rose up toward the blank sky. As he looked around, someone pushed past him fast, bumping into his shoulder.

"Excuse me," he said, annoyed at the skinny skater kid with his sideways trucker hat and blue hair.

"No problem," said the kid, glancing over his shoulder. Jesus, was that eyeliner? Ben stared at the face, but it turned away and ducked back under the brim. His eyes dropped down the length of the kid's body. It was a girl. He watched her slide through the door back toward the gym and the locker room. She was carrying a long skinny green plant in one hand, the root ball shedding crumbs of dirt on the tile floor as she went. The smell of cigarette smoke hung behind her. Cigarette smoke and something else. Ben inhaled deeply. Cinnamon.

Weird, but Ben shrugged it off. Stoners were weird. He sat down against the wall. It was cold but not too windy, and he was protected on either side by the high brick walls. He unzipped his backpack and pulled out a textbook. He opened it to a random page of French verb conjugations, afraid to look like he was just sitting there having some random freak-out.

He stared down at the incomprehensible lines of text on the paper. He felt like crying, but that wasn't an option—hadn't been for years. He did what he always did in these situations. He played the whole thing out to its worst conclusion in his head. He imagined touring that Shane kid around the school. What if he couldn't even speak right? What if he tried to sign to Ben? He imagined each of these possibilities, taking care to note the horror and disgust on his classmates' faces. He repeated this process over and over again, relishing the sick pit of churning acid his stomach had become. Then he imagined Tyler.

He knew what the look on Tyler's face would be. He would love the kid. He pictured him giving high fives and wrapping his arm around the kid's shoulders while introducing him to every hot girl who would, of course, be cooing as if Tyler had brought her a fluffy puppy instead of some freak who's not even a freshman. He tried to go back to the other image, the gut-stabbing one. But he couldn't. Just the thought of Tyler gave him a way to imagine a better outcome for the whole thing.

The door opened and Ben looked up to see Peter, their freshman equipment manager, struggling to pull out a net bag of soccer balls and another one of cones. He jumped up and stuffed the textbook back in his bag, glad to have a purpose again. He helped Peter bring the balls and cones out to the field.

When the team took the field, it was 3:15 and the wind was blowing harder than ever—an advantage for Ben since every-one would have a hard time hearing. Ben was trying to keep his mind on the game, trying not to imagine that Shane kid and his parents sitting in the bleachers, sad and lonely, by them-selves in some cold corner of the stands. Half the stands were full of crimson and white, the Chelmsford school colors. Their side was all black and yellow for the Easton Fighting Hornets. Will DeGrazio was running around in his bee costume, trying to get people fired up by cheering and attempting to start the wave. The crowd was a pretty good one already—certainly a better turnout than their usual weekday games. But it *was* the playoffs.

Shit, this was the playoffs! He shook his head and ran out to stand in goal and take some warm-up shots from the defense. The first two he saved easily, but then a low corner ball caught him by surprise and sailed just past the tips of his fingers into the open net. No one said anything as he jogged to the back of the net to grab the ball. But he could hear them thinking: it was a shot he should have had. Another ball went wide of the net, and he ran after it. It bounced against the black chain-link fence. As he scooped it up, he came face-to-face with Julie Snow. She was cradling a cup of hot chocolate in her red mitten–covered hands. Her cheeks were bright pink, and her hazel eyes seemed brighter. "Ben Wireman," she said, as though both amused and surprised to see him there. There was another girl standing with her.

He looked over his shoulder. Coach was working with the offense. He bounced the ball off his chest and down to his feet. "Don't act like you didn't know I'd be here," he said. It sounded stronger and more flirtatious than it had in his head.

"Darcy," said Julie, "this is Ben Wireman. He doesn't have a plan for college. Ben," she continued, "this is Darcy. She was my freshmen buddy last year. Now we're just friends."

Darcy rolled her eyes and smirked at the introduction. Then she met his eyes and seemed to hold his gaze a little longer than normal. She had freckles and dirty blonde hair, and she was definitely cute. She was wearing a light fleece and looked like at any moment she might start shaking. He was about to offer the girls his jacket when his parents appeared just behind them, waving frantically with excitement. "See you after the game," he said casually before his mother could yell something embarrassing like, "Good luck sweetie!" He nodded again at the girls before he kicked the ball to the defense and ran back toward the net.

Brandon Rosetti fired a line drive at the back corner of the net, which he leaped for and punched away. He didn't miss another shot during warm-ups. It felt like new blood was flowing through his veins. Talking to Julie and her cute sophomore friend had given him a transfusion of energy. After he dove for another ball, sending it wide of the net with just a touch of his fists, Coach called them into the huddle.

The first half of the game was pretty flat. Both teams played cautiously, trying to feel each other out and find a weakness. Ben only touched the ball twice, and once was when the defender kicked the ball back to him so he could send it past the midfield with a dropkick. Chelmsford had their best player marking Tyler, and the guy was sticking to him like glue. Tyler looked bored and almost angry when they came into the huddle for halftime.

Coach was intense but measured in his words, like always. "No more wasted time, guys. You know what happens when we waste time. It becomes a game not about who's the better team, but about who gets lucky in the last five minutes. That's not a great win, and if you lose, it's a lousy way to end a season. If you want this game, you need to come out and play like you want it." After that he talked specifically to the offense about how he wanted them to play. "Stop passing to Nuson.

Let that kid who's marking him get lazy, and then Tyler can free himself up." He clapped a hand on Tyler's shoulder. Tyler flinched as though Coach had struck him. If Coach noticed, he pretended not to. Ben stared at Tyler, willing him to remember his promise not to be an asshole to Coach, but Tyler wouldn't meet his eyes.

He cast a glance up into the stands to see if Tyler was right about Coach's boyfriend or whoever he was. He scanned the crowd. His parents caught his eye and waved frantically. Sitting one row below them were Julie and Darcy. Julie was talking to another senior girl, but Darcy was staring right at him. She smiled. Ben looked around him to see who she was smiling at. He looked back. Now she was grinning as though she could read his self-conscious action. He gave a little smile back.

Coach was talking to the defense now. Ben listened as Coach reminded the players about staying calm and feeding the ball forward. There wasn't that much to say. They were all playing well, just not well enough. No one was taking risks, and it would take risks to win the game. Ben was only half listening. None of this pertained to him. His job was not to take risks but to consider them and guard against them. His job was to be the most conservative player out there. The only time he had to take risks was when a game went to penalty kicks. And then it became a different kind of game entirely. Something bright red jumped out from the sea of black and yellow and caught his eye. It was Coach's friend in a long red scarf and a tan overcoat leaning against the fence. He was talking to Mrs. Rosetti, his arms crossed in front of his body to ward off the cold or possibly her advances. Ben instinctively tried to find Tyler's eyes but then realized that was ridiculous. What was his point? Whatever was going on with Tyler, it was about more than just Coach.

"Ben!" Coach was saying loudly now. Ben blushed. Had he missed something? Had Coach been trying to get his attention? "Don't get flat out there." Coach looked up at the time clock. Seven minutes left in the halftime break. "Everyone get out and get warm. Josh and Bret, go warm up Ben," Coach called to the two freshmen riding the bench for playoffs. The boys jumped up, clearly eager to do something besides shivering on the bench.

Both teams were more energized in the second half of the game. Twice the Chelmsford offense penetrated their half of the field. The first time they got a shot off, it was a slow dribbler—probably a pass gone missing—and Ben was able to scoop it up and send it off. The second time resulted in a corner kick: a perfectly placed ball that came down right in the middle of the pack. There weren't too many situations more dangerous for a goalie. But this time Brandon Rosetti got a head on it, and then the midfielders were able to clear the ball.

Midway through the half, Easton got a break. It was an indirect kick just fifty feet from the goal. The Chelmsford players lined up to make a wall. Ben walked forward as the entire defense marched up to push the play forward. Tyler lined up next to Andy Debias, who was taking the kick. The whistle blew, Andy tapped it, and Tyler blasted it over the wall. Ben's heart sank as the ball fell straight toward the goalie. But then the goalie did something unexpected. Instead of catching the ball and keeping control of the game, he punched it out. He punched it hard. The ball sailed back toward Tyler, who was running in. He jumped up, impossibly high up, and drove the ball into the back right corner of the net with his head.

The crowd erupted before Tyler's feet even touched the ground. Ben ran forward to join his team. They were all sprinting toward Tyler, lifting him up with the sheer force of bodies coming together in one place. They were jumping and chanting and shouting until the ref's whistle brought them back to earth. Ben dashed back to the goal, goading the crowd with his outstretched arms as he ran. The noise swelled again. Was there anything better? Was there any other place in his life where he allowed himself to enjoy this much focused attention?

The next few minutes were the most dangerous time in the game. The other team would expect them to relax with their one-goal lead, relax, and get lazy. Chelmsford took the kickoff and booted it past their midfield. They charged the ball. Their winger reached it before Brandon could get there. With a light touch, he slid past Brandon, and suddenly there was just Ben between him and the goal. Ben felt the adrenaline surge through his arms and fingers. He could see Brandon thundering just behind the Chelmsford winger, but he wasn't going to be fast enough. Ben came out of goal to cut off the angle. He bounced back and forth on his feet and watched the muscles in the other boy's chest. Was he going to pass? He glanced up, but his nearest teammate was behind him more than five yards. No, he was going to shoot. Ben came forward another foot. He watched the footwork, waiting for an indication of which way the ball would go. Then the kid dribbled just a tiny bit too hard. It was an opening. Ben dove, scooping the ball into his chest and tucking his head so that the kid and the teeth of his cleats sailed over Ben's head. He could hear the crowd explode before he even opened his eyes.

He jumped up, shaking off the clods of dirt, and sent a huge dropkick up the left side of the field. It dropped right in front of Tyler, who gave a little push off his defender and settled the ball neatly at his feet. He dribbled just a few feet and shot the ball neatly past the goalie into the bottom corner of the net.

After that, it was all over. The defense was flawless, and Ben didn't touch the ball for the rest of the game. In the last three minutes Andy Debias scored, making the final score three to nothing. When the whistle blew, Ben was walking on air as he watched his team run down to scoop him up and celebrate in the goal. It wasn't really *his* win, even though he did have that one save, but the team always celebrated in their own goal.

After they rolled around on the field, Coach came running out with Peter, who had water bottles and a bag of their warm-ups. Coach kept it quick. He was proud of them. Eastern Mass finals would be played on Saturday. They would have a light practice tomorrow after school. "Go home and get some rest," he said sternly. But he was smiling. The crowd was clearing out. Ben's parents gave him a little wave and pointed in the general direction of home. Julie was gone.

Ben fell in with Tyler as they began to jog their victory lap around the field, first toward the parking lot and then back to the main building. Ben glanced sideways at Tyler. His face was light, untroubled, almost gleeful, and Ben realized how long it had been since he'd seen Tyler this way. "Good game," he said.

"Great game," Tyler agreed. He had just run for eighty minutes, but he jogged as though it were nothing. He wasn't even breathing hard.

"Eastern finals," Ben said.

"Yup," Tyler said. "Might even get the old man out of his study for that one." Ben glanced up at the stands, but if anyone had been there for Tyler they were gone now. Tyler caught his glance. "My mom was here. And Jer, of course. He's the only reason she's here."

Ben knew better than to argue with this. Jeremiah was Tyler's little brother and his biggest fan. Six years was just enough for Tyler to appear like some half-god half-man to the sixth grader. But Jeremiah's adulation aside, sports just didn't matter very much in the Nuson household. Except for cricket, which the professor had developed an affinity for when he studied at Oxford. Sometimes he watched it on some obscure sports channel in their living room. It was embarrassingly pretentious.

"They'll come if we make it to States," Ben said.

"Does it matter?"

Yes, it does. Or it should. "Is everything cool there? With your parents?"

"Oh no," Tyler said, his face clouding over. "Not you too. It's fine. It's the same."

Ben thought about what that meant. About how little time Tyler spent at home and how often he was alone or hanging out with Jeremiah, the two of them making microwave pizza or spaghetti for dinner. When his mom was around, she was constantly checking her phone, and his dad seemed to reside permanently in the den or his study. Their dysfunction was in the complete absence of anything resembling a family, at least in a social sense. But Tyler was right; it had always been that way. It was not new, the way this cold, easily snappish, pissy version of Tyler was.

CHAPTER 7

If the soccer playoffs weren't on everyone's mind before, they certainly were the next day in school. Kids Ben didn't even know were slapping him on the back in the halls and talking about the "amazing save" he'd made. He didn't know whether to correct them or just accept the praise. Tyler laughed when he saw Ben's confusion apparently written all over his face. "You're overthinking it, bro," he said. There was even going to be a pep rally eighth period on Friday and a fan bus to take kids to Wentworth Community College, where the Eastern Mass final would be played on neutral turf.

Ben had double lunch on Thursday—which meant he had lunch and a study hall—and he and Tyler made plans to go to Colucci's for steak bombs to celebrate the win. He was waiting in the hallway for the Tyler Nuson fan club to clear out so they could go. He sat down on a bench and glanced at his phone, but he didn't really mind waiting. It was kind of like watching a National Geographic special on primate primping. Tyler was leaning against his locker. One of the twins was there (who knew which one) as well as a couple other sophomore girls and a junior girl who Tyler was sort of on-again off-again dating—if you could call repeated hookups at parties "dating." Megan

Sewell didn't hang on Tyler's every word like the other girls did. In fact, right then she was checking her phone as Tyler recounted the header goal.

Light was coming through the skylight above their heads, and it caught some of the red and golden highlights in Tyler's hair. His skin really was golden—not yellow like a kung fu comic book character but actually golden like pictures of summer wheat on cereal boxes or beer bottles. When he grinned he got a dimple on his left cheek. Were these things what made girls like him so much? Was it weird that he, Ben, was noticing? Someone sat down on the bench next to Ben. He flinched as though they could read his thoughts and quickly slid over.

"That's not very friendly." It was Darcy.

"Oh, hey," Ben said. "I didn't realize it was you." His eyes flicked over, up, and down. She was wearing a tight bluish-green V-neck sweater. A thin silver chain hung around her neck with a tiny silver horseshoe resting just above the dark shadow where her boobs came together. He looked back up to see if Tyler was ready yet.

Darcy followed his gaze. "So you and Tyler are like best friends, huh?"

"Uh huh," Ben said, although the title made him feel like a kindergartener.

"Since forever?" Darcy asked.

"Fourth grade," Ben said. He didn't mean to be short with her. It was just that he knew where this conversation was going. Girls were always being nice to him as a way to get to Tyler. Next she would ask if Tyler had a girlfriend, or if she was subtle she might ask if Tyler's girlfriend got in the way of their friendship. But it was really the same question.

"So you're probably used to all this, then," Darcy said.

"What do you mean?"

"The Tyler show. I mean, it seems like it's like this a lot. It must get annoying, all the waiting."

"Hang out with Julie much?"

"Huh?" Darcy said.

"Never mind." Ben wasn't sure how to respond. If he agreed with her he sounded like Tyler's sidekick, but if he disagreed he was obviously lying. But how to explain it to her in a way that didn't sound like he worshipped at the altar of Tyler Nuson? Tyler really liked people. He liked talking to them and hearing their stories. When they were around town, it was like hanging out with the mayor of Easton. Everyone knew Tyler. Whenever they drove into Cambridge to get a burger at Bartley's in Harvard Square, Tyler always wanted to stop and hear the street musicians. He wasn't the guy who stood at the back and shuffled on without leaving a buck after listening to a song. He wasn't the one who would listen to a whole set and give five dollars. Tyler would stand there for the better part of an hour, throw some money in the guy's guitar case, and then talk to the guy about where he performed and if he had an album. And it wasn't just music. Tyler genuinely wanted to know what people were up to.

Sometimes it was tiring. Sometimes Ben did just want to eat his damn burger in peace without hearing all about their waiter's audition to be a janitor in the latest Matt Damon action movie.

But he wasn't going to tell Darcy that, so he smiled and shrugged. Just then, Tyler broke away from the pack and sauntered over to where they were sitting.

"Steak bombs!" he hissed the word excitedly. "Who's this?"

he said, turning to smile in Darcy's direction. "Want a steak bomb?"

"Tyler, Darcy, Darcy, Tyler," Ben introduced them.

"So, you coming for steak bombs?" Tyler repeated.

Ben felt himself bristle. Why did he care if Tyler invited Darcy? Should he be the one?

"Thanks, but no," Darcy said. She stood up and shouldered her backpack. "I've got class. And, as it so happens, I'm a vegetarian."

"It's a really good steak bomb," Tyler said.

"That really came from a cow," Darcy replied.

"Moo," said Tyler sadly.

Darcy smirked. "See you later, Ben. Interesting to meet you, Tyler," she added.

"Did she sound a little sarcastic?" Tyler asked as they walked down the hallway toward the main entrance.

"I don't think she's as impressed with you as the rest of your public." For some reason Ben was pleased by this. He turned around to get another look at Darcy heading down the hall in the opposite direction.

"Well, that's a shame," Tyler said. "I'll have to do something about that." There was that bristly feeling again.

As they walked out to the car, Ben slapped his arms against his sides, questioning the decision to leave his coat in his locker. Tyler tossed his keys in the air, catching them behind his back. "There are going to be some sweet parties on Saturday after the game."

"*If* we win," Ben said.

"If we win," Tyler said, "the parties will be insane! Unhinged! But either way, there will be parties. Jessica Albright's parents are going out of town."

Ben shrugged. "I'm just thinking about the game."

Tyler turned and bowed deeply, his hands pressed together like some kind of yogi. "You are the better man," he intoned.

"Open the car, numbnuts. I'm freezing."

"Your wish is my command," Tyler said, and he clicked the button.

On the ride over, Ben thought about Tyler's reaction to Darcy. Tyler was used to getting attention from pretty much every girl who saw him. The story of how he became hot was something Ben called Ty-lore. In sixth and seventh grade they were still both pretty much dweebs. Tyler had some status as a good athlete, but neither of them talked to girls or even really paid much attention to them. They were both into video games, and that, along with endless hours of playing Pig or Horse or Around the World in Ben's driveway, would keep them occupied for the better part of a weekend.

All that changed the summer after seventh grade. Some of the guys started playing a pickup soccer game at Albermarle Field. They played five-on-five, and usually they had enough guys to get a mini tournament going. This was where Ben first learned one of the few valuable things he knew about girls. If all the boys were somewhere, girls would turn up. This and also, with a few exceptions, girls moved in packs, and although the packs had an internal decision-making process that was a complete mystery to him, the packs could make or break you. And one day, the pack made Tyler.

They were playing shirts and skins the way they always did. A few of the shirts made a six-foot goal on each side of the field. Ben played goalie because he liked to, and because it had the added advantage of making him the good guy. No one had to be cajoled into standing in net because he was there.

At the far end of the field, a group of girls was sitting. They were braiding each other's hair and pretending not to pay attention to the game. They had become a regular feature of the games now. None of the boys interacted with them, but their presence was now an accepted part of the scene and gave it an extra charge, something they didn't really have a name for yet. On this one particular afternoon, Tyler—a skin—booted the ball wide of the goal, right into the center of the girls' nest. There was some screeching and yelping as the ball bounced around them. Then Joanna Cote grabbed the ball, held it to her side, and planted a hand on her other hip. Tyler beckoned for her to throw the ball, but she shook her head no. Tyler walked closer and then closer. Now everyone on the field was watching the exchange. When he got close enough, they all watched as Joanna Cote reached out her hand and touched him. His back was to the rest of them. What did she touch? Everyone's mind buzzed with the question. Then it was over. She handed him the ball and sat down with her friends amidst an explosion of whispers and giggles. Tyler turned around and shrugged, but his face was red, and not just from running around.

After the game Joanna and two of her friends walked right up to Tyler, who was pulling his T-shirt back over his head. "See," Joanna said to her friends. "He's got a six-pack." She lifted the bottom of his T-shirt with one of her pink-polished fingernails. Everyone looked, even the boys. It was true. Tyler had a perfectly formed six-pack; the muscles around his hips and stomach rippled with definition. Ben tugged self-consciously at the bottom of his shirt. Were they going to check everyone?

Joanna, who had straight blonde hair and already wore eye makeup, cocked her head to one side and said, "We're going to the pool tomorrow." She chewed her gum, and Ben could see her tongue dancing delicately inside her mouth, playing with it like a seal might bounce a balloon on its nose.

When no one said anything, she looked directly at Tyler and said, "Are you going to come?"

Tyler looked at Ben. Ben shrugged. "I guess so," Tyler said.

Joanna didn't even glance at Ben. "Good," she said. "At, like, three." It definitely wasn't a question. She turned around and the three girls walked back to their friends, ponytails bobbing and butts shaking. Ben felt a surge within himself that usually came only from soccer or sometimes from certain parts of movies that made him clamp a pillow over his lap if he was watching at home with his family.

They hung out at the pool all summer. Joanna was the first girl Tyler ever kissed. Ben could still point out the exact spot where it happened, on the side of the pool building near the dumpsters. He had been just around the corner, waiting awkwardly with two of her friends. But it wasn't just Joanna. That was the summer Tyler became Tyler: good-looking, popular, funny, and athletic. He'd been that way all along, Ben supposed. But after that summer there was no going back.

Ben stole a sideways glance at Tyler in the car. He was drumming distractedly on the steering wheel as he scanned the street in front of Colucci's for parking. He didn't look like someone who was troubled by anything. Since that summer after seventh grade, Tyler had had a girlfriend here and there. But it never seemed to last more than a few weeks, and he could never get a good explanation from Tyler about why. After a while he just stopped asking about them. The story never changed much, and they were gone a few weeks later. Megan Sewell was the first one he could remember ever cracking the one-month mark—not that he was keeping track exactly, because that would be weird, wouldn't it?

They didn't say much until they ordered and sat down in one of the cracked red vinyl booths in the back of Colucci's general store and pizza place. The pizza place was mostly a takeout operation with a few booths making a halfhearted attempt at a restaurant in the back. Ben could smell the peppery steak grease sizzling on the flat grill and felt his stomach contract and gurgle in response. "What about Megan Sewell?" he asked.

"What about her?"

"Are you going to see her this weekend?"

Tyler shrugged. "Maybe. She said she might go to Jessica's party."

Ben shook his head and grinned. "So that's it, huh?"

The guy from behind the grill slapped their sandwiches down in front of them on two circular silver trays. "What's that supposed to mean?" Tyler took a big bite of his sub, and his eyes bugged out in appreciation.

"Well, it's been a while," Ben said. He popped a grilled onion that had slid out from the bun into his mouth. He bounced it around on his tongue until the heat dissipated. "You must like her, right?"

"Do *you*?" Tyler asked. He seemed annoyed.

Ben's first thought was that he didn't actually like Megan that much. He thought she was kind of aloof, maybe even a bit snobby. But he hadn't really hung out with her that much. She and Tyler always seemed to hook up at parties or get together, just the two of them. It occurred to him that he might be coming off as jealous, so he did something to lighten the mood.

"I asked you first," Ben said. He blew his straw wrapper at Tyler's face.

"Of course I like her," he finally said. "I mean, I wouldn't hang out with her if I didn't. She makes things pretty easy."

"That's beautiful," Ben said. He tried not to act annoyed. If there was something special about Megan, Tyler was clearly not going to tell him about it.

"What about you?" Tyler picked up the straw paper and flicked it back at him.

"Me and who?" Ben said.

"Whoever."

Ben gave a little cough. "I don't really think we're in the same, er, league as far as girls." He tried to keep his voice cool so they could stay in the world where it just hadn't happened, hadn't been convenient. And out of the place where he was a complete defective unworthy of a serious hookup with any girl ever.

"What?" Tyler smacked the table with his open palm. The guy behind the grill gave them a long stare. "Look at that face," Tyler said. "Seriously, look!"

Ben glanced at his reflection in the mirror over the beer coolers. When he saw that the flesh-colored plastic in his ears was covered, he looked a little longer. Shaggy brown hair, hazel eyes, the telltale red dot on his chin from an incoming zit.

"Dude, you're hot," Tyler said.

"Don't be an asshole."

"I'm not," Tyler said indignantly. "When am I ever an asshole? No wait, don't answer that. But seriously, you are a nice-looking guy. You act like a Sheldon, but you're not, you're like a Pitt or a Cruise. Seriously. You look like that guy in the vampire movies, whatshisface?"

Ben sighed.

"Edward Cullen!" Tyler shouted. "That guy!"

"Do I sparkle like diamonds?"

"You watched it!" Tyler shouted. This time the guy behind the counter put down his spatula and made like he was coming over. Tyler put his hands up in defeat and mouthed a silent *Sorry*. Ben laughed and took another bite of his sub. The last time he'd slept over at Tyler's house, Tyler had tried to get him to watch one of the Twilight movies. He had refused, opting instead for the latest in the Bourne sequence, *The Bourne Calamity* or something like that. Anyway, he'd given Tyler a lot of shit for trying to get him to watch it when really he'd already seen it with Shannan one weekend while she was home from school.

Now, the look of betrayal on Tyler's face only made him laugh harder, and a piece of gristle rocketed out of his mouth onto the floor. He looked over for a minute at the grill man, but he was busy with a customer. Ben scooped it up into a napkin thinking for a minute how, whether or not it was bullshit, he was glad that at least Tyler still seemed to prefer his company over one of the countless girls he hooked up with.

CHAPTER 8

"WE GOT THE SPIRIT! YEAH, YEAH! WE GOT THE SPIRIT! YEAH, YEAH!" The Easton High School Fighting Hornet cheerleaders were leading everyone in the gym in a popular cheer. Popular mostly because it involved the cheerleaders leaning forward and celebrating feats of athleticism by bouncing their boobs around.

"We got the tits!" Tyler shouted every time that part of the chant came up. They were standing up on the stage with the rest of the team in their uniforms on Friday, the day before the Eastern Mass final. They were supposed to be cheering along, but the clamor in the gymnasium was so overpowering that no one could hear Tyler's slight alteration to the lyrics. Ben and Brandon, on either side of Tyler, were trying not to crack up.

"We got some ass!" Tyler yelled as the cheerleaders bounced forward. This time Coach turned around and shot them all a look. Ben elbowed Tyler in the side. They started clapping again, slightly off from the rhythm of the cheerleaders. It didn't matter. Everyone was in a good mood. It was Friday and they were missing last period to stand around in the gym and get pumped up—it didn't really matter what for.

Ben was actually trying hard not to think too much about the actual game. When he did, he felt something between nausea and excitement.

Shannan was coming home from school for the game, and he was looking forward to having the weekend together. Besides the fact that she was his sister and he loved her, the house felt a little more complete when she was around. When it was just the three of them, Ben sometimes got the feeling he was keeping his parents back from something. Like the last customer in a restaurant, appreciated but not encouraged to linger over dessert.

"What are you doing tonight?" Tyler asked as they walked out of Plummer Gymnasium. Someone had propped open the outer doors, and the blast of cold November air felt great on Ben's red face and sweaty back. It must have been a thousand degrees in the gym by the end of the pep rally. The hallways were emptying out as kids headed to their lockers and then home, eager for the weekend to begin.

"Shannan's coming home. We're probably just going to have dinner and watch a stupid movie."

"That's cool," Tyler said.

Ben felt a pang of guilt. On any other night at his house, Tyler would be more than welcome, but Ben was looking forward to time alone with Shannan.

Was he being a douche about it? It's not like Tyler wasn't fed or had pants that ended five inches above his ankles like Danny Fisher, who had been in their elementary school class and had to take a food backpack home every weekend. Tyler lived in a big, beautiful house. He had two parents. But it was cold, a house that never seemed like a home to anyone—especially since the Nusons had outgrown the last of the nannies. Tyler and his brother drifted through the large high-ceilinged rooms like two ghosts passing time in a mausoleum.

It was only five or six years since the Nusons dismissed their last nanny. They were Mannies, actually. Usually college guys who lived in the in-law apartment attached to the back of the house, made some meals, did some laundry, and were responsible for supervising Tyler and Jeremiah when work kept Mrs. Nuson and the professor busy. Which was a lot. The Mannies were like built-in older brothers, except they were paid. Tyler hated the last one with a vehemence Ben didn't really understand. Besides being a bit obsessed with his car—to the point where he polished the red Mitsubishi with a cloth diaper every weekend—he had seemed to Ben to be an all right guy.

After Scott left, Tyler gave his parents an ultimatum: either leave him to watch Jeremiah in the afternoons and evenings, or pack them both off to boarding school. That was the last of The Mannies. About half the time, Tyler made dinner for the two of them—usually pizza, always served in front of the television. When the Nusons were around, his mom cooked and they ate in a formal dining room at a long glass table with high-backed crushed velvet chairs. Ben had been forced to sit through his fair share of those dinners. He always left feeling slightly confused as to whether the Nusons were actually parents or just a pair of badly cast actors trying their hand at a parental role.

"You need a ride?" Tyler asked, interrupting Ben's thoughts.

"Nah, I got my bike."

"All right then. Pick you up for the game?"

"Definitely," Ben said. He held his hand out and Tyler greased it with a little high-five handshake they had perfected over the years. They parted at the intersection of two hallways. Ben needed to grab some stuff out of his locker before riding home. The locker area was quiet on a Friday afternoon. A custodian was pushing one of those tall brooms down the hall, catching the flotsam of writing utensils and missing homework assignments.

When Ben came out of the locker row, someone brushed past him heading in the other direction. Ben caught a glimpse of blue hair and heard a single word uttered clearly and distinctively—almost like he'd said it inside his own head.

"Freak."

He whipped around, but the person had already gone through the double doors that led to a hallway of classrooms. He walked over to the small windows set into the doors and saw the same backwards trucker hat from the other day outside the gym. He shook his head and, glancing around first, pushed the test button on his hearing aids to make sure he was getting a clear sound. They were fine. Who the hell was trucker hat girl? By senior year, he was pretty sure he knew everyone by face or by name. She was probably one of the burnouts who hung out in the Bridge and were finishing high school on the five- or six-year plan. Who was *she* to call him a freak?

He got on his bike, his face still flushed from the gym and from a feeling he hadn't felt so strongly since middle school. As he rode home, the flush of embarrassment turned to intrigue and annoyance. He wasn't the freak. He belonged. Hell yeah, he'd worked hard to make sure of that. He decided if he saw her again, he'd make a point to look her right in the face and see if she had the balls, or whatever, to say it again. Then he deliberately put it out of his head. He needed to focus on the game tomorrow, not on some burnout, blue-haired weirdo.

It was hard not to be intimidated by Poly Prep. They were a city school, and their team looked different from the Greater Boston suburban schools Easton was used to playing. They were big, for one thing—more like football players than soccer players. And they had already done the Mohawks, and Ben could see why. It was definitely intimidating. Half their team was made up of African kids. Sudanese or Somali—they were recent immigrants to New England, and Ben knew they were amazing soccer players. Most of them had grown up with a ball at their feet, and they played with that same innate fluidity that Tyler did.

Ben tried not to watch them as their team ran a warm-up lap around the turf, but everyone was glancing past Coach as he gave them some instructions for warm-up. The steel bleachers at Wentworth College rose higher around the field and, combined with the tall steel light posts, gave the whole stadium more of a gladiatorial feel. The fans were pouring in dressed in Easton and Poly Prep colors. He looked for familiar faces in the crowd, something to anchor himself with, but couldn't find his parents or Shannan. He stared at the goal, reminding himself that it was the exact same size as the one they used at school.

"Hey!" Coach said suddenly. "You earned the right to be here. Play your game. Don't just defend against their game. I don't need heroics here. I just need you to play the game I've seen you play a million times, and you'll win. It's that simple."

At the half, they were tied one all. Both teams had scored early and been deadlocked ever since. Ben drank and spit water and jumped up and down, trying to stay loose. He pushed the thoughts of overtime and penalty kicks from his mind. He had to focus on the game that was now. If he thought too far ahead, then he would lose focus and make a stupid mistake. He glanced into the stands, and this time he saw his mom and dad and

Shannan. Shannan grinned and waved like a maniac. His dad mouthed, *Have fun.* Ben rolled his eyes back at him. He could see the crease between his dad's eyebrows from the field. His dad was a worrier. He had no business telling Ben to loosen up.

In the last ten minutes of the second half, Poly Prep turned up their game and made a couple big pushes down to their end. On one of their scoring attempts, they ended up with a corner kick, a beautifully lofted ball that landed right in the middle of the swarming pack of players. Someone got a head on it, but Ben got there with both fists and punched the ball out. A Poly Prep defender quickly rebounded, sending the ball back into the fray. Ben reached out to stop a hard low shot to the corner as a Poly Prep defender thundered toward him. He blocked the ball, bouncing it off the other team and then out to one side of the goal. But the player was running at full steam, stumbled, and tripped right over the top of him, crushing Ben's hand with the full force of his plastic molded cleat. The scream shot out of Ben's mouth as he felt a crunch of plastic against bone into hard packed ground. He staggered to his feet only to hear the play whistled, and then rolled to the ground holding his injured hand underneath his body.

Brandon Rosetti was there first, patting Ben's back and asking him repeatedly if he was okay. Ben could only groan. He wiggled his fingers gingerly, but the pain was like a bolt of lightning up his arm and into his gut. Next, Coach was there with the trainer. They were turning him over and trying to pull his arm away from his body to assess the damage. He focused in on Coach's face. There was a ref there too. "Looks like you're going to need a sub, Coach," he said.

"Give us a minute," Coach snapped. He helped Ben sit up and got him to extend his hand to the trainer, who held it gingerly in both hands, assessing the damage. There was already a series of red marks where the cleats had dented his palm.

"Can you try and close it for me, Ben?" the trainer asked.

Ben grimaced but slowly closed and opened the hand. He felt a glimmer of hope. The pain was bad, but moving it hadn't made it worse. The trainer looked at Coach. "Could be fractured," he said. The whole team was standing around him now. He could see Tyler's pink and yellow Adidas shin guards closest to Coach. Tyler knelt down so he was at Ben's eye level. He gave him a small smile and a chin nod.

Ben returned the nod—they both knew he would be okay. "Good thing you beat off with your left hand, Wireman," Tyler said.

"Christ, Nuson, get the team into a huddle," Coach said, gently shoving him away.

Coach looked back at the bench where their backup goalie was getting warmed up by the freshmen. Mayhew wasn't a bad goalie, but he had hardly seen any playing time this year. Coach mostly put him in at defense when they were already destroying another team. Coach looked back at Ben. "It's your call, Ben," he said.

Ben looked at the play clock and flexed his hand one more time. He didn't want to wimp out, but neither did he want to blow a save because his hand was compromised. He looked up, hoping to find Tyler—something in his face would tell him what to do—but Tyler was talking to the rest of the team. He decided his experience was more important to the game, even with a busted right hand. It hurt, but he could move it enough. "Wrap it up and leave me in."

The trainer cracked open his tackle box before Ben finished speaking. He wrapped Ben's hand tightly with tape so that Ben could only close it with extreme pressure. The rest of the team came over, giving him props for manning up and staying in the game. Still, they sounded a little nervous. He wiggled his fingers in their white athletic-tape cocoon. "I'm all right," he said. He knew he sounded less than reassuring.

Tyler looked around at the defense. "Get it out of here," he said. "Get it up and out of here, and then it doesn't cross midfield. We've got six minutes to wrap this up and get ourselves to States. Play like there's no overtime, no PKS. We're going to win it right now." Ben looked at Tyler. He knew Tyler was thinking of him. Just like he knew that it was his heart beating explosively in his chest. Like he understood what it meant in those war movies when guys talked about how they would risk their lives to save their buddies.

"Win on three," Coach said, and he put his hand out and everyone else put their hands in the middle.

The winning goal came in the last ten seconds of play. It was sophomore Matt Middlebury's first goal of the season. The team swarmed on the kid, jumping all over him and incurring a meaningless penalty from the ref for excessive celebration. Ben was more than relieved. Even though the defense had successfully kept him from touching the ball, the pain in his hand was increasing to a consistent stabbing sensation. Now when he tried to open and close his fingers, the pain surged.

After they doused Coach with Gatorade, Ben ran over to the fence, where he hugged his mom and dad and Shannan over the top of the black chain links. Dad, of course, wanted to take him to the ER immediately. "Dad," Ben said. "Phil said I could go home and ice it. He said I don't have to get it checked out right away. If it still really hurts tomorrow, then I promise I'll let you drive me to the doctor, okay?" His real motivation was to make it to the evening's promised festivities without any parental intervention. He could put up with whatever pain was necessary until tomorrow morning at least. He was pretty sure he wasn't going to feel anything tonight.

"All right, Ben," Dad relented. "We'll meet you outside the locker room?"

"Tyler can give me a ride, Dad." Ben smiled. His parents hadn't picked him up after soccer since sophomore year. He knew that his dad was just going into overprotective mode.

His dad looked at him as though puzzled by this answer. "Oh right, sure."

Ben clapped him on the shoulder with his good hand. "Can Tyler come for dinner tonight?" It would make things easier when they both slid out the door later.

"Sure," said his dad. "We can celebrate together!"

"Sounds good, Dad," Ben said. He ignored Shannan, who was rolling her eyes behind Dad's back and smirking. Surely thinking of how he and Tyler would really be celebrating later on.

The bus ride back to school was mayhem. When they pulled into school, Coach gave a quick reminder talk about the athletic contract and what he would personally do to anyone who made himself ineligible to play by getting caught like, in his words, "a drunken jackass."

"See?" Tyler said as they piled off the bus and jogged toward the locker room. "He didn't expressly forbid us from acting like drunken jackasses. He just told us not to get caught."

"I'm pretty sure that's not what he meant," Ben said. But he wasn't going to argue. Not now. Not when things were light and easy between them and everything seemed to be going their way.

CHAPTER 9

Jessica Albright's house was down a dirt road, about half a mile from the nearest neighbor. It was definitely going to be an epic night, Ben thought as he surveyed the scene. There were two kegs in the backyard when he and Tyler arrived around 9:30, the music was loud, and it seemed like half the school was there. This would be one of those parties that everyone would talk about later and you would feel really bad if you hadn't been there. Or you would just smile and nod like you had been. There was a different energy—as if these weren't the people they saw every day in the halls. They were all new people that night. They could be anyone.

They grabbed yellow plastic keg cups and got in line behind Whitney Morrison and Dana Reid. They were both cheerleaders. Whitney had soft brown eyes and light brown skin. She smiled at Ben and Tyler like she knew the whole party was kind of foolish and destined to end badly but what were they going to do about it anyway. Tyler was uncharacteristically quiet in the face of cute girls. Ben saw Lindsay Walker standing in line for the keg just a few people in front of them. He looked at Tyler, but his face was cold, impassive. Before Ben could come up with something to say, he heard their names being called from the front of the line.

"Boys! My boys!" It was Brandon Rosetti, and it sounded like he'd already had a few. He was at the front of the line, pumping the keg and working the crowd. Ben followed Tyler up to the front while Brandon shouted out a bunch of bullshit about their prowess on the soccer field. Brandon handed Tyler a full beer, sloshing some of it out onto the ground.

"Hey, no cutsies!" Ben turned around and saw Julie's sophomore friend standing behind him. She was pretending to look pissed.

"Hey," he said.

"Darcy," she said.

"I know," he lied. He *had* remembered it began with a D. He tried to think of something else to say. "Is Julie here?" he asked, then kicked himself as he saw a flicker of annoyance in her eyes.

"I don't know. I could probably find out if I could ever get my beer. But some people think they're big shots who get to cut the line."

"I hate those people," Ben said. Whoa, was he flirting with her? She did look cute tonight—her lips were all pink and sparkly. Brandon handed him a full beer, and he turned to offer it to Darcy. "Ladies first?"

"Thanks," she said, giving him a real smile. She took it and handed him her empty cup, which he pushed back into Brandon's hand for a refill.

"How's your hand?" she asked when they both had their beers and had moved away from the line. Tyler had already left, pulled away by one of the other soccer guys to haze Matt for his game-winning goal.

"It's okay," he said, holding up his fingers, which were pleasantly numb and still wrapped tightly in athletic tape. "A little cold, I guess." His glove wouldn't fit over the bandage, not that he would have left them on at the party anyway.

"You need, like, the opposite of fingerless gloves," she said. "Like, whatever happens to all the fingers when they make fingerless gloves? Are they just sitting in a factory somewhere being sad and purposeless?"

"I don't think they actually make the fingers and cut them off," Ben said. "They're probably just made that way in the first place."

Darcy looked at him with a half smile. "I know, Ben. I was just kidding. You're kind of serious, you know? You should try and lighten up."

"I'm not serious." He tried to say it lightly—like all along he'd known they were joking around. "What makes you think I'm serious?" He took a long pull on his beer. That would help—it had to help.

Darcy shrugged. "I don't know. It just seems like you're very careful, you know. Like you're always watching people and, you know, thinking about them."

"And that's bad?"

"Only if you don't know how to turn it off and just relax and have fun sometimes."

"I have fun," Ben said. But he brought his hand up to his winter hat—the orange one he bought from a traveling hippie flea market when he was visiting Shannan at UMaine. He knew just how it fit snugly over the top parts of his ears. Beside him, Darcy shivered and rubbed her arm with her free hand. "Want to go stand by the fire?" he asked. "I could try and be more fun over there."

Darcy laughed and then her teeth chattered, which was somehow incredibly cute. "Sure," she said. Her laughter made him feel warm and more certain of himself.

They stood by the fire pit for a while and chatted about little things. Soccer and the upcoming State final, classes, how Darcy hated her chemistry teacher. Ben was glad that the What-Are-You-Going-To-Do-Next-Year topic didn't come up. He figured sophomores didn't care that much about that sort of thing yet. Talking with Darcy was easy. And when they weren't talking it wasn't awkward either. They just watched other people and Darcy made some comments that were sarcastic but never that mean. She was still shivering a bit, and Ben thought about putting his arm around her—just to keep her warm—but knew he'd never have the guts. Tyler would have. And with Tyler it wouldn't have seemed sleazy either. It was the kind of thing he would do for anyone, really—not just a girl he thought was cute and kind of interesting. Did he feel that way about Darcy? He looked down. She was at least five inches shorter than he was.

"Knock it off, Ben," she said playfully.

"What?"

"You're thinking too much again."

"Sorry," he said and then in a robot voice, "No more thinking."

Darcy laughed. She reached up toward the back of his neck. "There's got to be a switch around her somewhere." He flinched even before she touched him and just as quickly wished he could take it back. Her hand fell lightly on his collar and then back at her side. "Sorry," she said. "I didn't mean—"

"No, I know you didn't," he said too quickly. It was awful. He searched his mind for something to say. What he hated most of all was that she felt bad about it. He was the awkward one, not her. But how to explain that without becoming even more awkward? Just then, one of her friends ran up and asked if she could steal Darcy away because she just *had* to talk to her.

Ben nodded numbly, but as she turned to go she reached for his frozen fingers and gave them a little squeeze.

"If I see any gloveless fingers lying around, I'll grab them for you."

"Thanks," he said.

Maybe it wasn't that bad. Maybe she didn't think he was a total loser after all. He didn't have too much more time to contemplate it. Someone threw a huge log onto the fire, and a spray of sparks shot up in the air. Some girls screamed. Some moron threw his beer on the fire, and it began to smoke like crazy. Coughing, he made his way back toward the house and the line for the keg. His cup was empty anyway.

Tyler intercepted him before he could get to the line. "Here," he said, thrusting a full cup in his hand. "I got this for you. Where'd you go?"

"I was talking to Darcy. You know, that friend of Julie's?"

Tyler stared at him blankly. "The one who doesn't like steak bombs." Or you, Ben felt like adding. The one girl who didn't topple over and faint in your presence.

Tyler squinted, "Smallish tits, nice ass?"

"Maybe," Ben said. "You're an idiot."

"But I'm your idiot," Tyler grinned and spread his arms wide like he was going to hug him. "Come on over. Let's both be idiots. Rosetti's got some game he learned at his brother's frat at UNH." Ben grimaced. Tyler always wanted in on whatever the game was. Sometimes he wondered if it bordered on a fear of being left out. But that was ridiculous, because no one ever wanted to leave Tyler Nuson out.

Ben took a big swig out of his cup and let Tyler drag him over to the side of the yard where the soccer team was lined up in two rows facing each other. He missed most of whatever explanation was given, but the basic premise of Boat Race seemed to be that you drank your beer as fast as you could without spilling and then put your cup on your head upside down. Then the next guy in line could drink, and so on until everyone was finished. The team to chug the fastest, with the least amount of spillage, was declared the winner. People started gathering around to watch, and Ben felt that nervous feeling he got in situations where he was unsure of the rules or expectations. He took another sip but Brandon, who was standing next to him on the seniors' side, whacked him in the arm. "That's cheating, dude," he said. Then more thoughtfully, "Sorry, is that your bad hand?" Ben shook his head.

"Come on!" Brandon yelled out to their line. "Come on, seniors. We gotta own this!"

Ben looked across at the sophomores and juniors on the other team. Next year some of them would be standing over here. They were already taking on the roles that would define them in school and on the team. Jason Chiazzo, who played defense, was a leader and a junior with a huge foot—he could boot the ball halfway up the field. Matt Middlebury was a really talented midfielder who played a lot like Tyler did: fluidly and with that same innate sense of where the ball was and where it was going. Ben looked around. No one was really like him, but that wasn't surprising. Goalies were outsiders by nature. It was probably the reason he felt so at home in the role. He never would have lined up for this game as a sophomore. He probably wouldn't have even come to the party. It was always Tyler who convinced him that the team meant it when they got invited to parties with upperclassmen.

The short sharp sound of a whistle pierced his thoughts. He looked quickly around. The guys at the front of each line had started pounding their beers, and everyone else was yelling and cheering them on. There were two more guys in front of him. He put his beer on the ground like everyone else and then leaned forward, waiting for the person behind him to tap him when it was his turn. When the tap came he didn't hesitate. He opened up the back of this throat and let the liquid pour down, barely tasting it. The last gulp he swallowed hard, and then he turned the cup upside down on his head. There were no drips—just a feeling of cold dampness where the edges of the cup pressed into the knit of his hat.

Tyler was the anchor—the last man in the line. He downed his beer easily, and the seniors won it with time to spare. Everyone cheered, but one of the sophomores demanded a rematch. There was a general shout of agreement, and they all rushed the keg to refill their cups. A couple of the sophomores looked a little unsteady as they charged over. Even though drinking did make him feel more at ease, he had always been cautious, even as an underclassman. More afraid of what he might do or say if he ever got truly out of control. Tyler's cheeks were bright red, but that was just something that happened to him when he drank. He said it was an Asian thing. Soon they were all lined up again, and the whistle blew. Seniors won again but this time only by a few seconds—however, all the sophomores and even a few of the juniors had spillage down the fronts of their jackets. Some of the juniors shouted for yet another rematch, but then someone heard that Danny Fisher—a kid who seemed to have an infinite supply of weed—was smoking everyone out. The soccer team began to drift and dissipate throughout the crowd. There was cheering coming from over by the keg, and Ben could see feet in the air. He shook his head. It *was* going to be an epic night.

Suddenly his fingers began to tingle. He held up his hand and wiggled them, and they didn't even hurt. Not even a twinge. He grinned, feeling the same warmth in his stomach. Yup, he was good and buzzed. It was that perfect time of the party, when everyone was having fun and no one was hurling in the bushes yet. Then the crowd sort of parted, and Ben saw Darcy walking toward him and he was really glad to see her. All thoughts of their awkward moment just a half hour earlier had vanished from his head. He smiled as he realized she was walking toward him with a purpose. And then she was right there in front of him, and she grabbed the collar of his jacket and pulled his head down until his mouth was pressed firmly against hers. He started to say something, but when he opened his mouth to speak her tongue was there—warm, and engaging his whole mouth.

In a move that was totally unlike him, he grabbed at the back of her jeans with his good hand, sliding it down to the curve of her ass. He felt her breathe heavy and warm into his mouth—which seemed like a good response. She kept walking, pushing him backwards, until he fell back onto a piece of outdoor furniture—one of those long chaise chairs with the squishy plastic cushions. Darcy fell forward on top of him. It was cold on his back and the backs of his legs, but everything else was warm.

Her tongue kept pushing into his mouth and he pushed back, mashing his mouth into hers. One of his legs was between hers and she was grinding on his thigh. He opened his eyes just for a second to see if anyone was watching them, but no one was. He glanced over at another couple similarly intertwined on another chair. He pulled his mouth away and sucked in a breath of the cold night air. His lips were buzzing, almost burning. "Um, do you want to go somewhere?" he asked.

Darcy laughed, wiped at her mouth with the back of her hand, and said, "Why?"

"Um, I don't know. Are you cold?"

"Not anymore."

So he kept kissing her. And then she was running her hand up and down his leg and over his dick on the outside of his jeans. Each time she did he shuddered uncontrollably because it felt so freaking good and because he felt like his jeans might split open with the sheer force of his hard-on. And then they just had to stop. Because if it wasn't going to go any further right there, they had to stop before he burst a blood vessel somewhere. Darcy looked up at him quizzically. "Uh oh," she said. "You're not having fun?"

"No," Ben said. "I mean, yes. I am definitely having fun. I just, well, you know me. Can't have too much fun all at once. Just need a little break from the fun for a second."

She smiled contentedly, almost smugly, as though pleased with her ability to reduce him to a quivering mass of sexual tension. They lay there for a while watching the party build up to a crescendo—a couple girls wearing only their underwear streaked by in a cacophony of screams and giggles—and then slowly start to mellow out. Ben drank his beer and then finished Darcy's, but somehow he didn't feel that drunk. If anything, he felt like he was seeing things more clearly than he ever had before. He could do this—be with a girl. He wasn't worried about the time because his parents knew he was staying at Tyler's, and Tyler's parents didn't care when they came home. But his butt felt like it was going numb, from either the cold or lack of movement, so when Tyler came over and proposed they do a shot for the road with the rest of the seniors, he was ready to get up and move. Darcy had to find her ride home and declined to join them, but she gave his hand another little squeeze before walking a bit unsteadily toward the house.

Tyler was already walking back into the yard. Ben gave him a glance but then jogged after Darcy.

"Hey," he said when he caught up to her. "You should give me your number or something." He hoped his voice was casual even as his heart threatened to pound right out of his chest.

"Okay," she said. She took his phone and entered her number, handing it back to him so he could read that she'd entered her name as Darcy Is Hot. He couldn't believe it could be this easy. He tried not to fast-forward to the idea of actually calling her—like, when he was sober.

"Okay, I'm going to go now, before you start thinking too much about all this," she said. He smiled at her and watched her walk away. But when he turned to find Tyler had gone ahead, he found he was glad that he hadn't been watched, that this moment had been achieved on his own for once.

CHAPTER 10

He couldn't remember agreeing to let Tyler drive, but then he couldn't remember arguing with him about it either. He sank into the seat and licked his lips to see if he still tasted Darcy's lip gloss.

"Pizza rolls at my house?" Tyler said.

"Sure."

"Pepperoni? Or no, wait, I noticed you're going vegetarian?" Tyler smirked and slapped the steering wheel. "Nice moves, man!"

Ben shrugged his shoulders, but he was grinning too. "Shut up," he said easily. "And you better not be lying about those pizza rolls."

"You get her number?"

"Yeah."

"Ahhhhhh!!!!!" Tyler yelled and laid into the horn, sending a blast of stale-sounding air into the darkened neighborhood.

"Cut it out!" Ben yelled. "We're going to get pulled over. Besides, it was just a hookup."

"But you got her number," Tyler said. "She gave it to you. Which means it could happen again. She wants it to happen again. That is not *just* a hookup."

Ben didn't really want him to shut up. That was exactly the kind of information Tyler was good for. And he didn't have to ask and risk looking like an inexperienced idiot. He could count on his uninjured hand the number of times he'd hooked up with a girl in high school, and this was by far the most promising in terms of potential for a repeat performance.

When they got to Tyler's house, they were locked out.

"Shit," Tyler said as he grappled for the key that was hidden underneath the back porch. "It's not there. Jer's dead. How many times do I have to tell him to put the damn thing back after he lets himself in?" Ben jumped up and down, trying to stay warm. They threw rocks at Jeremiah's window for a few minutes, but his bed was on the other side of the room and the kid was a notoriously sound sleeper. They tried the windows, but everything was locked down for winter. "Shit," Tyler said. "I do not want to wake the professor. Can we go to your house?"

"Hell no! Not like this. My parents would give us a breathalyzer. What about the apartment?" The Manny's apartment had a separate entrance back by the pool.

"No one's been in there in forever."

"So? Maybe it's open."

Tyler shrugged, so they walked around to try it. They found a sliding glass door that had been left unlatched and walked quickly into the spare, unheated space. There was a futon frame against one wall with a navy blue comforter pulled up over a bare mattress. A large flat-screen TV sat on a dresser of drawers, and a Ferrari poster featuring girls who were definitely not race car drivers hung slightly off-center on one wall.

"It's gross in here," Tyler muttered.

Ben followed behind him through the apartment and through the den into the main part of the Nusons' house. They went into the kitchen and concocted a disgusting booze-fueled feast of previously frozen potato products and pizza rolls. When Ben was on his fifteenth pizza roll, he pushed back from the counter, clutched his stomach, and groaned.

"Let's crash," he said.

They tiptoed through the too-big house to Tyler's room, which had a second bed always made up and pretty much reserved for Ben. Ben kicked off his shoes, threw his jeans and his jacket on the floor, and crawled underneath the covers. When he woke up a few hours later, the room was flooded with a pale light. It was still night, but it was snowing lightly and the sky was quilted with thick clouds. Tyler's bed was empty. Ben found his hearing aids stuffed into his jeans pocket—he didn't even remember taking them off—and walked down the long hallway to the bathroom, took a leak, and gulped water straight from the faucet. When he came back into the hallway, he thought he heard someone crying downstairs. Sometimes their neighbor's cat made a sound that was just like a baby crying, but this was different. It wasn't a high whine. There were distinct sobs. He stood poised at the top of the stairs, wondering if he should just go back to bed, but instead he followed the sound.

He went downstairs and the sound got louder. Ben passed through the den and saw that the door to The Manny's apartment was open a crack. He walked over to it and pressed his face into the opening. He could see Tyler hunched over on the edge of the futon. His head was against his knees, and his shoulders were shaking. Suddenly he stood up, reached back, and punched the wall. Grabbing his hand, he twisted around and pressed himself against the sliding door. Then Ben saw Tyler slide down to the floor and collapse against the glass. There was a look on his face Ben didn't recognize, even after all their years of friendship. If anything, he reminded Ben of Jeremiah: softer, younger, like when they told Jeremiah to get lost or shut him out of Tyler's room so they could pre-party with some stolen booze. Scared, vulnerable, sad, hurt. Why didn't he walk in and find out what was wrong? Ben couldn't move his feet forward. He didn't feel he had the right to. He didn't know this person weeping on the floor.

Outside, the most beautiful oversized flakes of snow were slowly drifting downward, each one with its perfect arrangement of geometric patterns. Ben watched them float down so close to Tyler, where he lay. Slowly Ben backed away from the door. He walked quietly back up the stairs and got into bed. He did not sleep for a long time. Finally, close to dawn, he must have dozed off. When he woke, Tyler was passed out in the bed across the room.

CHAPTER 11

Ben didn't mention what he had seen the night before. He wasn't sure *what* he had seen. But he thought about it.

He thought about it constantly that week before States. He searched Tyler's face for anything that would tell him if Tyler knew he'd been overheard. He looked for signs that Tyler wanted to talk, but there was nothing. He thought of all the questions: *Hey, are you okay?* or *What's going on?* He told himself that Tyler was keeping him out of this part of his life for a reason—even if Ben didn't quite know what it was. And a certainty took over this idea that he was being excluded. It bordered on resentment. It was enough to keep him from reaching out.

When he wasn't thinking about Tyler, he had the beautiful purples and yellows of his right hand to distract him. That it was only a deep bruise meant he was good to play in the State final. And then there was Darcy. He had tapped several texts into his phone since Saturday night but discarded them all as being too casual or too serious. Finally he settled on:

Hi

To which she responded:

Who is this?

Ben

Hi Ben

And then, horrifically, he was stuck, completely unsure of what his next move should be.

He finally saw her on Wednesday when he went looking for Tyler in the library. Tyler didn't usually hang out in the library, but it was their day for double lunch and Ben had checked everywhere else. He walked up and down the rows of books, walking through both of the computer labs—even though Tyler had his own laptop at home—and poked his head into the conference rooms where occasionally a study group or club met. That was where he saw Darcy again. She was sitting with a group of three other girls. Bio books and lab notebooks covered the surface of the table. He gave her a little wave and then beat a hasty retreat in the other direction. What if she thought he was looking for her? What *if* she thought that?

He stopped in his tracks. Wait, he wanted to see her, didn't he? God, he felt like an idiot. He was about to give up on Tyler and turn in his lunch money for a sad school cheeseburger and some soggy tater tots when he saw Darcy coming toward him down the aisle of books.

"Hey," she said. "Again."

"Hi."

"How was the rest of your hangover? I mean, weekend."

He smiled. "Not too bad, I guess." She was leaning against the bookshelf, blocking him from exiting the row. He glanced past her at the clock on the far wall.

"Oh," she said without moving, "do you have to go somewhere?"

"Just lunch," he said, realizing too late that the correct answer was no.

"Okay," said Darcy. "I had fun on Saturday."

"Yeah," he said. "Me too. I guess there's still hope for me," he joked.

"Maybe," she said, and she moved a step closer.

"AND THEN SHE DID IT?" Tyler shouted. They were changing in the locker room for practice.

"Yes," Ben said, but he hushed Tyler with his hand. "I don't need the whole team to know."

"She seriously stuck her hand down your pants?"

"Yup."

"Were you hard?"

"No! I was, like, completely shocked."

"But then you got hard?"

Ben shrugged. He was embarrassed about the next part. Truthfully, he hadn't known what to do. So he kissed her and she kissed him back and her hand was still in his pants, her wrist pinned between his stomach and the waistband of his jeans. He couldn't really enjoy it, though, because he was sure at any second Mrs. Passarelli, the school librarian, was going to come around the corner and ask if she could help him find anything in the stacks. She was a petite woman with a sweet smile and small, dark eyes. The kind who might shush you in church but then offer you a candy from her purse afterwards.

"So you just went for it right there in the library?"

Ben shrugged again. Honestly, he hadn't really enjoyed it that much. It was too weird to mix making out with Darcy and the World Religions section of the Easton High library.

"I like this girl," Tyler said appreciatively.

"Hey, where were you anyway?" Ben asked. "I was looking for your sorry ass so we could get some lunch."

Tyler's face darkened. "Oh, you know, just chatting with Mr. Higginbotham about my feelings."

"Why?" Ben asked. But he felt a surge of relief. Maybe Tyler could tell someone else what was bothering him.

"Because apparently I'm deeply screwed in the head."

"Who said that?"

"One guess."

For a second Ben had the irrational fear that he was the one who had gone to Guidance on Tyler's behalf.

"Coach," Tyler said before Ben could let the thought go any further.

"Oh." It was the perfect opener for him to ask Tyler about Saturday night or even just express some general concern about Tyler's moodiness lately.

But before he could say anything, Tyler sneered and said, "Some people don't know when to back off already."

Ben nodded; his question froze in his throat.

"Besides," Tyler said, more lightly now, "we're going to States. He should focus on bringing home that trophy."

CHAPTER 12

They lost States. Ben played, but it wouldn't have made much of a difference if he hadn't, since the rest of the team was so completely outmatched. If anything, Ben could feel good about keeping the score to a respectable 4–1 by blocking ten direct shots on goal.

Midway through the third quarter, Tyler was red-carded and ejected from the game for punching an opposing player in the chest. Ben couldn't see the events that led up to this, but he could hear Tyler screaming to the ref that the guy had his hands all over him all game. The fans on their side were quiet as Tyler stormed to the bench and kicked over a bunch of water bottles. After that display, Coach sent him to the bus for the rest of the game.

When Ben and the rest of the team finally climbed onto the school bus after watching the state trophy be presented to Longmeadow, Ben found Tyler, his head resting against the glass, his earbuds in his ears. Ben elbowed him when he sat down. "It was a good season," he said.

Tyler nodded, removing only one of his earbuds. "Yeah," he agreed. The bus started up, the loud diesel motor coughing and then roaring heavily to life. "Hey, I think I'm going to go out with Megan tonight." He held up his phone so Ben could see the text exchange.

"Brandon said he was going to have people over to watch *Apocalypse Now* or *Full Metal Jacket* in his basement," Ben said.

Tyler nodded. "You should go."

"I might." He was somewhat surprised that Tyler would choose to hang out with Megan after losing the game. He thought about offering to do something just the two of them, but he didn't. He had a feeling his offer would have been rejected anyway, and this made him sadder than losing States.

They didn't talk the rest of the way home. When Tyler dropped him off, Ben said, "Have fun with Megan," but Tyler was already fiddling with the radio. He felt crappy throughout dinner that night. His parents made a few weak attempts to console him about the loss, which he ignored by changing the subject.

"How's Tyler taking it?" his mom finally said.

"Fine, I guess," Ben said. "He's going out with Megan." He immediately hated how this might sound to his parents: jealous and petulant.

His parents kept up the conversation at dinner, rehashing some of the better moments from the game and from his four years of playing soccer at Easton. He was only half listening; he thought about calling Shannan but felt guilty about bugging her on a Saturday night. And he didn't want *her* to feel bad about the loss. She already felt terrible about missing the game. He thought about going over for the movie at Brandon's house, but that sounded even more depressing than sitting around by himself. He considered calling Darcy, but he doubted she liked him enough to tolerate his mopey mood.

After dinner his phone rang. He smiled when the picture of

Shannan he'd taken on last summer's trip to Martha's Vineyard popped up on his phone.

"Sorry about the game," she said before he could even say hello.

"Yeah."

"You all right?"

"Yeah."

"How's Tyler?"

"I don't know. He's fine too, I guess. Why is everyone in this family always so worried about Tyler?"

"Uh, I guess because he's been your best friend since fourth grade, jerk face."

But he was afraid. Afraid that his parents or Shannan understood something about Tyler that he was missing. Afraid to confront Tyler about what he'd seen that night at his house, and afraid that he might be a terrible friend for avoiding it. If Shannan had a similar falling-out with her friends senior year, he had been clueless about it. "Shannie," he said, "do you still talk to Marcy and Eva?"

"Sure, sometimes. I mean, we text. We don't actually talk that much."

"Did you think you would? I mean, when you were a senior?"

Shannan laughed. "You know what's funny? I think we were more worked up about it when we went from middle school to high school. Everyone wrote these super-dramatic things in the middle school yearbook like, 'Don't just be a face in the hall!' But by senior year? I mean, I think we just kind of accepted that we were all moving on. I don't actually miss them as much as I thought I would. Freshman year was harder. But it's weird how quickly high school starts to feel like the past.

I mean, I think of my friends here as *my friends*, you know what I mean?"

"Yeah," he said, trying hard to imagine a new group of friends he would think of as *his friends*.

"Are you worried about next year?"

"Not really," he lied. Sometimes he wondered how much Shannan and Mom talked about him behind his back.

"Do you want help with your essays?"

"No!" he said a little too forcefully.

"You know you do actually have to apply to go to college?"

"Yeah, yeah," he said, ignoring her sarcasm.

"Tyler's going to go to BU, right?"

"Yeah."

"Why don't you apply too?"

He laughed. "I think I can probably find my own place to go to college."

"Okay, whatever. It's just a place to start looking."

Shannan had to go study, but when they got off the phone Ben pulled up the BU home page on his phone. He couldn't do it, could he? He wasn't sure which made him feel like a bigger loser: following Tyler to college or going somewhere without him.

Finally, around eight, he got tired of thinking about it, made himself a bag of microwave popcorn, and put in the first of the Lord of the Rings movies. His mom walked past the living room and stood for a minute, watching a scene of bloody carnage between the Fellowship and the Orcs who were chasing them. "Which one is this?" she asked.

"The first one."

She reached down and grabbed a handful of popcorn. "I can never tell which is which."

"That's because you never watch the whole thing," Ben said.

"I just don't understand why they all have to kill each other all the time."

"They're on a quest, Mom." He wasn't annoyed, but he liked pretending that he was. "And they're not killing each other. They're killing Orcs and cave trolls and whatever other minions of Sauron are trying to destroy them and send Middle-earth into the dark ages."

"Well, I just wish they didn't have to be so bloody about it." She sat down on the arm of the couch and winced as Gimli drove his axe through a particularly nasty-looking Orc.

After a few more minutes of battle, she shook her head and stood up to leave. But then she reached back and rubbed her fingers on the top of Ben's shoulder blade. It was one of those moments when Ben could almost feel the things she wanted to say or ask—about soccer and Tyler and his lack of plans for the future.

He kept his eyes glued on the screen. It was easier to focus on Sam and Frodo making their way toward Mordor with the ring heavy around Frodo's neck.

He watched the first two movies and thought about putting in the final part of the trilogy, but he decided to go to bed instead. It seemed like he had been asleep for only a few minutes when there was a rapping on his window. The house was a single-story ranch, a fact Tyler frequently took advantage of when he needed somewhere to crash. Ben sat up, pushed the window open, and then flopped back down. Tyler knew where he kept the sleeping bag and the extra pillow. But Tyler wasn't there to sleep. He crawled into the room and perched at the end of Ben's bed, squatting and rubbing his hands together like he was sitting in front of a campfire.

"What?" Ben said. He reached for his hearing aids next to his bed, shoving them in and turning them on.

"Let's get tattoos," Tyler said. There was something different about his face. Where he had seemed scattered and inattentive after the game, he now had an intensity in his eyes, almost hyper-focused.

"Right now?"

"No," Tyler said. "You'll be eighteen in January, and my birthday's in February. Maybe over February vacation. Senior list," he added definitively, referencing the folded piece of notebook paper they had stuffed into the glove box of the Saab last summer, a compendium of all their pre-planned senior glories.

"I thought you were going skiing over break," Ben said. But he was glad to hear that Tyler hadn't forgotten or blown off all their plans.

"Oh yeah, right. Well, some other weekend then. But that's not the point."

"No," Ben said. "Apparently that's not the point at two in the freaking morning. Go to bed."

"No, I can't stay. I'm over at Megan's house. Her parents are gone for the weekend."

Ben sat up. Tyler looked okay. He didn't appear to be drunk or on anything. He just seemed wired. "If you're at Megan's house, why are you here?"

"Couldn't sleep. I thought I'd go for a drive. That's when I remembered about the tattoos. Remember, we talked about it last summer."

"Yeah," said Ben. "I remember." He lay back down on the pillow.

"So are you in?"

"Probably."

"Cool." But Tyler didn't seem ready to go. "Ben," he said. "Uh huh."

"Is there anything about yourself that you hate?"

Ben's eyes blinked wide open. He didn't even have to think. He didn't move his hands, but he felt them like ghost limbs reaching toward his ears. "Uh huh," he said.

"Is there anything about me that you hate?"

Ben didn't have to think about this one either. "Nope."

"Okay," Tyler said. He waited a moment and then lifted the latch on the window and was gone. It was only after Tyler left that Ben realized he had not returned the questions.

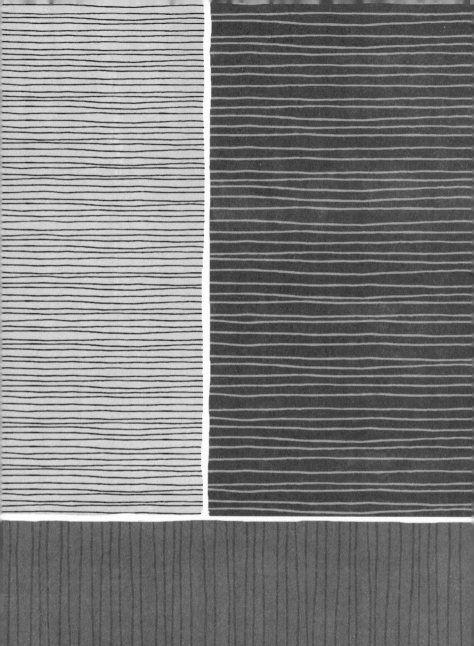

WINTER

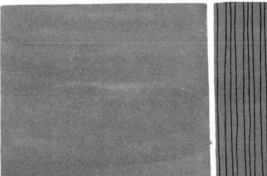
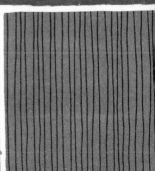

CHAPTER 13

Tyler was in Florida over Thanksgiving, and he came back to school glowing from his week on the beach—though he complained it was unbelievably boring despite screwing around with the granddaughter of one of his grandmother's bridge buddies. They texted about hanging out, but every time Ben suggested doing something, Tyler seemed to be busy. Ben knew Tyler's family didn't really do anything together, and he'd never had holiday commitments before.

Tyler seemed to be spending a lot of time at Megan's, but when Ben saw them in school together, Megan was forever on her phone and Tyler seemed okay with just standing near her while engaging his public. Finally, when Ben asked him about seeing the Hobbit movie on Saturday—something he figured was a definite—Tyler mumbled an excuse about Megan's family's Christmas party. Ben tried not to look surprised.

"She asked me a while ago," he said without meeting Ben's eyes.

"So are you going to meet her parents and everything?"

"Yeah," Tyler said. "I mean, I already have. They're not so bad. For parents." It was weird; Tyler had never hung out with the family of any girl he had dated in the past—not, like, intentionally anyway. He thought about seeing if Brandon Rosetti or one of the other guys from the team wanted to go, but they wouldn't get *The Hobbit* the way Tyler did. Waiting two weeks for Shannan to get home didn't feel like an option. So that was how he decided to ask Darcy on a date. He figured she probably didn't hate him, because being mauled by someone at a party and then being attacked by them in the library were pretty good signs that you weren't hated.

It seemed like a simple enough idea when he came up with it, but when he made a point of stopping near where she and some of her friends had their lockers, his heart picked up pace and his hands got sweaty. She seemed happy to see him and walked away from her friends when he asked her if she had a second to talk. When he asked her if she wanted to see *The Hobbit* with him that weekend, she seemed a little surprised but agreeable enough. He told her he could pick her up around 6:30. He breezed over his obsession with Peter Jackson and the other Tolkien movies and just hoped she wasn't one of those girls who liked to talk during a movie.

But when Saturday came around and he went online to get tickets, he kicked himself because both the seven and nine o'clock showings were sold out. He looked at the list of other movies, but there was nothing he wanted to see. Then, on a whim, he checked for earlier times and, without calling Darcy, paid for two tickets to the four-thirty showing. Luckily, when he called her to change plans, she didn't seem to care about the earlier showtime. He told his parents he was going to the movies when he asked for the car. They probably assumed he was going with Tyler, and he didn't volunteer that it was an actual girl he was taking along. This omission helped him ignore the feeling in his stomach that reminded him of a dying fish flopping around, gasping for air.

When he drove up to Darcy's house, she scooted out the front door before he could even stop the car, skittering down the front path but not falling on the icy sheen that coated the bricks. "I would have come up to get you," he said once she was sitting in the passenger seat. He caught a whiff of fruity perfume or maybe shampoo when she reached back for her seat belt and tossed her hair.

"No way. My grandparents are just sitting around looking for someone or something to criticize. My mom's hiding out in the kitchen—I think this is like the fourth batch of cookies she's made today—and my little brothers are in the basement playing video games. There's only so long I could hang out in my room pretending to do homework. I'm just glad no one's noticed that it's Saturday."

"Wow," Ben said. "How long are they here?"

"Until New Year's," Darcy said darkly.

"I hope you have a lot of homework."

"I think I'm going to flunk a test just so I can do some make-up work over the break."

"That's dedication."

"Yeah, right," Darcy said. She smiled at him and Ben noticed that she had a dusting of light purple eye shadow and mascara on. It seemed like a good sign.

She looked up, and for a moment he was embarrassed, thinking she could read his mind. But instead she said, "It's so nice to go out with someone who can drive. I can't even tell you how tired I am of begging my parents to take me places— or someone's douche-bag older brother. And I'm young for my grade, so I'm not going to have my license for forever."

"How young?" he asked.

"Don't worry," Darcy said. "I'm legal." Then she whacked his thigh. "Kidding, Ben, kidding! Speaking of age, though, do you always take girls out for afternoon movies? I mean, will we still make it for the early bird special at IHOP afterwards?"

"Ha, ha," Ben said. "I told you the other showings were sold out."

"Right, so, *The Hobbit.* Are they like Smurfs?"

"No," Ben said, "nothing like Smurfs." He sighed and then attempted to give Darcy a comprehensive overview of the history of Middle-earth. She was a good enough sport about it, asking clarifying questions about Elves and Wizards, if occasionally getting some things from Harry Potter mixed up with Tolkien. And it kept Ben from feeling that nervous feeling he got when he had to keep up conversation with, well, anyone besides Tyler, really.

The Hobbit movie was good, and Darcy seemed to like it enough. They ate popcorn and Sour Patch Kids and shared an enormous soda with two straws. Darcy didn't exactly react like his mom did to the violence, but she did jump every time one of the Orcs got disemboweled or a Warg came jumping out from behind a boulder. She even grabbed his hand once when it was resting on their shared armrest. At the end of the movie, Ben felt pretty good about things. It was only 7:30, and Darcy suggested they walk around the mall.

"So you didn't hate it?" he asked as they wandered past a Starbucks and a women's clothing store that looked like somewhere his mom or his teachers probably shopped.

"No, it was cute," Darcy said. "The Hobbits were cute," she clarified. "Some of the dwarves were kind of gross though.

I still don't really understand what they were trying to do. And it seemed like it kind of ended without them doing anything."

"Well, it's a trilogy, remember," Ben said.

"Oh, so there's more?"

"Yeah, there's two more," Ben said. "One plus two equals a trilogy."

"Thanks, Ben," she said sarcastically. "I'm sure something will happen in the next one," she added. "Ooh, can we go in there?" she pointed at the neon sign for Hot Closet.

"Sure, I guess." He walked in uneasily. Shannan always made fun of this store and the girls who went into it. Shannan wasn't a prude. She just thought the silver tank tops and hot pink frayed denim shorts they sold were kind of funny. She always said she could cut up her own pants if she wanted her ass to hang out the back of them.

He walked behind Darcy as she flipped the tags over on all the clothes, offering some appreciative oohs and ahhs at a black off-the-shoulder sweatshirt with the word "Hottie" written on it in neon green cursive. Then she found a bright blue thing that he thought was some kind of a scarf before he realized it was a skirt. "Do you mind if I try this on?" she said.

"No," he said, while thinking, *not if it means we're closer to getting out of here.* The dressing rooms were in the back of the store: a series of small closets with brightly colored, striped fabric covers for doors. It looked like they were going for kind of a beach vacation theme. He stood nervously outside, hoping that no one would think he was some kind of pervert. Then he heard Darcy whisper.

"Ben, come tell me what you think?"

"Are you coming out?"

"No way," she said and laughed. "Just stick your head in."

He glanced around once, but there were only two sales ladies, and they were in the front of the store putting together what looked like the most glitter-intensive holiday display ever. He took a step forward and peeked behind the curtain. The skirt did look good, but he only had a second to take it in before he realized that was all Darcy was wearing. She had one arm across her chest, covering her boobs, and then she was bare— all the way bare except for the tiny blue skirt. "Jesus," he said. And then she pulled him into the dressing room with her and pushed him down onto the white bench that was partially covered with cast-off clothes.

She laughed and straddled him, letting her hand fall away and her soft breasts press into his chest. Her mouth was on his mouth immediately, and he tried to return the intensity of her kiss but found it was a little too intense. He understood now why his eighth grade health teacher called it "sucking face." It felt somewhere between sexy and a vacuum cleaner. He put his hands on her thighs, but they were just so bare that he settled for her back just above the waistband of the tiny blue skirt. She raked her hands through his hair, avoiding the backs of his ears, and moved onto the hair at the back of his neck. She pulled there as she dove again and again toward the back of his throat. Her hand, firmly on the back of his neck, pointed his head upwards. When he looked up, he saw the tiny round camera perched just on top of the paperboard walls separating them from the next room. He jerked his head away suddenly.

"This is freaking you out," Darcy said.

"Um, yeah," he said. He pointed up toward the camera.

"Oh, that?" Darcy rolled her eyes. "There's no one watching. It's just like a deterrent or whatever." Her voice dropped to a whisper. "I've taken stuff from here like a million times without getting caught. I bet it's not even on."

Ben squinted, taking in this new piece of information. "Taken stuff, like stealing?"

"I mean, not a lot of stuff. But, you know, just like little things here and there. Oh great, now you're even more freaked out."

"No," Ben lied weakly. "I just. I think we should get out of here."

Darcy shrugged. "Okay," she said. "What do you think of the skirt?"

Ben grinned. "I think you could get arrested in it. But I like it."

"Sweet, me too." Then, as he watched, she pulled her jeans up right over the skirt and zipped them. He stepped out of the dressing room to avoid being called an accomplice and then lagged behind a few feet as Darcy sashayed brazenly out of the store, holding his breath as she passed through the security system.

It was only 8:30 when they got back in the car. Ben stared at the digital display as he maneuvered his way out of the mall parking lot. He didn't want to be rude, but he didn't know if the date was exactly over. "Do you want to hang out at my house for a while?" he offered.

"I should probably get back," Darcy said.

Ben nodded and then thought all the way back to Darcy's house about how he should take this information, wondering if he'd blown it somehow and trying to decide if he really cared. When he pulled up in front, she released her seat belt before the car had even stopped. "The old people," she said. "They're probably watching."

"Sure," he said. "Okay."

"Well, that was fun," Darcy said as she opened the door. "Thanks for the date, Ben." There was something in her tone he couldn't quite place. It wasn't sarcastic. More like amused. Like she was reciting lines rather than saying what she actually thought.

"Yeah," he said, for lack of anything better. "See you Monday."

She smiled and shut the door, and he wondered for a second if he should have offered to call her. But somehow he didn't think so. As soon as he pulled around the corner, he let out a big sigh, a whole bunch of tension-filled air he hadn't even known he was hanging on to. What was wrong with him? Darcy was cute, and he liked her enough, so far. It wasn't like he didn't respond to her when she kissed him. But it wasn't the same as that night at the party. The things that had seemed hot after a couple beers by the bonfire just seemed a little awkward at the mall or in the library. He wondered if it would be different if they were hanging out in his living room—somewhere a little more normal. He tried to imagine what they would talk about, but he got stuck.

At least the Hobbit movie was good. When he pulled into his driveway, he took out his phone to tell Tyler about the weird make-out session in the dressing room, but then he remembered Tyler was at Megan's family's Christmas party. He texted him:

Call me later—movies with library veggie girl. He thought Tyler might not remember who Darcy was.

He was surprised when his phone lit up almost immediately after he hit Send. "Dude, I had to call you," Tyler said, forgoing a more traditional greeting. "What did that chick do in the movie theater?"

Tyler laughed as Ben recounted the dressing room episode, and Ben found as he told it that it seemed more okay and less weird to him. "Where are you, anyway? I thought you were at the party."

"Yeah, I'm hiding out in Megan's brother's room for a few. Just killing some time until I can take off. It's just a bunch of her parents' friends and whatever."

"Where's Megan?"

"I don't know. Downstairs somewhere."

"Is she going to be pissed that you disappeared?"

There was a pause. "I don't know. Probably not. Why do you care?" Suddenly there was that cold hostility again.

"I don't really. Whatever." Ben tried to turn the conversation back to lightness. *Why do you hang out with this girl,* was what he wanted to know. *Why do you, when you don't seem to like her? Do you even like anyone anymore?* "Later, I guess," he said when the silence had stretched on for another awkward pause that felt like a year.

"Yeah, later," Tyler said, and the phone went silent. Ben sat in the car staring at the phone, which faded to black after a few minutes. His head was spinning like he'd just gotten off one of those centrifugal force rides that sticks you to the wall and drops the floor from under you. Why did this thing with Megan bother him so much? Why did he compare every relationship he had to his friendship with Tyler? Why was he afraid of not liking Darcy? Thinking of Darcy reminded him that apparently he was the kind of guy who thought about things too much. He resolved to be different—*but like what?* His brain practically shouted at him. *More shallow? Like Tyler?* All he had were questions and the gnawing feeling that somehow all this was related to his complete indecision and lack of motivation around life after high school.

Finally he bit the bullet and went inside. His mom was sitting at the kitchen table. She looked at him and cocked her head to the side. "Are you feeling all right?" she asked.

"Yeah, why?"

"I don't know; you look a little pale."

"It's winter, Mom, in New England. We're all a little pale."

"Okay, sorry. You're fine. How was the movie?"

"It was good." He hung his coat on the hook and went to root around in the fridge for something snackish.

"Did Tyler like it?"

He sighed. "I went with Darcy, this girl from school." He kept his face in the fridge so he didn't have to register his mother's look of surprise.

"Was it a date? This girl you went with?"

"Um, sort of. I guess so."

"Well, that's great!"

Ben shook his head in the refrigerator. Didn't parents know how to turn off the super-obvious enthusiasm? He peeked up over the egg tray. Mom was looking sheepish. "It was okay, Mom. It was an okay sort of date." He didn't have any desire to share details about the shopping portion of the date. He pulled a piece of tinfoil-wrapped pizza out of the fridge, unwrapped it, and took a bite.

His mother grimaced. "Don't you want to heat that up?"

"Nope," Ben said, his mouth already full of crust and cold cheese. He walked into the den and flopped down on the couch, calculating the days until Shannan was home again, and then wasted a couple hours playing Call of Duty with Brandon Rosetti.

When he went to bed, his head felt pinched as though he were wearing a too-small fitted hat, and he tried not to think about his mother's comment about how he looked like crap. And he found, as he tossed around beneath his sheets and comforter, that he was both too hot and chilled at the same time.

CHAPTER 14

As soon as Ben woke up, he knew something was wrong. First of all, it was a Sunday morning and his body had decided to wake him at five in the morning. Second, he was drenched, absolutely drenched, in sweat. His back and chest and even the insides of his legs were soaked and slippery. He rolled out of bed and staggered to the bathroom, where he pulled off his boxers and T-shirt and mopped himself off with a hand towel. He fumbled around in the medicine cabinet, wiping his palms off twice before getting the child safety lock off the container of ibuprofen. He swallowed two pills with a handful of water before staggering back down the hall and crashing into his bed.

He woke up hours later to his mother's cool hand on his shoulder. "Ben?" He could hear her, but her voice was fuzzy, distant. He clawed around on the nightstand for his hearing aids. He felt his mom place them in his hand. He slipped them in, but when he tried to open his eyes the world felt too bright to look at. He pulled the covers up over his head.

"Too early," he groaned.

"It's three in the afternoon, Ben. Did you go back out last night? I thought I heard you go to bed, but Dad and I went out to Home Depot this morning and you were still out cold."

"No, I didn't go out," he said. "I think maybe I'm sick."

Mom's cool hand snaked underneath the covers and found his forehead. Her hand was so blissfully cool. He closed his eyes and tried to will himself to become the hand, to live in the place where flesh was cool and comfortable. His own felt stretched and stiff and sore. "Jesus! Dan," his mom yelled, "get the thermometer!"

A few seconds later he heard the door open again. "What's going on, buddy?"

"It's just a fever, Dad. I took some ibuprofen or something. I just need to sleep some more and then I'll be fine." But he wasn't even convincing himself and was a tiny bit relieved to feel his mother push the rubber core of the digital thermometer to his temple. Both his parents stood over him. He could feel their anticipation like he imagined he could feel the digital pulse of the thermometer measuring the speed at which the atoms of his skin were moving and translating that into a numerical measurement of heat. It beeped.

"104," his mom said. "When did you take the ibuprofen?"

"I don't know," Ben said. "Early." Mom pressed a few more pills into his hand, which he downed with a glass of the most incredibly cool and delicious water.

"Can you eat anything?" she asked.

He shook his head. "I just want to sleep." As he drifted back into slumber, he could feel the worried whispers of his parents outside the door. He slept through the rest of the day and most of Monday.

Monday afternoon, his mom bundled him into his track pants and his soccer sweatshirt and hustled him out to a prewarmed car. He slept most of the way to the doctor's office. The doctor's waiting room was so bright, and the primary colors and burbling fish tank seemed like instruments of torture rather than cute throwbacks to his childhood. "How old do you have to be before you can get a real doctor?" he grumbled in the waiting room.

When the nurse called his name, he stood and shot a backwards glance at his mother when she tried to follow him. "I got this," he said.

"Well, just make sure he doesn't tell you it's a cold virus. I really don't think it's a cold."

"Thanks, Mom."

Dr. Ellsworth's exam was quick and painless. At one point, Ben almost nodded off as the doctor listened to his chest and felt his lymph nodes. "It could be a virus, Ben," he said. "But we'll have you do the blood draw for mono just to be sure. There's a lot of nasty stuff going around right now."

"My mom made me come in."

Dr. Ellsworth smiled. "That's pretty common."

The test came back positive for mono, and after briefly researching the topic online, Ben realized he was completely screwed. He had to get extensions on all of his semester finals, and he was bedbound for a week and housebound for another.

During that first week, whole days seemed to pass in a blink and then two hours might crawl by in infinitesimal increments—the approximate length of commercials on the low-budget cable channels. Ben floated in and out of consciousness, getting so bored with TV that he tried to read, but he found it too draining and the words began to undulate on the pages. On one semi-lucid afternoon, Tyler stopped by and sat at the end of his bed.

"Your mom said as long as we don't make out I can't get it," he joked.

"I'm not really in the mood anyway," Ben said. He lay there while Tyler told him about some random gossip at school. Apparently one of the Driver's Ed teachers was arrested for peeping in windows.

"Perv," Ben said.

"Yeah," Tyler agreed.

"What have you been up to?"

Tyler shrugged. He looked almost self-conscious. "Not much. Hanging out with Megan a lot, I guess."

"Huh," Ben said. He watched the afternoon light sparkle on the wall above his bed. He was pretty sure he was hallucinating at least part of it. "Do you love her?" He wasn't even sure the words had come from his mouth. It seemed he could see them in the air like the specks of light against his wall.

Tyler made a choking sound and then gave a small, constrained laugh. "No," he said. "I don't think so."

"Oh," Ben said. "How do you know?" He felt like the words were just floating out of his mouth on their own.

"I don't know. I don't feel that way about her. Not like—"

Tyler paused. Ben looked at Tyler, taking in without discomfort how uncomfortable Tyler looked.

"Not like Jer, or you." He was quiet for a minute. "That's weird, right? Those are the only examples I can think of."

"Not weird," Ben said. He shook his head and closed his eyes against the spinning sensation it produced.

"I can't ever imagine her knowing me like you do. Is that gay?"

Ben shrugged. He wasn't really sure what Tyler was so afraid of. What did he really have to worry about? The more anyone got to know Tyler Nuson, the more they loved him. "It's okay to have flaws," he said, thinking of his hearing. He felt a bit angry being the one to explain this to Tyler, who seemed to have none of his own. But Tyler didn't pick up on his tone. There was more Ben wanted to say. More he thought he probably should say if he were a really good friend. But he was so tired. He let his eyes flutter shut. When he opened them again, it was dusk and Tyler was gone.

CHAPTER 15

Even small excursions to the Rite Aid—or on one daring night, pizza with his family—left him completely drained. Christmas came and went in the same fashion. The only difference was that Shannan was home and humored him by playing a lot of Risk and Stratego. Tyler was away, but they texted back and forth about the ski conditions and whatever else was going on where he was, since Ben didn't have much to report. They said nothing about Megan, and Ben even began to wonder if he had imagined most of their last strange conversation. Finally, a week into the new semester, he started getting some energy back.

He still had finals to make up and two new second semester electives that he hadn't even been to yet. One was Tennis, a gym class reserved for juniors and seniors. No big deal there; he already knew how to play. The other was Popular Culture Since the 1960s, a history elective known as a blow-off. The class was supposed to cover the time period from the 1960s to the present, but each year the students reported that they never seemed to get much past the Vietnam War. The teacher, Mr. Kapstein, routinely brought his guitar to class to play folk songs reminiscent of the period. He liked to punctuate his lectures with little bits of The Beatles or Bob Dylan.

The class was famous for the television assignment: a twenty-four hour period in which the students were required to watch TV on one of the major networks without changing the channel or turning it off. They were required to log every show and every commercial. It was legend around Easton. But it was another week before he could make it to that class, since it was eighth period, the very end of his day. He was exhausted and had contemplated calling home for a ride, but he decided to tough it out to at least make an appearance and see what he had missed.

Kapstein's room was in a weird location, at the end of the foreign language hallway. Ben eyed the posters of the Spanish countryside and French cheese as he dragged himself along, dreaming about a siesta in a sun-warmed hammock. Darcy came out of a classroom on the left, a pile of books pressed against her chest. He felt somewhat safer seeing that her hands were full. She smiled and gave him a little finger-wave without shifting her books around too much. They were moving in opposite directions, which made things less awkward, but he wondered if she was blowing him off and if he even cared.

Exhausted by the day, he collapsed into a seat at the back of Kapstein's class. He thought for a minute that he was early, because everyone was out of their seat and milling around. Slowly he realized they were partnering up and then sitting down together. And when everyone was in place, there was only one person standing in the room without a partner. And she had blue hair. It was awkward as hell, but the girl didn't seem to look uncomfortable. She stood with one knee bent, her weight back on her hips and her hands at her sides. *Hips* was really a misnomer. She was built like a skinny boy—and were those actually boys' jeans she was wearing? The rest of her clothes— the red-and-black checked shirt and the black suede vest, the dark blue combat boots, and that backwards trucker hat—made her look like the lead singer of an indie band—either that or someone in line at a soup kitchen.

"Okay," Kapstein called out. "Who doesn't have a partner?"

The girl lifted her hand halfway; her elbow still locked in at her waist. She didn't even turn around. "Well," Kapstein said hesitantly. Teachers had to hate this part—pairing up the losers with each other. "Hey!" he said excitedly, his eyes lighting on Ben. "You must be Ben." Ben nodded. "Welcome to the way-back machine!" Ben just stared at him. His bushy eyebrows were speckled with gray hair and seemed to be dancing up and down on his forehead. "So, this is great," he said, clapping his hands too loudly. "You two can work together, and then everyone has someone."

Then Kapstein shot back to his desk and began to type furiously on his computer, leaving the two of them to sort out the pairing of the less-than-desirables. The girl took two steps toward Ben and flung herself down into the desk in front of him. She sat facing sideways and said, "What's up, freak?"

Ben was stunned. So he hadn't imagined it. She wasn't even trying to hide it. She had just said it to his face. His cheeks burned with embarrassment, or maybe it was the fever kicking back up. "What the hell is wrong with you?" he said.

"Ah, a lot of things. Too many to list, probably."

"Why do you keep calling me that?" he hissed.

"I dunno," she said. She turned and looked him straight on. She had a light spattering of brown freckles on her forehead and cheeks. Her eyes were a dark green or hazel color and almond-shaped. "Why? You don't think you're a freak?" Before he could answer, she added, "I think we're all freaks."

Ben shook his head and got up from his chair. He walked

purposefully to the front of the room and stood in front of Kapstein's L-shaped desk until the teacher swiveled to face him. "Is there anyone else I can be partners with?" Ben asked.

Kapstein sighed. "It's really a two-person project. I used to have kids do it in groups, but there was too much cheating. People seemed to miss out on the point of the project that way. What's wrong with . . . ?" He paused, searching the class roster for a name. "Her?"

Ben set his jaw. "I just don't think it's going to work out."

"Well, you haven't really given it a try." Kapstein looked at him. Ben stared back. They both knew what was what. Kapstein turned back to his computer, and Ben stalked back to his desk. It seemed he was stuck with her.

"Tough luck, huh?" the girl said when he sat back down.

"Whatever." He was still trying to think of a way out of this situation. The idea of bringing this girl to his house for an entire day—or worse, spending a whole day at whatever weird hipster world she inhabited—was so beyond him at that point.

He sighed. "I guess I should get your number or something." He pulled out his phone. "What's your name?"

"Ilona."

"Ilana?"

"Nope, wrong again, jockstrap."

He put the phone down. "Have I done something to piss you off?" he asked. "Like in a previous life? Did I run over your cat?"

"I hate cats," Ilona said. "So if you ran over one of the six or seven that live in my house, I would probably make you a cake. But 'Thanks for running over my cat' is hard to write with frosting, so it would probably just say 'Thanks.'"

"If you hate cats, why do you have six or seven of them?"

"Because Judy likes cats."

"Who's Judy?"

"She is the witch-in-residence, a Satan-worshipping, utter nutcase. Also, though not definitively proven with DNA evidence, known as my mother."

Ben shook his head. He had no response. "How do you spell it?"

"Judy?"

"No, *your* name. Whatever it is."

"Ah-lone-ah," she sounded out and then fed him the letters. "Yup, get it out. Say it. Ilona—a loner."

"I wasn't going to say that," Ben said, although he had thought it.

"Coward."

He shook his head and tapped her number into his phone. "Do you want mine?"

"Nah, I don't have a phone."

"Seriously? So what's this number?"

"Home phone. But I make an effort to be home as infrequently as possible, so we should probably just agree on a date now."

"Anytime in the next two weeks, right?"

Ilona nodded.

"How about next Friday, then?" Ben said, figuring that would give him enough time to find a way out of the project, or the whole class if necessary.

"Whatever, fine with me." She seemed annoyed, like she knew what his game was.

Ben made it through about ten more minutes of class before signing himself out to the nurse's office to call his dad and go home. Once home, he barely kicked his shoes off before falling asleep facedown in his bed.

When he woke up, the sky was dark and his phone was buzzing. It was Tyler. He felt a surge of annoyance; he'd hardly heard from him, and now, when he was completely depleted, now Tyler wanted to talk?

"Hey," Tyler said.

"Hey," Ben said back.

"I've been texting you."

"I was asleep."

"You want to see the Hobbit movie with me?"

"Tonight?"

"Yeah."

Ben tried to gauge his own level of exhaustion and annoyance. Being sick, Tyler's weirdness—it all seemed to blend together in a way that made it difficult for him to know how he felt. He wondered whether he'd even be able to make it past the front door without his mom giving him the full-scale inquisition about his health. But wait, it was her chorus night, and she wouldn't be back until nine.

"Yeah, all right. I already saw it with Darcy."

"Oh," Tyler said.

"But I'll see it again, I guess." He wanted his voice to sound cool and indifferent, though it was not at all how he felt. The less time he spent with Tyler, the more he felt the known parts of the friendship slipping away from him.

"Cool. Pick you up in twenty."

His dad seemed nervous about letting him go out, but Ben convinced him that he wasn't even sick anymore, just tired, and he let him go without too much hassle.

As soon as Ben slid into the leather seat of the Saab, things felt right and good again. He was back. The seat heaters were just starting to kick on, so only the very center of his seat, right below his butt, was warm. Tyler, as usual, was fiddling with the radio. "Hey," he said without looking up. "You're better, huh?" He held out his hand at an angle. Ben grabbed it in an odd sort of handshake hug.

"Mostly," he said.

Tyler pulled away from the curb, drumming his fingers on the steering wheel without connection to any particular song. At the end of the street, he turned right instead of left toward the movie theater.

"Gas?" Ben asked.

"What? No." There was a pause. "Megan's coming. I gotta pick her up."

Was Tyler actually going to pretend this was normal? They never hung out with girls, even the ones Tyler was sort of or not really dating. Suddenly the fatigue of the day seemed to have him by the shoulders, rocking him gently, asking him what the hell he was thinking, leaving the house at this hour. Was he overreacting? "So you guys are still hanging out a lot?" he tried to ask casually.

Why the hell couldn't he ask what he wanted to ask? Why couldn't he just say, why the hell is she coming? Ben remembered that Danny Fisher, in sixth grade, before he'd reworked himself into a well-liked weed supplier, had been a dirty kid—the kind that even the other kids could tell was being neglected. He always wore the same gray sweatpants and SpongeBob T-shirt to school. Danny was assigned to work with Roz Peterson on a pairs project—a moon-faced girl who chewed the ends of her hair into wet, pointy spikes. After receiving the assignment, he stood up in front of the whole class and said, "Why the fuck do I have to work with her?" It was the one stand-out memory of sixth grade. Ben remembered being shocked by

Danny's complete disregard for all norms and expectations, but mostly he was just in awe of Danny for standing up and saying exactly what he thought. He wished he could do that now.

"I guess so," Tyler said. He seemed nervous, agitated.

"I've barely seen you since soccer ended." Immediately Ben regretted the way he sounded, whiny and needy.

"I'm glad it's over," Tyler said. "And I'm sick of everyone asking me about it. It's so freakin' gay. Life goes on, you know. Soccer's over. Find something else to care about."

"Whoa," Ben said, "aren't you still going to play club in the spring?"

Tyler looked at him oddly. "Of course," he said, and Ben thought perhaps he'd missed the point entirely.

They stopped in front of a large brick colonial house with a winding pathway up to a large front door, framed by columns and decorated with tasteful white lights and pine garlands. Megan came out the front door as soon as they pulled up. Ben considered moving to the backseat but didn't. Megan was on her phone. She looked up briefly when she got in the backseat and then immediately went back to it. Tyler barely even greeted her. Ben didn't understand. This girl seemed so indifferent. Or maybe she didn't say anything and that was the whole point? Maybe that was exactly why Tyler had chosen her.

The car was silent all the way to the movies except for the light tapping of Megan's texting. Finally Tyler adjusted the radio to one of his favorite hip-hop stations. Ben kept expecting her to explain what was so important, some girl crisis or something. When they pulled into a parking spot at the Cinemagic, Megan put her phone away and they walked in together. Tyler sat in the middle, and if Ben didn't lean too far forward, he could easily pretend it was just the two of them. But before the movie started, he deliberately leaned forward and asked Megan how her Christmas break had been. So at least Tyler couldn't say later that *he* had been the one being rude.

"Oh," she said as if this were a difficult or surprising question. "It was okay. Kind of boring though, you know." Ben nodded. But there was something weird about her response. It seemed like she was talking a bit too loudly.

"Did you go away or anything?" he asked, not because he cared but because he wanted to test his hypothesis.

"No," she said. Yup, definitely too loud. "No, I didn't," she reiterated, and this time he noticed that she was over-mouthing her words. Did Tyler notice? He was staring at the screen where a stupid trivia question about Steve Carell was flashing while dancing bags of popcorn wiggled in the background. Megan pulled out her phone again, and Ben leaned back. Maybe he was being paranoid. But he was paranoid for good reason. This girl had barely spoken to him, and she'd already hit two of his top three most annoying habits:

1. Speaking too loudly
2. Over-mouthing your words
3. Making excessive eye contact

At least he didn't have to worry about number three. The only thing Megan seemed interested in making eye contact with was her phone.

After the movie, he ducked into the bathroom to take a piss. When he came out, Megan and Tyler were having an animated discussion about something. Tyler even pushed her playfully, but when he approached the conversation dropped.

"What's so funny?" he asked.

"I don't like Orcs," Megan said and rolled her eyes.

Ben shrugged. "No one likes Orcs."

"See?" Megan said. "They're so nasty and their teeth are, like, all black and disgusting."

"Yeah," Tyler interrupted. "Dental care in Middle-earth was really subpar."

Megan whacked him with, of course, her phone. "Shut up! I'm serious. And why does he have to make the battle scenes so bloody and loud? All the gushing and chopping." She looked at Ben. "You're lucky that—" And then she stopped. "I mean, maybe . . ." Her voice trailed off.

Ben stared at her. He braced himself, waiting for the explosion from Tyler in his defense. This girl was history. But Tyler's face gave nothing away, no emotion at all.

"Let's get out of here," Tyler said.

Ben waited for Tyler to say something on the ride home, something that would clear the sour burning feeling from the back of his throat, but Tyler was quiet. And then Tyler took Ben home first. That was the final humiliation. The fact that his house was, in fact, slightly closer to the movie theater meant nothing. He got out of the car and shut the door maybe a hair too close to a slam.

He went straight to his room and sat down in the darkness. He tried to put together what was making him feel so crappy. It wasn't just Megan. It was all the Megans and Ilonas and Darcys of the world: the people who seemed so determined to call him out when all he wanted to do was quietly blend in. Was it so wrong not to want to be an individual all the time? And the one person who always made him feel part of things, who put him at ease and made him feel perfectly accepted—that person seemed lost to him and, truthfully, had been for some time.

CHAPTER 16

"Absolutely not," was Mrs. Watson's response when Ben went to see her about dropping Kapstein's class. The college counselor was glaring at him over the top of his transcript. "You're fine on credits, but you don't have any other electives. And let's not pretend that Tennis counts for anything. Colleges are going to look at this and wonder about someone who drops a class during senior year." He must have looked especially dejected, because she softened her tone slightly. "Is this a personal thing with Mr. Kapstein? Most kids love his class."

"No, it's not that."

"Well, do you think you can tough it out for the semester?"

"Yeah, probably." Not that he had much choice.

She stared down at his transcript for a minute, looking puzzled. "Ben, when was the last time we checked in about your applications?"

"I don't know."

"Well, I don't have a list of your schools. Where are you applying?"

"I don't know. UMass, I guess."

"Ben," Mrs. Watson said, "have you even started getting

recommendations or filling out the application? The deadlines are coming up."

"I know, I know," he said. "But I don't think I'm applying early decision or action or whatever."

Mrs. Watson gave him a puzzled look. "Ben, those deadlines were several weeks ago. You're looking at regular admissions at this point. Some of them are as early as next week."

"Oh."

"Would you like me to schedule a meeting with your parents?" It did not sound like a question.

"No!" he said too forcefully. "I mean, why?"

"It might be helpful to get your college ball rolling. I don't want to see you limit yourself here." The idea of his future as a rolling ball was amusing. His future, to him, seemed more like a giant concrete block of inertia.

"Look, I'm going to apply to UMass and probably a couple other ones too." He got up. Meeting over. He hadn't even gotten out of Kapstein's class.

Mrs. Watson was still wearing her concerned face. "Okay, well, I'm going to check in with you next week and find out how it's going."

"Okay," he said and ducked out of the office. He briefly considered going to see Abby Simmons about Kapstein but then reconsidered. However awful working with Ilona turned out to be, it wasn't worth letting Abby Simmons in on any of the details of his personal life. He tried to forget about it until the next day when Ilona tracked him down in the hallway.

"Hey, freakshow!" He ignored her even though he could tell she was walking fast to catch up to him. He was on the way to gym and was almost to the boys' locker room, but this time she shouted it so that he had to turn around.

"What do you want?"

"Did you complain about me to guidance?"

"No," he said. It was mostly true.

"Huh, well, maybe it was Kapstein then. Because this morning in the middle of my period two class, I got yanked out to guidance. Mrs. Watson said Kapstein thought you and I might be having some kind of an issue." Ben tried to control the heat that was rising from his chest. How much worse could this get? "She asked if I was your girlfriend." Ben couldn't control the snort of disbelief that rocketed out of his nose and mouth. "Yeah," Ilona drew out the word. "I thought it was funny too." She tugged the collar of her flannel shirt up over her collarbone and shoulders. It looked like she was wearing a black tank top underneath instead of a bra. "So we're cool for next Friday?"

"I guess so."

"Don't act too thrilled."

He took a deep breath. "Look, will you stop calling me that?"

"What? Freakshow?"

"Yeah, freak, freakshow, jockstrap, whatever. Just stop with the weird names, okay. I don't care what you call your friends, but it's not cool with me."

"All right." She held her hands up like she was putting down a weapon. "Sorry," she added more quietly.

He exhaled loudly, the relief of saying something directly. But the force of his breath caused a coughing fit so strong that he had to throw down his backpack and run for the nearest water fountain.

"Wow," she said. "You're still really sick!"

"Thanks for noticing." She was standing over him, and he couldn't figure out why she didn't just walk away.

"So you're really going to gym like that?"

He swallowed a mouthful of water, stood up, and nodded. "I guess so."

"Dude, just skip it. I'm sure you could get someone to write you a note. Actually, screw that. Just go down there looking like that, and tell them you're too sick to play. Or you could do what I do, and just tell them you have cramps." She grabbed at her middle and the shiny blue leather belt slung around her jeans. "But I don't think that would work for you." She started tapping her foot against the tile.

He didn't say anything, just waited for her to leave. He gave a tired glance at the locker room. It was the last place he wanted to be right now.

"So, do you want to go or not?" she said.

"Go where?"

"Oh, oops," she snorted. "I thought I already said it. Get a cup of coffee or something."

"I don't have a car." This seemed easier than saying no.

"I have some in my locker," Ilona said.

"Coffee?"

"Yeah, come on." He hung back, a little conscious that he could be seen as going somewhere with her and not sure if he was committing to that yet.

But unable to summon a reasonable argument, Ben found himself back at the Bridge with Ilona. "I don't know why we have to come out here to drink coffee," he muttered. It was a warmish day for January, probably thirty-four degrees, but it was still cold enough to send his breath out in steamy puffs.

"Well, it's a little more than coffee." She pulled a tall plaid thermos from her backpack and unscrewed the two plastic cups from the top.

"What is it?" As soon as she pulled the stopper off the top, he could smell the alcohol that wafted toward his nose on a cloud of steam.

"Just a little something extra to help perk you up." She passed him a plastic cup half-filled with coffee and whatever she had spiked it with. It did smell incredible— the bitter, burned, roasted coffee and the sweet tang of an alcohol he couldn't name. "Come on, sit down over here by the vent. It's not so bad." There was an old blue gym mat squished into a crevice between two sections of brick. Just above the mat, an enormous vent was blasting warm air. Ben sat down with a thunk. The liquid in his cup sloshed forward and back, almost cresting over the side of the cup. He leaned against the bricks, which were surprisingly warm. She was right; it wasn't so bad there. He took a sip. The liquid was hot and the alcohol buzzed the back of his throat without burning.

"That's good," he said.

"It should be. It's some fancy brandy."

"I don't think you're supposed to put that in coffee."

"Yeah, you're right," Ilona said. "But it's funny. Every time I try and bring the bottle to school to drink it straight, someone gives me shit about it. Teachers—they're so uptight."

"That's not what I meant."

"I know."

He took another sip. Either the booze or the coffee or some combination of the two was making him feel warm right down to his toes, which he was particularly enjoying wiggling around in his socks. "So are you, like, a booze expert or something?"

"Nah, I'm just going through my dad's stash."

"Is he away?"

"Oh yes. Like, permanently."

"Sorry," Ben said quickly. Despite his initial judgments about Ilona, he was, in fact, curious to know more about her.

"Oh, he's not dead." Ilona laughed. Her laugh sounded a bit like a cough and seemed to come out in short bursts from one side of her mouth. "No, but he's long gone. He left Judy years ago." Ben nodded. "But luckily he left his booze collection too, and he's got decent taste." Ilona opened up the thermos again and refilled her cup. She gestured toward Ben, and he held out his cup for her to top off.

"Where is he?"

"North Shore. He lives in some giant castle right on the beach in Marblehead."

"He didn't go very far."

"He works for Blacksmith-Waterson. So I guess he's close to that. Make sense; it's the only thing he appears to care about. They're a defense company, so I don't even really know what he does except he's got crazy security clearance. He can probably see us right now with one of his super spy cams."

Ben held up his plastic thermos cup like he was toasting. "Thanks for the drink," he said.

"No problem, son," Ilona said in a deep voice, "just keep your hands off my daughter."

Ben flinched. Surely he had not given Ilona the idea he was interested in her in *that* way.

"Kidding," Ilona said, "he probably doesn't even know I'm in high school or that half my friends are guys. I mean last year when I *had* friends. I swear he still thinks I'm ten years old. You know what he sent me last year for my birthday?" She didn't wait for a response. "Headbands. Ignoring the complete lack of personality in the gift, not to mention the cheapness.

Headbands? They were purple with blue flowers and rhinestone shit on them."

"Huh," Ben said.

"I gave them to my boss's daughter. She thought they were great. She's seven."

"Where do you work?" Ben asked.

"Uh-uh," Ilona said. "I get to ask a question now."

"All right, shoot." He looked at his cup and took a sip to dissipate the nervous energy.

"Your parents, they're together?"

"Yeah."

"Thought so. You have that look."

"What's that?"

"Well loved."

"What do you mean by that?"

Ilona grabbed his bag. "Someone had your initials monogrammed on your backpack for Christ's sake."

"That was my grandmother," Ben said. He waited for the familiar rush of blood to his cheeks that always accompanied this kind of direct confrontation. Maybe it was the alcohol, but it didn't come.

"Proves my point even more. Look, they're together. They both have jobs—careers, probably the kind they care about where they do good things for people. And probably you're the youngest. Maybe you have an older brother."

"Sister."

"See. I knew you were a youngest. You have a little bit of that woe-is-me, center of attention thing going on." She held a finger up when he started to protest. "Takes one to know one. It's all right. We're allowed to be brats, at least a little bit. I mean, we're kind of afterthoughts, really. The whole

'Oh my God, we had a kid' thing was over by the time we rolled around."

Ben didn't know what to say. He didn't know if there was anything he could say. He had been pretty sure going anywhere with Ilona would be a complete disaster, and he was totally surprised that he liked her peculiar and honest take on things. Something about the knowledge that she was the bigger weirdo made him feel like he had nothing to prove to her.

"Where do you work? You said you gave the headbands to your boss's daughter. Where?"

"Broadway Gardens."

"In the winter?"

"All year, actually. I mean, I have a lot more hours in the summer, but there's still stuff to do in the winter. They have greenhouses. They do roses and shit for Valentine's Day."

"Do you like it there?"

Ilona looked at him. He wondered for a second how he had ever mistaken her for a boy. Her eyes and her soft upturn of a nose, her lips that seemed unnaturally pink though it was clear she wasn't wearing makeup—these were all very feminine things. "I love it," she said. "If I could live there, I would."

"What happened to your friends?"

Ilona jumped to her feet. "Nope," she said.

Ben stood up too, but when he was on his feet his eyes seemed to slide to the back of his skull. He stepped awkwardly sideways to catch himself.

"Lightweight?" Ilona said, smirking.

Ben ignored her. "What did you mean, *nope*?"

She waved her hands around in front of her face. "I just meant, you know, enough getting-to-know-you chatter for one day." She seemed uncomfortable for a second, and then, just as quickly, the sarcasm in her voice was back. "I mean, we have to hang out for a whole twenty-four hours next week. What if we run out of things to say? Awkward!"

"Yeah, well, I have class now anyway," Ben said.

"Oh, me too. I have class too."

There was that sarcasm again, but he hadn't meant it as an excuse, just a fact. "So, thanks for the coffee."

"What time? On Friday, I mean. We could blow off the whole day, but Judy doesn't work until the afternoon so unless you want her in our face the entire time, being annoying and trying to change the channel, I suggest we wait until after school. Is that cool?"

"Sure," Ben said. He thought about offering his house as a location potentially free of all whack-job parental intervention but reconsidered. Talking to Ilona had been pretty cool, and he wasn't dreading the assignment as much, or even at all, now. But everything about her was a little wild and risky, and after her spot-on observations about his parents and his backpack, he wasn't sure he was ready to expose his house or his family to her critical eye.

CHAPTER 17

"What are you doing tonight?" Tyler had the cardboard center from a roll of masking tape, and he was hitting it back and forth from hand to hand. He was leaning back against the lockers while Ben contemplated what he actually needed to take home for the weekend.

"I've got that thing for my pop culture class—twenty-four hours of TV."

"Oh, right. Did you ever get out of doing it with that girl?"

"No, but it's all right. She's not as bad as I thought she was."

Tyler looked at him with a raised eyebrow.

"No!" Ben said. "Not like that. Just, you know, tolerable."

"A lot can happen in twenty-four hours."

"Yeah, but not that. What are you up to?"

Tyler shrugged. "I don't know. Megan's going skiing with her family. I don't know. I feel like I could really get faced tonight. You know, go all out." He shrugged again. "But whatever, I'll probably just watch a movie and blaze one by myself."

"You can come watch TV at Ilona's," Ben said, half seriously.

Tyler sneered. "That's her name? Ilona? Like a-loner? HA! That's classic."

Tyler had been his best friend since fourth grade. Ilona was a girl he barely knew. But Ben felt inexplicably defensive. "Ilona Pierce," he said. "She lives right over on Hawthorne Street." He knew the number but he didn't give it, hoping that Tyler would forget he'd even half offered.

For a second Tyler looked like he actually might be considering it. "Nah," he finally said. "Just text me if there's anything good on. Or if she tries to break your ankles and tie you up in the basement."

"Right," Ben said and shouldered his backpack. He had spent a long time deciding what to pack but settled for a clean T-shirt and boxers, because it seemed like you should have those things, a toothbrush, and extra batteries for his hearing aids. He had already planned how he would change them in the bathroom and what time he would do it to be sure he didn't get caught in a lapse. He had never even changed them in front of Tyler. Once he had tucked an extra battery behind a bottle of hydrogen peroxide in the very back of the medicine cabinet in Tyler's bathroom for backup. It was probably dead by now anyway.

He was actually kind of nervous about how the whole thing was going to go. Mom had flipped out when he explained what he was doing. She threatened to call Kapstein and demand that he be excused from the project on account of his health, and she only relented when he promised that he and Ilona had agreed to take shifts and actually get some sleep. So there had been an out after all—an easy out. And he hadn't taken it. He wasn't entirely dreading spending more time with Ilona, crazy mother and cats and all. It was weird, but there it was.

They met outside school after the last bell and walked, without saying much, toward Hawthorne Street. It was only three blocks from school. There were some big houses interspersed with multi-families. His mom always said no one wanted to buy so close to the school because of the noise and potential for break-ins.

Ilona's house was surrounded by a high wooden fence with gray peeling paint and shaded by two enormous pine trees in the front yard. They walked down her driveway, which was heavily rutted with frozen puddles. Ben heard the scraping of a shovel on ice. Ilona exhaled loudly. "Jesus, I guess she hasn't left for work yet. Well, at least I warned you." On the porch, hacking away at the gritty snow frozen on the buckling wooden boards, was a woman in a navy blue leotard, pink tights, and knee-high snow boots. Ben only recognized it as a leotard because he remembered them from Shannan's gymnastics days. This woman, who Ben assumed was the infamous Judy Pierce, was also wearing a pair of enormous yellow headphones with a metal antenna jutting out the back.

"What are those?" Ben whispered as they stood at the edge of the porch.

"Nineties portable music device. Judy pretty much stopped updating everything in the nineties—her clothes, her car, her social life. She's, like, frozen there with Milli Vanilli and Ace of Base."

"Who?"

"Exactly." Ilona frowned. "Come on. I think we can just walk past her and she won't even notice." But as soon as they stepped onto the porch, the boards shifted and creaked loudly. Judy swung around, heavy metal shovel in hand.

"Hi, kids!" she shouted over the music that was piped into her ears. She pulled the headphones down around her neck. Her shoulder-length brown hair had an inch of gray at the scalp, and a single pink roller still dangled just above her shoulder.

"Judy," Ilona said, "you've got a thing there." She pointed to her shoulder.

"Don't call me that, Ilona," Judy said. She batted at the roller like it was an annoying insect that wouldn't leave her alone.

"Why not, Judy?"

"Call me Mom. Your friends are going to think it's weird. They're going to think you don't like me."

"I don't like you, Judy," Ilona said.

Ben tried not to smile and shifted his weight back and forth between his feet.

"Ilona!" Judy squawked.

"Judy!" Ilona opened the door and walked through, leaving her mother standing on the porch with one hand on her hip and the other on her shovel. Ben smiled apologetically and followed her in.

The hallway was dark with two closed doors immediately on either side of the entryway. There was a long, threadbare oriental rug running the length of the hall, and overhead was a box-shaped chandelier with two missing panes of glass and a single browning bulb. At the end of the hallway, a staircase wound up to the left, and just below it was a big closet. As they passed, Ben recoiled at the sour smell of unchanged cat litter. Ilona pulled the closet door shut.

The hallway emptied into a large room that was part kitchen and part living room. The kitchen section was behind a large island with a sink and several cabinets. On the other side of the island, there was a light brown leather sectional facing an enormous flat screen TV. A huge long-haired brown and black cat waddled out of the room when they entered. A smaller black one sprung off the couch when Ilona hissed at it. Behind the

TV, a wall of steamed-up windows created a small greenhouse space that was filled with plants. Ben set his backpack down and watched as Ilona pressed her fingers into the dirt and turned some leaves over to examine the undersides. She pulled a few browning leaves off and flicked them onto the floor behind her.

Then, for no apparent reason, she let out a string of expletives that made Ben's eyes pop. "Judy!" Ilona yelled. "I'm going to kill your freaking cats!" Ben walked over to her and saw a grape-sized turd in the pot of one of the larger plants, something with thick green leaves and yellow and green striped stems. Ilona went behind the island and came out with a plastic bag. She proceeded to pull out the cat shit and tie off the bag, which she tucked into an oversized leather purse that was sitting on one of the stools at the end of the kitchen island.

"That's disgusting," Ben said.

"Yup," Ilona agreed. "So," she said, changing the subject, "what's going to be our poison?"

"What do you mean?" A girl who put cat shit in her mother's purse might seriously consider drinking Drano.

"What channel?"

"Oh," Ben said, relieved. "I don't care. You pick."

"Whatever," Ilona said. "It has to be a major network, and they're all the same anyway." She jabbed at the remote control with her thumb. At two thirty they began their twenty-four hour television binge. It started slow. There was a soap opera on, so Ben mostly tuned out, playing on his phone and paying attention only when he had to write down the commercials during the breaks. He agreed to take the first shift while Ilona disappeared down into the basement. After a little while, he heard the rush of water and thump of a washing machine. When she came up she was wearing only a black tank top and a pair of green boxer shorts with black dice printed on them. "Sorry," she said, "all my clothes are dirty." She threw herself down on the other end of the sectional. He could tell she didn't shave her armpits. At least the hair there wasn't blue.

He decided he didn't care. And it wasn't really that weird. Girls at the beach wore less all the time. But of course they weren't at the beach. He was sitting on the cracked leather couch with a girl he barely knew. The soap opera ended, and the first of several afternoon talk shows came on. He didn't recognize the host, but Ilona seemed to think she had been a child star on some nineties sitcom.

Ben jumped when there was a gasp behind him.

"Oh, that's Melody Waters from *Family Diner*!" Judy exclaimed excitedly.

Ilona gave him an I-told-you-so look. Judy had shed the leotard—apparently that was only for snow shoveling—and was now wearing hospital scrubs and a long beige overcoat. She had removed the pink curler from her hair. With her eyes still glued to the television, she walked over to where Ilona was curled up and dropped several twenty-dollar bills on her. "Make sure you and your friend eat some dinner," she said.

Ilona picked up the money. "This is a lot of cash, Judy. Are we supposed to get some strippers too?"

"Ilona!" Judy said, sounding exasperated.

"Judy!" Ilona mimicked her tone.

"I'm working the overnight, so behave yourself, both of you." She paused for a minute and watched as Melody Waters offered a tissue to a woman who had just learned that her father wasn't her real father. "Your parents are okay with this?" she asked Ben without moving her eyes from the screen.

Ben nodded. "It's fine."

Judy looked relieved. "Okay, well, you have the money for dinner and—"

"Just go, Judy," Ilona interrupted. "You're going to be late."

Judy left and then came back in one more time for her purse. Then it was quiet in the house. "Is she a nurse?" Ben asked.

Ilona snorted. "Judy? No. She works in a halfway house for girls who are crazy. Like, crazy-crazy," she clarified. "Like they hear voices and shit. It's pretty ironic, actually, since Judy is a half step away from batshit herself. Kind of like the blind leading the blind." Ben felt himself bristle the way he always did when any kind of disability was mentioned as part of regular conversation. Ilona cocked her head as though she'd noticed his reaction. He pretended to study a framed print of some flowers on the wall behind her head, and she didn't say anything.

About halfway through *Dr. Phil*, Ben felt his eyes begin to glaze over. He realized something else as well: this project would be incredibly easy to fake. All he and Ilona would have to do was agree to check the TV every few hours and write down whatever crap was on, along with some made-up commercials. It was easy to see who they were marketing to. During the soap operas and talk shows, the commercials were all for cleaning products and diet foods. Later, during the basketball game—a bright spot in their evening lineup—it would be all beer commercials and trucks. How hard was that to predict? But he didn't suggest it, and neither did Ilona.

At the end of *Dr. Phil*, the first round of the news came on, and Ilona got up and started tending to her plants again. Ben was impressed by the care she took in inspecting and pruning each one. She carried a quart-sized yogurt container with her, and this time she dropped the dead leaves and twigs into it.

Each plant got doused with a spray bottle of water—first the roots, then the leaves. There had to be twenty or thirty different plants in an eight foot by eight foot area. He considered this in comparison to Ilona's treatment of her mother. He still wasn't sure what to make of it—how much was an act meant for his benefit? Down on her knees, prodding at the dirt inside a large orange plastic pot, Ben noticed the tattoo on the back of her upper thigh.

"What's that?" he asked.

"What?"

"Your tattoo. What is it?"

Ilona pulled the leg of her boxers up so they hugged the right side of her butt. Ben tried to just look at the tattoo. It was a moon rising over some kind of field.

"*Tsukino*," Ilona said. "It means 'moon field' in Japanese. My dad's half, so I'm mixed. It was his mother's family name before she got married." Ben was surprised even though, now that he looked more closely, her eyelids did have a smaller fold to them and her skin was slightly browner than most for this time of year. "I went through a phase," she added by way of explanation.

"Well, at least her name didn't mean, like, 'pig's ass' or something."

Ilona gave him a look as though he had said something unexpectedly clever. "Good thing."

"It looks cool. Tyler and I talked about getting one. Maybe this winter sometime."

"Huh," said Ilona. "You're not going to get the same one, are you?" When he didn't answer right away, she said, "Ugh, don't do that. Just don't do that. I don't even think married people should do that. Although I'm not exactly an expert on what married people do, having spent very few of my formative years around any of them."

"I don't know. I mean, we hadn't really decided anything."

Ilona looked over her shoulder at him. "A tattoo is an individual decision. I mean, there's nothing more individual than your body, right? Why would you want to mark it up exactly like someone else's? I mean, what's the point of that?"

"Is that why you have blue hair?" Ben asked, stung for some reason. "Because you're *such* an individual?"

Ilona put down her bucket of plant clippings and came over to the couch. The spray bottle swung in her hands, its nozzle hanging on one finger. "You don't like my hair?"

"I didn't say that. I just don't know why some people have to try so hard to be weird. To be different," he corrected. The news went to commercials, and for the next six minutes they stared at the TV. Ben pretended to be really focused on writing down what they were and tried to ignore the hot feeling in his head and his chest. He could always leave, he reminded himself. This project could easily be faked.

When the news came back on, Ilona held up the spray bottle like a gun and said, "Why are you trying so hard to be like everyone else?"

"I'm not!" he said. "I mean, I don't mean that I'm not trying. And if I am, so what? I'm not like everyone else, and I just think that if I could be—I mean, if I were like everyone else—I would be happy with that."

Ilona narrowed her eyes. "This is about *that*?" She gestured to her ears. "Jesus. I mean. I thought I was a freak about some stuff, but you are, like, way beyond me. You really think your hearing is what makes you different from everybody else? You think, like, you're over there in the weirdo category and everyone else, I mean everyone else with no obvious abnormalities, is over here feeling all normal and good about themselves?"

Ben didn't say anything. She was pissing him off, but at the same time, he wanted—no, he needed—to hear what she was going to say. "You are deluded," she continued. "We are all freaks. Everyone." She lay back on the couch. "And the sooner you figure that out, the sooner you can let yourself off the hook for having ears that don't work exactly right or whatever. Or if it really bothers you that much, don't wear the things."

Ben huffed.

"Seriously, you can hear a little, right? So don't wear them and then see if you feel all perfect and fulfilled inside. Do what you want, but accept it: there is no normal." She sprayed him with the squirt bottle. A jet of water hit him smack in the middle of his chest. "Bull's-eye," said Ilona, and she blew on the top of the bottle like it was a gun.

Ben pulled at the damp T-shirt and sniffed it. Just water. Who the hell was she to talk about normal? "Are you going to put some clothes on?" he finally asked.

"Nope," Ilona said. "I'm going to stay just like this, with my weird blue hair and my boxer shorts. Deal with it," she said, and grinned.

CHAPTER 18

After the evening news they smoked their first bowl. It was a blue-green glass pipe, and Ilona packed it like a pro. Then they giggled their way through *Jeopardy* and a celebrity news show, which managed to show about three minutes of content for every five minutes of commercials.

"Who watches this crap?" Ben complained.

"Shut up," Ilona said. "I want to know Michelle Obama's trainer's top ten tips for toned arms." They both snickered as the impossibly fit blonde woman in the bright red dress tried a series of arm movements while another woman in fitness gear talked her through it. "What do you think aliens would think if they were watching this? I mean, what do you think they would think about our planet?"

"Uh, that we're shallow and incredibly stupid," Ben said.

"And that we have impossibly toned arms!"

"Yeah," Ben agreed, "that's like the goal of our entire society. The people with the best arm definition get all the money and live like kings."

Ilona snorted. "That's good."

He liked making her laugh. He liked that she was lying on the sofa and that her shirt was riding up a bit, showing her stomach, and she didn't care. He liked that a few minutes ago she blew her nose really loudly and burped without saying excuse me. "I'm hungry," he said. "How long did they say for the pizza?"

"Twenty minutes."

"But that was like an hour ago," Ben complained.

"Uh-uh, it was like five minutes ago. You can check in the cabinet to see if there's anything edible." She pointed behind her head at the tall cabinet at the end of the island. Ben pulled himself off the couch, threw the clipboard with their notes to Ilona, and found the cabinet. An orange and white striped cat sprung out at him when he opened the door and sent his heart racing. Inside there were a few cans of tuna, a large can of baked beans, and a pretzel bag with only a few pretzel sticks swimming in a mound of leftover salt chunks in the bottom of the bag. He shook the bag for the rattling sound.

"Not much?" Ilona asked.

"Nothing," Ben said.

"Yeah, Judy's not much of a homemaker. Every couple of weeks she'll throw a bunch of money at me and tell me to go shopping, but I usually blow it on takeout. My car's got a flat anyway. I watched a YouTube video on how to fix it but almost killed myself when I tried to jack the car up. So there's that."

"What do the cats eat?"

"Cat food," Ilona said. "But when it runs out, Judy just feeds them whatever. It's really gross. You should see what happens when the pizza guy comes. It's like they think it's for them." The buzzer sounded on the washing machine, and Ilona hopped up and went through the door to the basement. When she came back up, she had thrown a pair of black skinny jeans over her boxers. "I know you're disappointed," she said.

The doorbell finally rang when Ilona was upstairs gathering up more laundry. Ben scooped up the money on the couch and headed for the front door. Sure enough, there were five cats assembled in the front hallway and two more making their way down the stairs. The ones by the door were rubbing themselves against the door frame. He had to nudge them out of the way with his foot to open the door.

The pizza delivery guy had jet-black hair under his red uniform cap and a lip ring. He gave Ben a weird look but took his money. "Where's Ilona?"

"Upstairs," Ben said. It seemed all right to give the information out to someone who already knew her name.

"Oh," the guy said as he fumbled for the correct change. Ben handed him back a few bucks for a tip. "Well, just tell her Pete said 'what's up.'"

"No problem," Ben said, shutting the door quickly to stop any of the cats from finding their way out.

He didn't wait for Ilona before he dove at the pizza. "Such manners," she said when she came back into the room. She threw a paper plate at him like a Frisbee.

"Shorry," he mumbled with his mouth full of hot salty cheese. The pot was having the usual effect of making everything in his mouth taste incredible. The pizza was electric; the rich, slightly sour tang of the tomatoes, the chewy yeasty crust, and that cheese. When he managed to swallow enough so that he didn't feel like he was going to tear his face off from hunger, he passed along Pete's message.

Ilona rolled her eyes.

"Not one of your 'missing friends'?"

"Fortunately, no. Pete the Pizza Guy just happens to be the delivery dude at the only place in this town that makes anything that's slightly better than what you can get in the frozen foods aisle."

"Which you can't get to anyway, because your car has a flat."

"Point," Ilona said. "For whatever reason, he thinks this means we have some kind of 'relationship' beyond that he brings the pizza and I eat the pizza."

"That's good," Ben said. And then without really knowing why, he added, "He's too old for you anyway." He grimaced as soon as he said it and waited for Ilona to bust his balls about the comment, but she didn't.

"That's kind of a problem I have."

"With pizza guys?"

"No, with older guys."

"Oh," Ben said. "You go out with a lot of older guys?"

"Not really, but I have a lot of friends who are older guys. Basically all my friends were seniors and now they're all gone."

"At college?"

"Mostly. A couple of them just moved to New York to start a band and wait tables and be a cliché."

Ben smirked, wanting Ilona to think he was at least cool enough to get it. His phone buzzed in his pocket. He jumped at the sudden sensation against his thigh. It was Tyler wanting to know what he was up to. He texted back, "24 hours TV," to which Tyler responded, "forgot" and "ski tomorrow Wachusett?" Ben texted back that he wouldn't be done until the middle of the afternoon. Then there was nothing. Was Tyler annoyed? It was an assignment; he couldn't just bail. He didn't even really want to.

Wachusett was a tiny ski mountain about forty minutes from Easton, but calling it a mountain was being extremely generous with the term. When Ben was little, he took his first ski lessons there. He remembered how excited he was to follow Shannan over to the ski school area for the day. He also remembered that when his mom had signed him up, the instructor asked him what grade he was in. The helmet he was forced to wear made it nearly impossible for him to hear anything, so he didn't respond, unsure of what the question was. His parents usually filled in for him in these kinds of situations anyway. But when he pulled his helmet off to ask if he and Shannan could eat in the snack bar for lunch, he heard the ski school instructor's next question loud and clear.

"Is he slow?" she was asking his mother.

Even his mother had not understood at first. "Well, he's still learning the snowplow, but I think he's pretty comfortable moving on the hill . . ." Her voice had trailed off as she made sense of the question. It had never occurred to Ben that anyone might think there was anything wrong with him besides a little hiccup in his hearing. That's what Dr. Usarian had called it when he explained it to Ben. It didn't sound so bad, even though he didn't like the way the plastic pieces felt in his ears. It had been nice to know he wasn't missing anything anymore.

But this was the first time he realized the way other people saw his hearing aids—as more than just a hiccup. He put on his helmet, retreating into the padded silence, and pushed over to where Shannan was waiting to ride with him up the bunny slope.

"Hellooooo," Ilona said. She threw a little piece of crust at him. "Commercials?" It took him a minute to understand. Then he picked up the clipboard and started recording again.

"Who was that?" she asked.

"Tyler wants to ski tomorrow."

"So are you going to go?"

"Probably not." He had to grip and regrip the pen. It felt so slick between his fingers, not gross and sweaty, but shiny and smooth. It had to be the pot, because his whole body was sort of numb and buzzing and Ilona's words and even his own thoughts sounded slower and more meaningful. He was working pretty hard to stay mellow and not freak out about his buzz. *Wheel of Fortune* was almost over, and some medical science thriller was about to come on. Probably not the best thing to watch while he was blazing—he'd probably end up thinking he had some mutated megavirus.

"Tyler Nuson, huh?" Ilona asked, and Ben nodded. "I had a class with him freshman year. I think it was French. Yeah, it totally was, because I remember the teacher—she looked like she was right out of college. Anyway, she really liked Tyler. It was kind of gross, actually. I don't think he even came to class half the time. But whenever he did show up, she practically humped his leg."

Ben smiled, feeling like his lips were as wide as his face. He remembered Tyler talking about Madame Catrina—that's what she wanted her students to call her—and how she would write him excuse notes for other classes as long as he showed up and acted like he really needed her help with some girl problem he was having. "Whatever happened to her?" He managed to choke out the words.

Ilona shrugged. "I don't know. They probably recycled her down at the teacher factory and turned her into some middle-aged lady with super pointy boobs and wool slacks." She let the hard *A* in the last word ring out like she knew how weird a word *slacks* was.

"Slacks," Ben repeated softly. It made the sides of mouth

crinkle. He licked there. It was salty from the crust and cheese. When he looked up, Ilona was looking at him smugly.

"You are baked," she announced.

Ben didn't even try to deny it. He just raised his eyebrows and pretended to concentrate on the clipboard. "Slacks," he whispered.

"So what's his deal anyway?"

"Who?"

"Tyler? Your BFF?"

"What do you mean?"

"I don't know. He's too perfect to be perfect. You know what I mean?"

"No, I don't," Ben said shortly. The tack this conversation was taking was crushing his buzz.

"Come on, he's gotta have some deep dark secrets, right?"

"You don't know what you're talking about," Ben said. But he suddenly felt woozy and paranoid—like maybe Ilona did know something he didn't.

"Whatever," Ilona said. "I'm sure you know him better than I do." But her tone was skeptical, and her words seemed to peck at his self-doubt. Ben's phone buzzed again. This time he didn't check it.

It was Tyler. He was sure of it. But he didn't feel the need to drop everything and read the message. He didn't feel like he should or he had to, or even really that he wanted to. It was shocking, really, an alien feeling he couldn't remember experiencing before.

It was only ten o'clock, but it felt like four in the morning. They each had a beer and started playing a game where they had to drink every time the news anchor said "really" or "truly." Ben told himself it was only the one beer and after that

148

he would stop drinking. But there was really nothing else to do, and the Fritos Ilona had ordered with the pizza made him so thirsty and the PBR just went down so easily.

"Ugh," he said after the news was over and the late night shows came on.

"Yeah," Ilona agreed. "This is gross. How many people do you think get wasted doing this?"

"All of them," Ben said.

"Even Hannah Greenberg?"

Ben grinned. Hannah sat in the front and took notes on everything Kapstein said on her Macbook Air. He was pretty sure she even wrote down the lyrics to the folk songs he played on the off chance they might make an appearance on a quiz— not that Kapstein gave any quizzes. "What's she even doing in that class?"

Ilona threw her head back. "I heard she tried to take all AP classes and guidance told her she couldn't—like they were afraid she'd end up a complete stressed-out nutcase. Oops, too late! So it was either this or a study hall, and she probably wanted a little something extra for her college application." Ilona pumped her fist in the air.

"Oh, shit," Ben said. "Can we please not talk about college?"

"What's college?"

A little while later he felt something soft and warm land on him. He opened his eyes—unaware that he had been dozing— and found that a soft plaid blanket had been tossed on him.

"Wake me up after the show," he said, waving a hand at the TV. "I'll take the next shift."

"Sure."

But when he woke up there was a yellow streak at the horizon and the sky, though dark, was a deep navy instead of black.

He wiped a strand of drool from his cheek and sat up, bending to one side to see if he could crack the stuck places in his back and side. Ilona was sitting on the other end of the couch, smacking loudly on a piece of gum and twirling what looked like a black leather keychain around and around on her finger. "You let me sleep," Ben said. His voice was accusing and grateful.

"You seemed tired."

"You didn't have to."

"No shit." Ilona stood up and went to the fridge, where she poured herself a glass of orange juice. When she came back to the couch, she picked up the clipboard and tossed it to Ben. He threw the blanket over to her, and she lay down and pulled it up over her head. Within minutes her breathing became deep and even. Ben blinked a few times and stared at the workout routine that was being performed somewhere on a tropical beach or, more likely, in front of a tropical-beach green screen.

A little after two thirty, she walked him to the front door where they both blinked at the bright sunlight reflecting off the dirty snow in Ilona's yard. Her spiky hair was flat on top, and her bangs were pushed into her eyes. She blew them out of the way with a sharp puff. "Well, that wasn't so bad," she said. He shook his head and looked down at his shoes. When he looked up, Ilona was holding out her fist. He pounded down, took a step back, and turned to go. Then he turned back to give a little wave. Ilona looked amused.

"See ya," he said.

He went home and fell asleep until the buzzing of his phone woke him at 7:30. It was Tyler, and he sounded annoyed. "Where have you been?"

"Sleeping," Ben answered groggily.

"You never texted me back."

"Sorry, I fell asleep."

"At that weird girl's house?"

"Yeah."

"Sketch, dude. You don't even know her."

"Neither do you," Ben said. *Why are you being an asshole?* But instead he said, "Hey, listen, can I call you tomorrow or something? I've gotta crash. I feel like shit."

"Yeah, later," Tyler said, and Ben heard the click of disconnection. He went downstairs and ate a bowl of cereal before climbing back up and passing out again—this time under his covers and without his clothes on.

He didn't call Tyler the next day. He didn't consciously not call him; he just seemed not to get around to it. He was busy filling out his application for UMass, which suddenly felt like a pressing, needful thing to do.

CHAPTER 19

The following week, there was a chance thaw and for a period of five days the thermometer shot up to the mid-forties during the day. A lot of the snow melted, and the frozen ground turned to a muddy mess of dirt and slush.

One afternoon, Ben, who was slowly getting his energy back and no longer had to take a nap after school, borrowed his father's car and drove over to Ilona's house, where the drifts piled around her jeep had melted enough to access the back of the vehicle. It was unlocked, as he had expected it might be, and there were no other cars in the driveway. He changed the flat on her car and put the donut on, regretting that he didn't have the know-how to actually fix the tire or the cash to replace it.

He was just finishing up when she came outside onto the porch. "You didn't have to do that," she said. She was wearing a red-and-black checked hunting vest over dark green skinny jeans.

He smiled. "No shit."

"Come in and have some juice."

He followed her inside, down the dark hallway, and into the room where they spent twenty-four hours watching TV the week before. She poured him a dark brown tumbler full of orange juice. Ben held up the glass and clinked it against Ilona's. "Just juice?"

"You want something stronger?"

"No, juice is good." He looked around the kitchen. There were several days' worth of dirty dishes stacked up in the sink and a pile of clean, or maybe dirty, laundry sitting on the couch. The dining room table, visible over Ilona's shoulder, was covered with old editions of the *Easton Tab*, the local free weekly— some still in their plastic sleeves—and other assorted mail.

"Want to play Boggle?" Ilona asked.

"Sure. Why not?"

"Because I'm going to whip your ass and make you cry like a baby, that's why not."

"Huh." Ben said, "I'm not afraid of you."

"You should be."

He stayed until dinnertime, playing round after round of Boggle. Ilona was pretty good, but he held his own and managed to win a few games too.

"I should go," he said after checking the time. He had told his dad he'd have the car back by dinnertime. He thought about his parents, who were probably cooking dinner and listening to NPR or the bluegrass station on Pandora. He tried not to think about it in comparison to the dirty dishes or the empty refrigerator at Ilona's house. "See you tomorrow?"

"Yup," Ilona said.

She caught up with him the next day before Kapstein's class, which she convinced him to ditch. And just about every other day for the next week, he found himself playing Boggle and drinking or smoking a little weed with Ilona on her couch.

On Wednesday, as he was about to duck out of the building, he ran into Tyler. As soon as Ben saw him, he had the strangest urge to hide. Not because he didn't want to see him, but because he didn't want to be faced with the decision to include him or not. It turned out that Tyler was on his way to a dentist appointment and couldn't have come anyway, but it left Ben with a funny feeling as he walked down the street to meet Ilona at her house.

He kicked a large chunk of ice, which skittered ahead of him as he walked, thinking that he should really know how he felt about this new friendship before it went any further. It was similar to his friendship with Tyler in that he felt really unselfconscious; he was surprised at how easily this had happened. But it was different too. Besides Ilona being a girl, he never felt like he owed her anything for being his friend. She wasn't required to hang out with him because they had some long history together. This was the part that made him feel funny, because it was a new realization about his friendship with Tyler.

He let himself in and was just getting comfortable lying down on the couch when he heard footsteps in the hall. He assumed it was Ilona. So when Judy sat down on the couch next to him and reached for the green glass bowl, he jumped into an upright sitting position.

To his complete shock, Judy knocked the shwag out of the bottom of the bowl onto the coffee table and proceeded to pack a fresh bowl with Ilona's weed. She lit it and hit it and then offered it to him.

"No thank you, Mrs. Pierce," he stammered.

"God dammit, Judy," Ilona said when she entered the room. "What did I tell you about smoking my weed!"

"Don't curse at me, Ilona," Judy said. She turned up the volume on the TV. It was an afternoon talk show—something about vaccines and autism.

"*Damn* is not a curse word, Judy," Ilona said, her voice dripping with disdain. "Shit and fuck are curse words."

"Ilona!" Judy said, but then she dropped it, like maybe she'd lost interest in the whole thing. She leaned back against the couch and put the bowl down beside her. "I'm trying to watch this," she told the room.

Ilona rolled her eyes and beckoned Ben with her chin. "Let's go upstairs." Ben was glad to get out of the room. He never really knew what to make of Ilona's volatile, disgruntled-roommate-type relationship with her mother.

Ilona's room was at the far end of the hall upstairs, next to a small window seat overlooking the front yard. Ben tried not to look at the molding bread and a bowl of what might have been cereal decomposing on the faded cushions. "Ta da," she said as she shoved the door open against a small mountain of clothes pressed between the door and the wall. The room was dominated by an enormous wrought-iron bed frame with peeling white paint. The bed, which was vaulted three and a half feet off the floor, was a receptacle for even more clothes, a pale pink comforter, and some twisted sheets coming up at the corners of the mattress. A stack of very unused-looking spiral notebooks and textbooks leaned precariously against the footboard. Two walls had windows. On the third there were two closets, both with doors ajar and spewing more clothes onto the floor, which was visible only in patches. On the wall above the bed, there was a large water stain and an unfinished mural. "Your work?" Ben asked about the mural.

"One of the Calvins did that," Ilona said. "Stoners never finish anything."

"Calvins? You have two friends named Calvin?" He felt a twinge of jealousy about these other friends who now had names. Other friends who had been in Ilona's bedroom before him.

"Uh-uh," Ilona said, "Twins. Harris and Elwyn. Harris painted it the summer before last. Judy was on a cross-country bike tour with her boyfriend, so they were pretty much living here."

At the end of the bed, there was a dresser. The drawers were open and empty. "You don't believe in them?" he asked of the under-utilized furniture.

"Nope, just lazy." She climbed up onto the bed and pitched some of the books down to the floor. Ben sat on the floor and leaned against the mattresses for lack of anywhere else to go. Tucked behind a pile of clothes in front of him was a low bookshelf. He cocked his head to the side and read the titles. "You have the Lord of the Rings?" he said, unable to hide the excitement in his voice.

"No!" Ilona said. "They're probably my brother's. He ran out of room on his bookshelves and clearly doesn't respect my domain."

"He lives here?"

Ilona waved her hand. "No, he's older-older. Done with college. Lives in DC, working his balls off for some save-the-planet group."

Ben pushed the mound of clothes aside with his foot so he could pull out a rather fancy leather-bound edition of the first book in the trilogy. He flipped open to the title page. "'For Haakon, from Dad.' Your parents don't believe in regular names," he observed.

"Same mother, different dads," Ilona explained. "But yeah."

"So you've really never read this?"

Ilona sighed. "No, should I?"

Ben smiled. He opened to the first page and began to read. At first Ilona groaned and complained a lot—especially when a new character was introduced. "How am I supposed to keep track of all these people?" she grumbled.

"Hobbits, not people."

"Sandwich and Froyo. It sounds like the food court at the mall."

"It's Samwise and Frodo," Ben said. "Do you want me to stop?"

Ilona said nothing, so Ben kept reading. He read until his throat got hoarse. Ilona got him a drink from the tiny closet-sized bathroom tucked in next to the wall of closets. The water was cool, though the plastic cup tasted faintly of toothpaste. Ilona curled up on her side and seemed to be waiting for him to continue. He was sitting on the bed now, his shoes resting carefully on one of the exposed corners of mattress—not on the sheets or comforter. It might have felt weird had there been anywhere else in the room to sit, but there wasn't. He read until the sun coming through the thick pine boughs outside her window cast an orange glaze against the wall. He heard the car door and the engine turn over when Judy left for work, but he didn't stop reading. He peeked over Ilona's shoulder a few times to see if she had fallen asleep, but each time her eyes were wide open, though her breath was steady and even. He didn't stop reading until his mom texted, asking in a roundabout way where he was and if he planned on coming home for dinner.

"I should go," he said. "The elves are about to sing again anyway."

Ilona made a face. "He could have left that part out. I don't care how much you geek out on this, you can't tell me you think the elf songs are interesting."

"I think it's interesting that Tolkien went to all the trouble to create them. You know, he made up all the languages and everything. This whole place was real to him. You should keep reading." He couldn't explain to her how important the books were to him, not without her busting out laughing. He wasn't even sure he could put it into words, but it was the importance of a quest—something bigger and more important than the boring everyday details of his life. There were rules to be followed and brave acts to be committed, and above all, there was the possibility of total destruction if the quest was not completed. No matter how many times he read the books or watched the movies, he was hooked by the journey of Sam and Frodo and, above all else, by their loyalty and, yes, love that withstood every trial. But no, he didn't really think Ilona would get that.

"I won't," Ilona said matter-of-factly. "Unless you want to come back and read more. I could probably handle that. Pick me up at work tomorrow. I'll get some money off Judy for pizza."

CHAPTER 20

The wind chimes on the back of the door made a tinkling sound when Ben stepped into the shop at Broadway Gardens. A woman came out of the back room. She had a pair of reading glasses on her face and another pair perched up on her head. There were two pens and one pencil sticking out at various angles from the back of her ponytail. Her eyes crinkled up as she assessed Ben. "Are you Ilona's friend?" Ben nodded. "She's in the back. Through here," she said and gestured behind her. "I think she's just finishing up."

Ben walked behind the counter and through the storeroom and a hanging door of thick plastic strips. As soon as he stepped through, the air felt warm and thick. There were green things everywhere: plants with thick leaves hanging in baskets from the ceiling, and a carpet of tiny green sprouts in plastic pots that covered the rows and rows of benches in front of him. At the end of one of these long benches, he saw Ilona staring down at a plant with a few orange blossoms and yellowing leaves.

Ilona looked up when she heard him, but her face looked concerned. "This isn't good," she said, holding up a few of the yellowing leaves. "These are roses, and Valentine's Day is less than two weeks away." Ben smiled. He couldn't help himself.

It was one thing to see Ilona in her green Broadway Gardens polo shirt, but then when she started talking about the health of roses for Valentine's Day? Had he entered another dimension? She rolled her eyes. He didn't even have to say anything. "Don't think I give a shit about anyone getting their sweetie some flowers and candy. I care about Diane." Ben assumed this was the woman out front. "Their profit margin around here is so thin to begin with. If this is some kind of fungus or bug infestation, it could mean the difference between being open next season or not."

Ben just smiled. Ilona looked annoyed. "Why are you still smiling?"

"It's just refreshing to hear that you care about something."

"Shut your piehole," Ilona said. She stuffed a few of the leaves in her pocket. "I'll figure it out later," she mumbled.

Ben waited in the store, staring at the bird feeder displays, while Ilona went into the staff room to get her stuff. The woman with the pens in her ponytail came in and out a few times, each time smiling at him in a way that made him feel he was being assessed. When Ilona finally came out, she had on a tight blue wool sweater pulled over the green polo and a puffy red vest, skinny jeans, and boots. Her face was still flushed from the heat of the greenhouse. With her blue hair, Ben couldn't exactly call her pretty, but she was something. Striking, he decided. Ilona was striking.

"I care about stuff," she said when they pulled out of the parking lot.

"Okay," Ben said.

They were quiet for a little while until Ilona said, "Are you going to read me that book again?"

"Did you get the pizza money?"

"Sure," Ilona said. "Judy puts out like a sophomore slut."

Ben coughed into his hand. He wasn't sure if he should laugh or defend somebody—the sophomores or Judy. Ben had told his parents he planned to be out for dinner, so they ate pizza on Ilona's bed while Ben read Tolkien in between chewing bites of crust. This time he felt a little more awkward about being in bed with Ilona; there *were* actually other places in the house they could have been since Judy wasn't home. But Ilona chewed loudly and clawed at a piece of tomato stuck in her teeth before flicking it on the floor. There was definitely nothing romantic coming from her end, he assured himself.

"You think we'll have a snow day tomorrow?" Ilona asked.

"It's supposed to snow?"

"Where have you been? All the radio stations have been blabbing on about it for hours—nor'easter, six to twelve inches and all that crap."

"Since when do you listen to the radio?" Ben asked. "That seems awfully mainstream."

"Since they have it on at the Greenhouse, asshole," Ilona said. "Besides, I like some of it. I like to dance."

"Oh, the mysteries of Ilona Pierce."

"Oh, the mysteries of Ben Wireman," she retorted.

"I'm not mysterious."

"Oh really? What do I know about you? You've met Judy and you've seen my crazy crack house of a home. You've even been to my work. What do I know about you?"

"You can come over sometime," Ben offered lamely. He knew how it sounded. He hoped Ilona couldn't hear his ambivalence. It wasn't her exactly; it was the idea of letting anyone in. But Ilona just shook her head. "If it snows tomorrow, let's have a reading marathon. Like, all day, no breaks."

"All right," he said. But the next day, when it seemed the storm had missed them, he was a little relieved. It was really cool to relive the story, to experience it with someone else who was reading it—or hearing it, in this case—for the first time. And even though the marathon sounded fun, it would have meant it was over faster.

On his way to English class, he caught up with Tyler in the hall. "Hey," he said.

"Where've you been?" Tyler asked. "You're never around anymore."

Ben's first reaction was to think, "Me? Look who's talking!" But instead he shrugged. It wasn't a big deal. So why couldn't he just say it? What was he afraid Tyler might say? "I've been hanging out with Ilona. A lot, I guess."

Tyler looked surprised but didn't make any of the snide comments Ben had been anticipating. "So she turned out to be pretty cool, huh?"

"Yeah, I guess she did."

"What do you guys do? I mean, when you're hanging out?"

Ben searched his face for any sign that Tyler was insinuating something. But he seemed truly curious. Ben felt a little guilty for assuming that his friend, who was rarely judgmental, would be so now. And now that Ben was looking at him, really looking at him, he realized he didn't look very good. There was a shine that was missing. His hair looked flat, maybe even unwashed, and there were circles underneath his eyes. As though he could sense Ben's gaze, Tyler pulled a hat out from his back pocket and jammed it on his head. He stood up straighter, puffing his chest out slightly.

"We just hang out," Ben said. "Sometimes we smoke up." And then, because Tyler looked genuinely interested, he added, "I've been reading *Lord of the Rings* to her."

"No shit? And she likes it?"

"Uh, not sure about that. I mean, I think she does. But she doesn't want to admit it."

"That's cool," Tyler said. Suddenly the door opened behind him, and Ben was surprised to see Mr. Higginbotham standing there until he realized that he and Tyler were, in fact, standing in front of the guidance office.

"I'm ready for you, Mr. Nuson," Mr. Higginbotham said before disappearing back into his office.

Ben gave Tyler a questioning look.

"College stuff," Tyler said.

"I thought you were going to BU?"

"I am," Tyler said. "I mean, pretty much I am. I failed some classes last semester, so guidance wanted to meet with me. Whatever, I'll bring my grades up. It's a new semester, right?"

It was weird. He'd never known Tyler to fail a class, much less several at once. "It's kind of a big deal though, senior year. At least that's what everyone says." The words felt strange coming out of his mouth—awkward, like trying to talk with those cardboard pieces they put in your mouth at the dentist. Who was he to lecture anyone in a cautionary way about the future?

"It'll all work out though," Tyler said.

It was a comment he'd heard Tyler make with ease hundreds of times. But Ben thought it was the least self-assured he'd ever sounded. He felt a pang of guilt. How did he not know that Tyler was failing classes? And then, just as quickly, the feeling turned to resentment. How could he know, when Tyler shared nothing about the darkness that was threatening yet another part of his life? He took a deep breath, searching for something to say that would let Tyler know he was there for him, even if he hadn't exactly been around much lately. But then Higginbotham coughed loudly, and before Ben could say anything, Tyler gave a halfhearted smile and ducked into the guidance counselor's office.

Last period classes were cancelled because the snow had finally started to fall. It was floating down in thick quarter-sized flakes that were piling up in a sticky fashion on the sidewalks and streets. The buses left early, and all afternoon activities were called off. Ilona was waiting by his locker when he went to get his backpack and jacket. "One ring to rule them?" she asked by way of a greeting.

"Can't, my mom wants me around to shovel." Ilona looked annoyed, so he brought up the text on his phone and read it to her. "'If you can stay up all night watching television for school, then you can get your butt home to help your father shovel.'"

"Later then?"

"Yeah, maybe. Okay, probably," he conceded. "But first you have to admit something."

"What?"

"You like the book," Ben said smugly.

Ilona rolled her eyes. "Of course I like the book. It's good."

For some reason her words took him back to that day with Tyler, the day he asked him why he had always been picked first when Tyler was captain. Of course it was Tolkien's book, not his, but somehow this approval from Ilona amounted to the same thing.

"Except for the elf songs," Ilona added.

"Nobody likes the elf songs," Ben admitted.

CHAPTER 21

Ben left a note thumbtacked to Ilona's front door. Call me when you get home. I'm waiting until midnight and then calling the police. Inconsiderate asshole.

Now that he looked at the note, he realized the last two words could be read as either an accusation or a signature. When he wrote them, he was flushed with anger and fear. Now it was just fear gnawing at his gut as he walked away from the front porch and got into his car.

When he had gotten to Ilona's house earlier that night, Judy was on a tirade. Apparently she had discovered one of the little "presents" Ilona had bagged up and left in her purse. Ben walked in to hear something made of glass shattering against the floor. He had been on the verge of turning around and heading home when Ilona came charging down the hallway, her boots unlaced, her jacket dragging on the floor. She grabbed him by the hand and pulled him out the door behind her.

At first he walked toward his car, but Ilona gave him a look and said, "I need to walk."

"Okay," Ben said. "Let's walk." He grabbed his hat and gloves from the passenger seat, and they set out into the road where the snowplows had recently passed, leaving a flattened area of snow that squeaked against the bottoms of their boots. At the end of her street, they turned right down Walnut Street, a road that became more rural after a few blocks and eventually dead-ended in front of a foundry. There were railroad tracks that ran across the road just before the foundry, but the snow had long since covered them, leaving only an outline under the white blanket.

By the time they reached the tracks, Ilona's anger had cooled and she was speaking, although in small fragments only. Ben didn't push her. The snow was still falling but in small crystalline fragments that sparkled under the orange street-light over their heads.

"Let's go that way," Ilona suggested, pointing down the tracks to their right.

A gust of wind blew the icy fragments into his face, blinding him momentarily. "Come on, Ilona. Let's go get some hot chocolate or something. We can warm it up with something extra if you want."

She looked up at him. Her blue bangs stuck out from one side of her black woolen cap that looked like something a trash collector might wear. "Where?"

"I don't know. I'm sure Dunkin' Donuts is open or Cumberland Farms or something. Come on."

Ilona's eyes hardened. "Nah," she said. "I'm going for a walk. This dumps out behind Broadway." She paused and looked at him critically. "It must be nice to visit crazy instead of living there."

"What the hell is that supposed to mean? Aren't we all freaks according to you?" As soon as he said it he regretted his tone, which was less-than-sympathetic due more to the snow accumulating in the heels of his shoes than to any real annoyance with her.

She waved him along and said, "Don't you have some luggage to go get monogrammed or something? Go on, get out of here!"

"You're being ridiculous," he called out. "It's a long way to Broadway." Ilona started walking away from him. "I'm going to get my car," he called after her. There was no response. God, she was stubborn. He tried again. "I'll pick you up at Broadway if you really want to walk there." She gave him a thumbs-up without turning around. He stood and watched her as she faded into the dusky swirl of falling snow. Twice he started walking after her, and twice he turned around again. As soon as he made up his mind for good, he started jogging back to his car.

He sat in the car in the parking lot of Broadway Gardens for an hour, staring into the darkness where the tracks were, willing Ilona to come walking out of the blur that was the falling snow and the bare silhouettes of the trees. He drove around the empty lot in slow circles, his eyes watering from peering into the darkness at the edge of the light cast by the streetlights. He even got out and walked the perimeter of the shop and greenhouse, hoping to find a light on and Ilona inside. Finally, he drove back to her house. Feeling like a stalker, he crept around to the living room, where he saw Judy asleep on the couch. Ilona's room was dark. He looked at his watch; there was no way she could have made it here before him. He left his note and drove away to wait, pissed at himself for letting her push him away with the stupid comment about the monogrammed luggage.

When his phone finally buzzed, he picked it up quickly without glancing down to see who it was. "Hello, Ben," a formal voice said. "This is Mr. Nuson. Tyler's father," the voice added after a pause.

"Oh," Ben said, "hi."

"I'm sorry to bother you. But I was wondering if you had seen or heard from Tyler today?"

Tyler was missing? For a second Ben was completely confused. Then his thoughts snapped into place. "Um, just at school. Is something wrong?"

"I hope not. He was supposed to have dinner with us tonight, and he never showed up. I'm sure he just lost track of time, but it's getting late and, well, I'm sure you're aware that we're having some weather . . ." His voice trailed off. Ben looked down at his phone. It was after ten. "I don't suppose you know the name of that girl he's been seeing?"

Ben felt a surge of annoyance. Mr. Nuson never knew anything about Tyler. He was at best a distant houseguest. But he managed to keep this out of his voice and say, "Megan Sewell, but I don't know her number. Sorry," he added.

"No, that's something. Thank you. Well, I don't need to keep you. I'm sure Tyler will turn up momentarily. But if you do hear from him, would you please ask him to call." There was something in his voice that Ben had never heard before. After Mr. Nuson clicked off into silence, he realized what it was: vulnerability.

When he turned onto his street, only a few minutes later, his phone beeped again. It was a text from Tyler.

Sup?

where r u?

Galaxy rm

Soccer field? Ben was sure he'd read it wrong or autocorrect had mangled the message.

can u come?

His heart jumped in his chest. *b there in 5*

The Galaxy Room was what they called the little press box above the bleachers at the soccer field. It was a small unheated space where the game's announcer could sit and give the commentary on the game. They could blast music over the sound system when they were warming up, so they had all been in there at one time or another. They called it the Galaxy Room because someone had painted the ceiling black and affixed it with glow-in-the-dark planets and stars. Ben didn't know how Tyler had gotten hold of the key—the idea of him being there was weirder than weird. But he had asked for Ben to come, not Megan or anybody else.

He left the car on while he ran into his house. He explained briefly to his parents where he was going, mumbling something about Tyler having problems, going missing, and calling him. He paused long enough to acknowledge the look of genuine concern on his parents' faces and to appreciate their trust when they cautioned him only about driving slowly on the snowy roads. There was no mention of curfew or annoyance at tying up the use of the car.

He went to Cumberland Farms for a bag of Cheetos and a couple of grape sodas. He wasn't sure if he was buying them for Tyler or to assure himself that no absence or awkwardness could change the foundation of their friendship. Still, he checked his phone every few minutes for a message from Ilona, and in the back of his mind there was a creeping question: what if they both needed him at the same time?

Ben looked around for the Saab, but there were no other cars in the third lot near the soccer field. The field was quiet and cold, and coming in from the parking lot it was completely pristine: not a single footstep marred the expanse of white snow, which meant Tyler had been in the Galaxy Room for a while. By himself. What the hell was going on?

He opened the door slowly at the top of the stairs. The room inside was dark except for a small light over the sound system. Tyler was sitting in the chair overlooking the field, his head in his hands. Ben closed the door quietly behind him. He shook the bag of Cheetos slightly, and Tyler turned at the sound. His face was tear-streaked, and he made no attempt to hide it. It reminded Ben of the time in sixth grade when Tyler got hurt while they were skiing. It was icy and they were going full-on down a black diamond. Tyler hit a patch of ice and skidded off the trail into a patch of trees. Ben, going more cautiously behind him, was able to stop and follow his trail. Tyler was holding his arm, which was bent at an unnatural angle, and sobbing, "It hurts!" He remembered the way he said it—the pain in his voice as if no one in the world had ever been hurt like this before.

It was the same look Tyler had now as he stared up at Ben. Helpless and lost. Ben glanced around the small room. Tyler's backpack was in the corner, along with some balled-up sandwich crusts and a bag of chips, probably from the cafeteria. "What's going on?" Ben asked softly. But Tyler just held up his hands, palms up, like everything that was bothering him was there—this weight that was invisible, even as it was crushing him. So Ben sat down in the chair next to him. He opened one of the grape sodas and pushed it over toward Tyler. He opened the other soda and the bag of Cheetos and popped a couple in his mouth. He wasn't even hungry, but he didn't know what else to do. He wanted to tell Tyler that he wasn't going anywhere. That he was there for whatever this was and however long it took. But then he thought that Tyler must have known that was true or he wouldn't have called.

After several long minutes of silence, Tyler took a swig of grape soda. They looked out at the field blanketed in white, the soft mounds of the bleachers like a layered wedding cake. "We should have won States," Tyler said. "If we had won States, then I would have stayed up. I wouldn't be down here. I wouldn't be failing school or thinking about ways to off myself all the time." His voice cracked.

Ben felt these last words like a kick in the gut. Was he serious? Would anyone ever joke about such a thing? Even though he couldn't quite contemplate the full meaning of the words—the idea of a bloodied, battered, lifeless Tyler—he could hear the pain and self-loathing in his voice. He felt a fat, helpless tear forming in the corner of his eye.

"I don't understand," Ben said weakly. "Why? I mean, you'll do better next semester. You hardly ever have to study anyway." But he knew even as he said it that he was pulling on the wrong thread—this was not the one that would cause the knotted ball of string that was Tyler to unravel into something that was clear and made sense.

"But I don't care. I just don't care about any of it. I mean, I never used to care much. I just wanted to do okay and go to BU, and I thought everything else would kind of figure itself out after that. But I don't even care about that anymore. I wake up in the morning, and all I can think about is how easy it would be hang myself in the closet. Easier than getting dressed. Easier than taking a shower and getting clean and putting on my fucking happy face so the rest of the world can think I'm okay. Because once I did that, it would all be over."

Ben didn't interrupt. Tyler's pain was visceral, almost

palpable in hot waves coming off him. He wanted to put a hand on his shoulder or on his back, but he felt that Tyler was burning and untouchable. "What is it?" Ben said cautiously. "What is it that you want to have over?"

Tyler looked up at him, his face contorted. "You know," he said. "You were there. I did it to you, too." Tyler was staring at him, and his expression begged for understanding. Ben searched his brain, desperate for the key that would unlock his own memory.

"The basement. The haunted house." Tyler's voice cracked again, his face a mask of shame.

Ben's cheeks flushed with the memory. That was it? That was what was torturing Tyler? He began to smile and then swallowed the smile in case Tyler thought he was being mocked. But Tyler didn't notice.

"But that wasn't anything," Ben said softly. "We were just screwing around."

Tyler looked at him incredulously, almost scornfully. "How can you say that?"

"Because it wasn't a big deal." At least not the way Ben remembered it—just something they used to do that first lonely year of middle school. There was this elaborately constructed haunted house that Scott the Manny had built in the basement, made from two or three generations of broken furniture in the basement. One of them would hide behind a battered sofa or chair and jump out at the other as he walked through. They would wrestle on the mattresses in the basement. Sometimes Tyler would press his hand over Ben's mouth and pretend to make out with him by tonguing the back of his own hand. They would talk about the girls in their class. And there in the dark, side by side, they would jerk off.

Sometimes Scott would start down the stairs; in the middle of the game they would see his Samba soccer flats and his hairy calves waiting to tell them to go play outside or eat the snack he had prepared. And that was pretty much it. If he knew what they were doing, he never said anything directly, but he always seemed a little amused when they emerged from the basement red-faced and sweaty.

Ben hadn't thought about it much at all since they graduated to actual girls. It had probably only been a few months that this had gone on at all, and he figured it was just a thing boys did, like the famed circle jerks that everyone who went away to summer camp talked about. He was going to say this to Tyler, but when he saw the look on Tyler's face he couldn't speak.

"That wasn't completely fucked up to you?" Tyler practically hissed the words at Ben.

"No. I mean, that's what you do. That's what kids do. That's what I always thought."

"That didn't completely mess up your head?" Ben shook his head again. "Because I can't get over it. I mean, I did that to you. What kind of a pervert makes up a game like that? And I made you do it."

"No," Ben said suddenly and firmly, more sure of anything than he'd been all night. "No, you didn't." And just like that, he placed a hand on Tyler's back. It wasn't burning like he'd imagined, just shaking with the force of his ragged breaths, like the thumping rumble of a clothes dryer turning over a pair of sneakers inside. He left his hand there until Tyler's breaths slowed and eased.

"I always thought that somehow you must hate me. And sometimes I even hated you because you acted like you didn't.

I thought you were just messing with me, waiting to get me back some day."

"You really thought that?" This admission was somehow even more shocking. All through high school he had imagined that Tyler felt some degree of pity for him and that this was what caused Tyler to drag their friendship on even after he had rocketed to popularity.

"No," Tyler said, "not most of the time. But sometimes."

"Well, that's not going to happen," Ben said. "Not from me."

Tyler stood up and pressed his head against the glass separating them from the snow and the bleachers. His breath made an opaque ring in front of his mouth. He stared out into the night.

"So that's it?" Ben said. "That's what's been bothering you?"

Tyler turned his head so he was looking at Ben. His cheek pressed against the glass still. He looked tired and weak. He shrugged ever so slightly. "Mostly."

"Well, what else is there?" Ben said and immediately regretted the sound of his voice. It was too demanding. He would scare Tyler off.

He was right. Tyler sighed. "I'm actually really tired. You think you could give me a ride to my car?"

Ben was caught off guard. A door that was closed for so long had opened, and now he felt afraid that if he let it close, Tyler might never allow it to open again. But what choice did he have? "Sure, yeah. I mean, if that's what you want to do."

"I just want to go home," Tyler said. And the exhaustion on his face, the shadows beneath his eyes, and hair that hung flat in his eyes proved it was true.

They pulled the door to the Galaxy Room shut behind them, and Tyler followed Ben down the stairs. Ben noticed his footprints from before, which were almost filled in, making it look like someone in soft slippers had padded through the snow.

In the car, they both shook a bit while the heater blew gusts of cold, stale air on them. "Were your parents pissed about you taking the car out tonight?" Tyler asked. It was clear he was trying to get the conversation onto more normal ground.

"Actually, I was out already." Though it seemed like days or even weeks ago.

"Doing what?" Tyler asked between his chattering teeth.

"I went for a walk with Ilona."

"In the snow?"

"Yeah."

"Hey," Tyler said suddenly.

"Yeah?"

"You think I could hang out with you guys sometime?"

"Sure. Whenever." It seemed possible, suddenly. He felt closer to Tyler now than he had in a long time, and he couldn't help but think of Ilona and her theory of the flawed freakishness of the universe.

"Cool."

Tyler's house was dark when he dropped him off, but the door was unlocked. When he finally got home to his own house, he opened his parents' bedroom door a crack to tell them he was home safely.

"Tyler okay?" his dad asked.

"Yeah," Ben said. He smiled as his father gave a sleepy wave.

Brushing his teeth in the bathroom, his phone buzzed in his pocket. There was a text from an unknown number. Two words.

Sorry Ilona.

CHAPTER 22

"That's messed up," Ilona said. They were sitting side by side, leaning against the lockers and sharing one of the cafeteria's cinnamon buns, a concoction so laden with icing that Ben was pretty sure he could feel his heart speed up from the sugar.

"Yeah," Ben said, "he told me kind of what was bothering him, and then we left. But there's more, I know there's more to it."

"Are you going to tell me what he *did* say?"

Ben looked around. It was weird even talking about Tyler at school. "Not here."

"But you will tell me?"

"Yeah, if you tell me why you blew me off the other night."

"I wasn't blowing you off."

"Oh, really? Because the way I remember it, I said I'd meet you over at Broadway and then you never showed up. So how is that not blowing me off?"

"I didn't think you were really going to go."

"What? You thought I was just going to leave you wandering around in the snow at night?"

"So, yeah, I realized there was an easier route back to my house, and I took it. I wasn't thinking about you, all right? I said

176

I was sorry. Anyway, I'm just not used to people who do what they say they're going to do."

"Up until that last part, I was going to say that was the world's worst apology."

"And now?" She was licking the icing off her fingers.

"Your tiny hint of emotional vulnerability got you some points."

"Hey, Ben," a voice came from above. He looked up to see Kitty Hudson staring down at him. Her stick-straight blonde hair covered her hearing aids. She blew her bangs out of her eyes, which were darting back and forth nervously.

"Hey," he said cautiously.

"Have you seen Miss Simmons?" He shook his head. Didn't she realize how assiduously he avoided all contact with Abby Simmons?

"I need batteries."

Immediately he felt his face go hot. He looked down, willing her to disappear, fall through the floor, have a bomb land on her, anything to make this moment end. Anything so he could go back to feeling like he was normal. "I don't know where she is," he said coldly. Kitty looked really upset. She stood there for another few seconds, gazing up the hall in one direction and then another. Then she walked off without saying anything else.

"Well, that was friendly," Ilona remarked.

"I don't know why she asked me about it. She knows I think Miss Simmons is a tool. I'm never around those people anyway."

"*Those* people?"

"Whatever," Ben said. "You know what I mean."

"I know you have a serious hang-up about something that no one else gives a shit about," Ilona said.

"If you really believed that, you wouldn't have blue hair."

"I stand corrected. No one *who matters* gives a shit about it." Ben said nothing back. After a few seconds of semi-awkward silence, he looked over to find Ilona studying him.

"What?"

"You do know that you're hot, right?" He blushed furiously and stared down the hall at Kitty Hudson, who was scurrying in the direction of the main office. "I'm not sure you're like Ryan Gosling hot, but you've got those killer eyelashes and—" She sighed. "And if I'm going to lay it all on the line, a totally gorgeous mouth. Like, seriously, do you wear lip liner?"

"Shut up," Ben said.

"Why?"

"'Cause you're screwing with me."

Ilona leaned over and stuck her head in his lap so that he couldn't look anywhere but up at the skylight, where a pep rally balloon was wedged between a metal beam and the ceiling. "I would," she said. And then, with drawn out emphasis, "Screw with you." He jerked out from under her head so that she had to sit up quickly to avoid cracking her skull on the floor.

"Shut up," he said, quietly but not meanly.

Ilona rolled her eyes and changed the subject before he could fully flesh out in his mind the possibility of screwing with her. "So when are we going to hang out with Tyler?" she asked.

Figures, he thought. That was the way these conversations usually went. "You want to?"

"Why not?"

"I don't know. I thought you thought he was kind of a jerk."

"Well, I did. But you find something redeeming about him, and you're a halfway decent person."

"Thanks," Ben said wryly.

"Besides, I love a good secret."

"This isn't really a *good* secret," Ben said.

"Well, whatever it is. I'll get it out of him."

"How do you plan to do that?"

"Easy. I'll get him drunk."

"I don't know," Ben said. He and Ilona were friends now—that much was clear—but they always hung out just the two of them, and he wasn't sure what it would mean to mix her in with the other parts of his life—especially right now when Tyler was such a mess.

"Don't be such a try-hard," Ilona said. "I'm not going to interrogate him or anything. We're just going to get together and have some drinks, and if this big secret of his comes up, well then, so be it. If he doesn't want to talk about it, *I'm* not going to bring it up." She held her hand against her chest as though she were being wrongly accused. "Besides, the guy totally reached out to you. He *wants* to tell you what's going on."

Ben shook his head. "Why do I think this is a bad idea?"

"Because you're a pessimist," Ilona said. "Besides, it wasn't my idea, or your idea. It was Tyler's idea."

"I guess so," Ben said. There was another part of his reluctance to include Tyler in his activities with Ilona: a creeping feeling, a dark and shameful fear, that she might prefer Tyler to himself.

CHAPTER 23

It was Friday night, and they were sitting on Ilona's bed, well into Ben's tattered copy of *The Return of the King*. He had a nice leather-bound set that his parents had given him on his thirteenth birthday, which he left at home because he knew Ilona would enjoy making fun of it as much as she did the monogrammed initials on his backpack. He was reading the scene before Minas Tirith goes into battle against the forces of Sauron when Ilona busted out laughing.

"What?"

"Read that last part again."

"It's the deep breath before the plunge," he read—Gandalf's words to Pippin the Hobbit. But Ilona just kept laughing.

"Has it ever occurred to you," she said while gasping for breath, "that this book is the gayest thing ever?"

"Shut up." He rolled his eyes and shut the book.

"Oh, come on," Ilona said. "Don't get all pissy about it. But I mean, seriously. Sam and Frodo are off on this quest together, which is basically a lovefest, and then Golem, like, comes between them so they break up for a while. And where are the lady Hobbits? Or the lady wizards or whatever? There's like one girl for every thirty guys in this book."

"It's not a romance book," Ben said, annoyed that he was even entering the conversation to defend Tolkien. "They're fighting to save Middle-earth. They don't have time to stop and talk about girls."

"Or maybe they don't care about girls. Maybe that's why Sam follows Frodo into, like, the eye of hell. Because he loves him?" She raised her eyebrows suggestively.

"He does love him. But not like that." His voice was rising now, and the more irritated he got, the more entertained Ilona seemed. "Don't corrupt my favorite book of all time with your stupid feminist theories," he said, slamming the book down.

"Homosexuality is not corrupt, Ben," Ilona said condescendingly. "It's a perfectly good way to get off."

"I don't have anything against people being gay," Ben growled. "I just happen to think that this is not a book about gay people."

"Okay," Ilona said, "suit yourself. Are you going to keep reading or not?"

He scowled at her lying on her bed wearing a T-shirt with a picture of a squirrel playing the drums on it. She was sucking on a Ring Pop. "Where did you get that?"

"I don't know. Judy brought them home from the grocery store. These and frozen waffles, iceberg lettuce, and a big family-sized bottle of blue cheese dressing. I told you; she's crazy. Now are you going to read or not?"

"You can be very irritating sometimes," Ben said.

"Yeah, yeah. Read the book, monkey boy."

He opened up the book and flipped through it, trying to find where he'd left off. He was coming to one of his favorite parts before the battle for Minas Tirith. Gandalf tells Pippin not to be afraid because all we have to do is decide what to do with the time that is given to us. At least, it used to be one of his favorite parts. Now it seemed sort of oversimplified. Maybe it was simpler when you were going to war.

Suddenly Ilona sat up. "Wait a minute," she said, pulling the Ring Pop from her mouth with a resounding popping noise. "That's what this is about, isn't it?"

"What?" Ben asked nervously.

"This thing with Tyler. This is a gay thing, isn't it? Oh, wow. Is he in love with you? Did you guys hook up?"

Ben couldn't speak. He couldn't speak because he couldn't possibly deny all the things she was saying at once. But they were all wrong. They were all wrong, weren't they? And Ilona wouldn't stop talking. "Wow, this explains why you are so uptight about everything with him. I get it now. It's not that big a deal, you know? I mean, to me it's not."

She wouldn't give him a chance to explain what had happened. He could feel his face reddening. His cheeks were burning hot and almost tingling. Now Ilona was standing up on her bed. She was jumping up and down. He couldn't even hear what she was saying because of the racket her bed made when she jumped on it. There were wheezing springs and clunks from the iron frame rocking against the wooden floor.

Finally she stopped. She stopped because someone was shouting stop. *He* was shouting stop. She gave one last jump and landed next to him. Her cheeks were flushed and her eyes were bright and her collarbones seemed impossibly pronounced. And he realized as he slammed the book down over his lap that he was completely sprung. A moment ago he was shouting at her, and now there was nothing but silence and the soft sighs of the down comforter settling. He stared at her glowing face and the dusting of freckles on the tops of her cheeks. How could he be seeing her like this just now when she was suggesting that, in fact, it was Tyler he was in love with?

"That's not what happened," he said. And then he told her everything.

"Huh," she said when he finished explaining.

"What?" He was already regretting his honesty and fearing all sorts of horrible repercussions.

"Well," she said slowly. "I just didn't think guys really did that. I mean girls do, like, practice on each other and stuff." Ben stared down at the book in his lap, wondering if he could just pick it up and go back to Middle-earth—just pretend none of this had ever been spoken. "It's not that big a deal," she said.

"Yeah, that's what I said." How could it be such a big deal to Tyler and not to him? Did his lack of horror at the whole thing mean something more? Like being gay? He felt pretty sure that wasn't it. He was a part of this thing that had plagued and threatened to destroy his best friend, and it hadn't bothered *him*. Or was there more he wasn't willing to face?

"But it is to Tyler," Ilona said.

The doorbell rang.

CHAPTER 24

They had planned it this way; they were all going to hang out at Ilona's house. But still, it was different to actually see Tyler standing on the porch looking up at the outside light with its purple and orange Halloween bulbs lingering months after the holiday. Tyler followed Ben who followed Ilona down the hall toward the kitchen. "It's weird in here," Tyler said. Ben thought he caught a whiff of something on Tyler's breath.

"Are you drunk already?"

"Nah. Just warmed up a little at home. So what's the plan?"

Ben panicked. There was no plan. This was what he and Ilona did. They just kind of hung out, got buzzed or high and, well, just hung out. He should have picked up a movie. This whole thing was too forced and way too awkward. He took a deep breath, but before he could speak, Ilona said, "Dance party?"

Tyler got a strange kind of twisted half-smile on his face. "Sure," he said. "Why not?" It didn't surprise Ben that Tyler would go along with this idea. It was more surprising that Ilona would suggest it. When he did catch her eye, she gave him a funny look and a shrug of the shoulders. Then again, he didn't really know what kinds of things Ilona did with her other friends, when she had them.

Ilona searched around in the cabinets under the sink. She came up with a 750-milliliter bottle of Jose Cuervo tequila and a half-gallon jug of Fridays restaurant margarita mix. "I think Judy was trying to hide these from me. She should know better than that." She placed the two bottles on the counter and opened the freezer. She pulled out seven empty ice trays and lined them up on the counter. The trays contained a few chips of ice and bits of brown freezer detritus. "Ew," she said.

Tyler unscrewed the cap to the tequila and took a swig. He chased it with a swallow of the margarita mix, grimaced, and burped loudly. "Margarita in my mouth."

"Not classy," Ilona said, "but very functional."

"Where are we going to have this party?" Tyler looked around the room.

Ilona shrugged. "Did you have something in mind?"

"What's in there?" Tyler asked. There was a tall five-panel wooden door off the kitchen that led to some other part of the house Ben hadn't been in before.

"That was Grandpa Chapin's room," Ilona said. "Judy's father used to live here with us. It was his house, really. So I guess you could say we lived with him. Whatever. He never let any of us into his special room when he was alive. Judy kind of left it the way it was when he died. It's just a bunch of books and stuff."

"Cool," Tyler said. "Let's go in there."

Ilona stared at Tyler. She didn't look bothered by the idea of partying in her Grandpa's old reading room, but there was something else in her eyes. "Cool," she said, without looking away. "We need outfits."

Tyler reached over and took another swing of tequila. He passed the bottle, and Ben knocked back a large sip that burned down the back of his throat.

"Sure," Tyler said. "What do you got?"

"Haakon's got some stuff. Follow me." Ilona took the bottle from Ben and took a big sip without flinching. They followed her up the stairs.

"Who's Haakon?" Tyler whispered.

"Her brother," Ben said, glad to have an answer for something. "He doesn't live here though."

Haakon was really into either fencing or medieval Renaissance fairs, or possibly both. His closet was filled with capes and weird suit jackets made from various shiny fabrics, with long draping sleeves or exaggerated pointy collars. There were a number of unusual-looking animal masks and several wooden weapons—heavy swords and a mace. Ben flipped the light switch on the wall several times, but nothing happened, so they had only the light from the hallway to guide them in their search. Ben grabbed what he thought was a soft brown jacket. It turned out to be dark red velvet with a black satin collar. Tyler pulled out a black cape with silver studs covering the shoulders. He giggled a bit as he threw it over his shoulders. Propping open the closet door was a small stone gargoyle statue with huge ears, fairy wings, and a pointed tongue sagging out of its stone maw.

"I'm taking this guy with us," Tyler said, tucking the stone figure under one arm.

They stepped out into the hall, and there was Ilona. She was wearing silver. Her entire outfit was silver. Was it a pantsuit? Ben wasn't even sure. There was a ruffle of fabric over one shoulder and a section cut out in the middle that showed her stomach. And the legs were short. They came only to the middle of her calves. The more Ben looked at her, the more he thought that wasn't intentional.

"What is that?" Tyler asked.

"Ice-dancing costume."

"You're an ice skater?" Ben asked.

"Ice dancer," she said. "From when I was five until I turned thirteen and quit."

"Wow," Tyler said appreciatively.

"I know," Ilona said. "Come on. Let's go start a fire."

Ben thought she was kidding, but as soon as she pushed open the wooden door into her grandfather's room he realized she wasn't. The room was unheated, with bare wooden floors and threadbare furniture that might have been nice when it was new—about two hundred years ago. There were two small lamps, one by a tall wingback chair and the other on the mantle of a large fieldstone fireplace. His shoulders shook with the cold, so he reached for another pull of tequila.

Ilona handed them a canvas wood carrier and gave them vague directions to a woodshed in the backyard. When they came back loaded down with the driest and least moldy pieces, she had a small fire going with twigs and some crumpled paper. When the blaze began to take, she fed it with pieces of a torn-up cardboard box before adding the first of the logs. Ben squatted down by the hearth and looked around the room.

The upholstery on the chairs and couch was sagging and faded, but the wooden legs were carved with elegant designs and edged with brass studs. The walls were bookshelves floor-to-ceiling, some aching and bending under the weight of the enormous tomes they held. All the spines were dark colors with letters that glinted in the flickering light. There was a long narrow marble-topped table near the windows that was covered with even bigger books: atlases and what looked like art books. The heavy curtains—dark green or blue; it was hard to say which in the dim light—had a Swiss cheese–array of holes in them, from age or maybe actual moths.

Once Ilona had the fire going and giving out a respectable amount of heat, Ben edged away from the hearth and leaned against the legs of one of the wingback chairs. Tyler did the same so that they were in the space but not fully inhabiting it—which seemed respectful to the dead man whose possessions and spirit seemed to linger. Ilona produced three amber-colored tumblers from a tall glass-front cabinet and set them down in front of the bottle of tequila. Ben tried not to think about the fact that a dead guy might have been the last one to drink from them. He knew from Bio that most viruses and bacteria couldn't survive more than a few minutes away from a host, and he hoped the tequila would kill off any other disease-causing interlopers.

They drank the tequila straight, taking periodic swigs from the bottle of margarita mix—the cloying sweetness of which seemed to fade the more liquor they consumed. "Where did you get that?" Ilona asked Tyler, pointing to the stone goblin sitting next to him by the fire.

"Your brother's room," Tyler replied.

Ilona reached back onto a shelf behind her and pulled down another figurine—this one wooden and shaped like a small totem pole. "Here's a friend for him," she said. But the wooden figure didn't want to stand in its place, so Ilona held it in her hand as she drained the last of the tequila from her glass. "Drink up, bitches," she said.

That was when Ben gave up any hope of staying in control on this particular evening. Usually he liked to pace himself and stay just a bit more sober than whomever he was drinking with. But he knew Ilona well enough to know she would never let that happen. So he raised his glass, clinked it with Tyler's, and drank down the rest of what she had poured. Then he placed it on the floor for Ilona to measure out their refills.

Before she handed them their second drink she said, "You can crash here if you want. Judy won't be back until tomorrow."

"My parents think I'm staying at Tyler's," Ben said.

"And mine don't care," Tyler added. "I just told them I'd be out."

"Huh," Ilona said. "My kind of people." Midway through their third or fourth round—Ben was losing track as the walls began to spin when he turned his head—Ilona lifted the wooden figurine to her mouth like a microphone and said, "What is Tyler Nuson planning to do after high school? Inquiring minds want to know."

Tyler scowled. "I thought this was a dance party."

Ilona tossed the wooden figure back onto one of the couches. "Have it your way," she said easily. Ben was oddly pleased at his evasion of the question, and not just because it was one he himself hated it so much. He was glad that Tyler wasn't going to open up so easily. "Check this out," Ilona said. She was standing next to a tall wooden cabinet. She pulled, and it creaked and moved on wheels a bit farther out into the room. Ilona opened the top of the cabinet, and Ben stood up to get a better look. The room tilted a bit. He was looking at a really old record player.

"Does that thing work?" Tyler asked.

Ilona nodded and opened the lower half of the cabinet to reveal rows of records. "At least it used to."

She pulled a record out and shook the large plastic disc out of the cardboard sleeve. The record player crackled to life and made a noise like fabric ripping as the needle swung into place. The song that came on was warm and full of horns. The melody was vaguely familiar, but Ben couldn't place it. "What is this?" he asked Ilona.

"This, you miserable excuse for a human being, is the late, great Otis Redding."

"Was he famous?" Ben asked.

"Legend."

"I don't know if you can dance to it," Tyler said.

"Then you're not drunk enough," Ilona said.

Tyler raised his eyebrows and then his glass. Ben pulled himself to standing and then flopped back down onto one of the couches, sending a plume of dust up around him. He ignored it and stretched out, propping his feet up on the worn wooden arm. The music wasn't exactly danceable, but his feet were moving with the melody. Tyler was sitting on the floor, his feet spread out in front of him like an old puppet splayed out and useless without someone to manipulate him. "Why'd you quit skating?" he asked out of nowhere.

"I'll trade you," Ilona said.

"Trade me what?"

"The answer to your question for the answer to one of mine."

"Okay," Tyler said. Ben would have asked what her question was first. He figured the reason she stopped ice dancing had something to do with Judy. Maybe she was a stage mom or whatever. But he was wrong.

"So I was twelve, right? Well, ten when I started working with a partner, this red-haired kid named Oliver Sammick. I loved that kid. Like, I really loved him. I used to pretend that we were characters from a Disney movie. We used to skate to the music from *Beauty and the Beast*, and I always used to pretend that he was a prince and I was . . ." she stopped. "Anyway, we were doing really well together, placing in competitions and stuff. But then I grew. And all of a sudden I was like four inches taller than him. It was kind of weird. So he dropped me as a partner. But I thought it was just because I was too tall and that when he grew we could skate together again. Then one day after practice, I heard his mom talking to one of the other moms about his new partner—this tiny little twig of a blonde girl named Ashley Eversbee. And wasn't it so great that Oliver had a partner who wasn't quite so unusual and exotic."

"Ouch," Tyler said.

"Yeah, I mean, it was his mom. It wasn't like it was him. But then that was all I could think about. You know, like, maybe the boys would get taller, but I was never going to stop looking like this." She was leaning over the back of the sofa where Ben was lying. "So I quit before anyone else could reject me. Probably a good decision anyway. It's not like ice dancing really matches my personality."

"Maybe," Tyler said. "But who knows? I mean, maybe if you'd have kept up you'd be a completely different person."

Ilona gave him a withering look. "Like tiny and blonde?"

"No," Tyler said, "probably not. But maybe one decision can change everything about the future. Maybe it would have taken you in a completely different direction."

"I don't think so," Ilona said.

"Why not?" Tyler asked.

The whole conversation was making Ben a little uncomfortable. He felt like there was an entire subtext he might be missing. He thought about pointing out that if Frodo and Sam had never trusted Golem, they would not have been able to return the ring to Mordor. But on the other hand, trusting Golem had not served them well through the entire journey, so maybe it was a bad example.

"Because I don't think life is like that," Ilona said. "I don't think there are forks in the road and paths not taken. You make a million decisions every day that add up to who you are. It's not like one decision carries that much weight."

They were both staring at her. Ben was thinking that, really, she had said, much more succinctly and without the use of Middle-earth as a reference point, exactly what he'd been thinking. "What? Why are you looking at me like that?"

"Deep thoughts," Tyler said.

"Oh, shut it," Ilona said, her eyes squinting at Tyler like she was fixating on a target. "Are you a virgin?"

Ben coughed. Now they were both staring at Tyler.

"No," Tyler said.

"Really? How'd that happen?"

"That's another question," Tyler said evenly.

"Damn," Ilona said. "I should have phrased it, 'In what way are you not a virgin?'"

"Too late now," Tyler said.

The record player scratched to a stop, and the silence was deafening. A thousand things were racing through Ben's drunken carousel mind. How was it possible that he was finding out about this critical event in Tyler's life just now? And only because Ilona had asked? He was curious, angry, and hurt—feelings that balled up in his chest and burned like indigestion. The next song came on with a blast of horns and a faster rhythm. "Want to dance?" Ilona asked. She had gone over to the record player to fiddle with it, so it wasn't really clear who she was talking to.

"One more drink," Ben said. He didn't want to think or feel anything right then.

"Sure, why not?" Tyler said nearly at the same time. Of course he would assume she was talking to him. Tyler put his glass down carefully on the floor and stood up, wobbling a little at first.

Ilona could really dance. Tyler just kind of stood there and swayed until she grabbed his hands and began to lead him around the room in back of the couch. Otis Redding was screaming something about try a little tenderness. Ben leaned back into the couch pillows, trying to figure out exactly what he was feeling.

Jealousy. It was undeniably there, but of who? And why? Was this about Ilona? He glanced up as she pulled herself under Tyler's arm and spun out perfectly in time with the song. Tyler moved like somebody's middle-aged uncle pulled onto the floor to dance in a movie wedding scene. He liked that Ilona made Tyler look awkward. It was the virgin thing that was bothering him. I mean, why hadn't Tyler told him? Wasn't that the kind of thing you told your best friend?

He didn't think either of them had ever been serious enough with any girl to make that happen. Was it Megan? For some reason that thought made him want to throw up. Or maybe it was the tequila. He sat up suddenly, trying to swallow the feeling. She didn't love Tyler. He was immediately embarrassed by this thought. It didn't have to be about love. It was just something you did. Something to get over with—at least the first time. All that flowers-and-candles stuff was for Hollywood and girls' imaginations. But somehow, when it was Tyler, he wanted it to mean something. He wanted that for him. He had to check himself given the amount of liquor he'd ingested. Were any of these thoughts enough to make him gay? He didn't think so. He didn't want to be the one with Tyler, but he wanted love for him—in some form, anyway. He looked up, and both Tyler and Ilona were staring at him.

"What?" he said.

"Where the hell did you go?" Ilona asked. Tyler just looked amused.

"I gotta piss," Ben said and stood up too quickly. He stepped forward into one of the end tables, grabbing the lamp before it teetered off and crashed onto the floor.

"Watch out," Ilona said, "we just put that there like four decades ago." Ben turned around to flip her off but then had to step hard to the right to avoid crashing into one of the bookcases. He managed to stagger out to the bathroom without hitting any more furniture.

About ten seconds after he zipped up, there was urgent knocking on the bathroom door. "Jesus," he said, "just a second." He slowly washed his hands, relishing the way the warm water slid over them and thinking about how drunk he was. He looked in the mirror. He was wearing his orange snuggie hat inside because it was still arctic in the reading room, even with the fire. His eyes were dull and glassy, and was that a zit coming in on this forehead? He leaned forward to inspect the red spot when the door flew open and Ilona squeezed past him. "Ever hear of privacy?"

"I really have to go," she said, pulling one arm out of her silver jumpsuit. "And getting out of this thing is like peeling out of a wetsuit." She looked up at him. "Are you staying for the show?"

Ben looked at her collarbones and her bare shoulders. Her cheeks were bright red, and her blue and black hair was spilling into her eyes. He leaned back against the sink to see what she'd do. Ilona stared at him and then yanked one side of the jumpsuit down. Ben felt his eyes go wide. Immediately he stared up at the ceiling, and then without looking down he pivoted slowly around toward the door. Except at the last second, just before she was out of his peripheral vision, he saw just a flash of the dark pink flesh of a nipple. And he was pretty sure Ilona saw him do it.

He walked back to the reading room feeling strangely proud.

"What?" Tyler said.

"Boob." It was all he could say.

He picked the stone gargoyle off the floor and pressed his cheek against the cool rock surface. He followed his feet, which were doing their best to follow the rhythm around the room, dancing with the small granite lawn creature. He was only partially aware of Tyler dancing next to him. Now he was over by the window where Tyler was unhooking a tired-looking length of velvet rope from the curtains. It had gold tassels on the end. Tyler swung it over his head like a lasso and then behind his back like it was a towel. At first Ben thought he was going to bust up laughing and fall onto the sofa. But then he saw Tyler's face. He was so serious. Like he was really trying to make something out of this dance with the rope. Then he had it around his neck like a scarf and through his legs for the old butt-floss move.

Ilona walked in. "And then it got weird," she said, assessing the scene in the living room. Ben didn't care. He didn't put down the gnome. In fact, he clutched it tighter as he whirled around the living room. He stopped in front of the tequila bottle and lifted it up. There was less than two inches of clear liquid sloshing back and forth in the firelight. He slugged it out of the bottle and, leaving his stone partner behind, danced over to Tyler and thrust the bottle in his face. Tyler drank and passed it to Ilona. Then Tyler threw the velvet curtain sash around Ben's shoulders and twisted him up as he danced around him. He turned around and pulled the cord so that Ben twisted and spun. Now the whole room was spinning and it didn't seem like it would ever stop. Ben stared down at his shoes, trying to find a horizon point, some way to center himself, but staring down made him feel even woozier so he focused on the only things he *could* focus on. There was the bottle being passed around and rapidly emptied, the stone figure tucked once again under his arm and magically giving him permission to dance unself-consciously, and the faces: Tyler's and Ilona's, laughing and dancing, glassy-eyed and dizzy, each lost in their own private ecstasy.

"You all need to stop moving," Tyler finally said. He was slumped against the legs of one of the high-backed chairs. Ilona was lying on the couch and Ben was leaning against it. The fire was dwindling down to a few black logs speckled with bright orange jewels. Tyler repeated himself, and Ben knew exactly what he meant because everything around him was spinning.

He was grinning and he didn't know why. He reached up and poked his cheeks. His face felt like a rubber mask. He was smiling at Tyler, at the velvet rope dance, and at the greatness of a friend who would follow along and dance with inanimate objects. Tyler would always be one to play along. When they were in elementary school, they had made up a secret handshake. It was a thirty-second-long series of moves that ended with a cool-guy head toss and a finger point. Their first year of middle school, an eighth grader had seen them doing it on the bus and called them fags.

Ben had wanted to melt down into the seat and die, but not Tyler. Tyler just shrugged his shoulders and flipped the kid off when their bus driver, Mrs. DeGrinney, wasn't looking. Did Tyler remember this stuff? And did he remember it the same way Ben did? Probably not. He stared over at Tyler, who was spinning a small wooden splint around and around with one finger, and felt a sudden surge of empathy—almost enough to start crying. Ben held onto these things, every last tiny humiliation, as proof that he wasn't worthy and all the while thinking that everything just bumped and glided off his best friend with ease. But it was not the truth of things. Even in his drunken haze, he could feel that the cloud in Tyler's life had not been lifted. He wondered what it would take. He also wondered, in his tequila-induced stupor, how you were supposed to love another guy without wondering if you loved each other in some way that society would think was wrong? It seemed heavier and larger than his friendship with Tyler, and yet the question lay at the center of a swirling tornado of confusion and love.

Tyler was staring out into space now. Ilona was rubbing the shiny silver fabric of her pantsuit and humming softly to herself. The song was a slow one. He could feel the energy draining out of them. Ben stood up suddenly. He wasn't ready for the party to be over. With booze-saturated boldness he walked over to where Ilona was lying and grabbed her hand to pull her up to dance. She surprised him with the force of her return grip. Before he could lift her up, she pulled hard and he fell down on top of her, his chin resting on her chest, his eyes neatly in line with a small scar underneath her chin.

"Hi," he said. "Want to dance?"

Tyler looked up from his place on the floor. "Whoa," he said, "should I leave you two alone?"

"No," Ilona said, "apparently Ben would like to dance." She was smirking and Ben thought about how unfair it was that the male of the species had an instant physical and visible reaction to lying between the legs of the female. Especially a female in a shiny silver jumpsuit who, not even an hour ago, had flashed her nipple at you. Ben conjured his "go-to" thought for situations like these, which was the one time he'd come home late and walked in on his parents. Ugh. The effect was instantaneous. He stood and pulled up a smirking Ilona alongside him.

Being close to Ilona was strange—but he didn't dislike it, and he didn't pull away. They danced, leaning against each other until the music stopped and the only sound was the soft thump-thump of the record player spinning without contacting the needle. The fire was just a smoldering heap of ashes, and Tyler was gone from the room.

They found Tyler asleep on the sectional, his face smushed awkwardly against one of the arms. His mouth was open, and his breathing was interrupted by the sharp inhalations of tiny hiccup breaths. Ilona mumbled something about blankets and left Ben standing there watching his friend sleep. When was the last time he'd seen Tyler in such a deep peaceful slumber? He felt a sudden tenderness and protectiveness toward his friend.

And then, it did hit him. He knew the last part after all, and he didn't have to wait for Tyler to tell him. The game, the haunted house, all of it. It was not something Tyler would have come up with on his own. He didn't start the games, even though he'd always played along. Ben felt a horrible rotten roiling in his stomach. He blinked several times, hoping that would clear his thoughts. He needed to be sure before he could ever say anything to Tyler. And yet he was sure—as sure as he'd ever been of anything. The feet on the stairs, the smug looks, and Tyler's burning dislike for the guy who was supposed to be a surrogate parent. Ben stood there over his sleeping friend, feeling his own helplessness to do anything to make it better.

Ilona reappeared with stacks of small plaid navy blue and purple blankets. "A lifetime of Judy's air travel kleptomania comes in handy." Ben shook one out over Tyler's chest and then another to cover his feet. Ilona looked at him funny—he didn't quite know why, but she just shook her head and swayed out of the room when he sat down on the couch next to Tyler. He felt somehow that his vigilance was necessary. And even after he covered himself with a few of the blankets and his breath began to come slower and steadier and his eyelids felt weighted with sand, he kept trying to see Tyler. When he finally did fall asleep, his dreams were full of missed connections and things just a tiny bit out of reach.

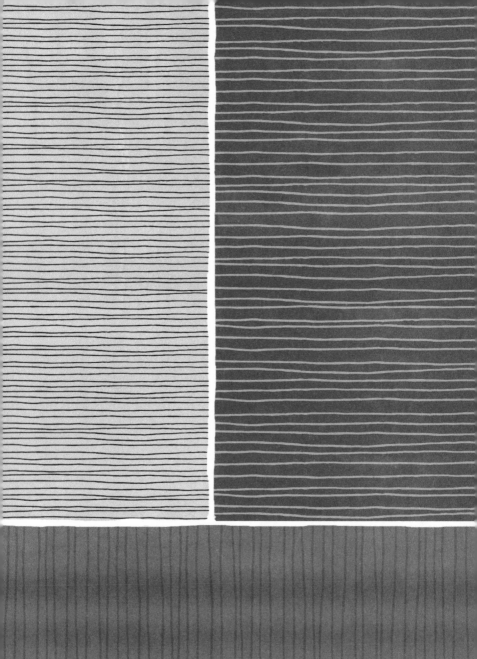

SPRING

CHAPTER 25

For a couple weeks after the drunken dance party, Ben agonized about whether to say what he thought he knew to Tyler. The hardest part was that things were better between them than they had been all school year. Their conversation was easy and light. They went for long conditioning runs around the golf course and through the park near Tyler's house, and they had their club team, which practiced two nights under the lights at the community college.

One afternoon before a run, as they waited in Tyler's car for a rain squall to pass them by, Tyler brought up that debaucherous night at Ilona's house. "I'm glad I hung out with you guys," he said as they watched the fat drops explode on the windshield.

"Yeah?"

"Yeah." Tyler was playing with the seat belt buckle. "I think I was afraid you were going somewhere without me."

Ben turned this over in his mind. "What would you think if I applied to BU too?" he blurted out.

Tyler made a noise in his throat that was somewhere between a cough and a snort. "Don't do that," he said.

"Why not?"

"Because it's a meathead school and you're not a meathead."

Ben sat there, stunned. In all the versions of this conversation he had played out in his head, he had never encountered this one. Tyler's flat-out dismissal of his idea. "Neither are you."

"I don't know what I am," Tyler said quietly. And then his voice brightened a little but it still sounded forced. "Look, it's my free ride. I can live with it. But I mean, what if you got there and you hated it? And I would be wondering all the time if you hated it but weren't saying anything because you didn't want me to feel bad."

Ben wanted to tell him that was ridiculous. That he would do what he wanted regardless of how Tyler felt about it. But he couldn't say it, mostly because he wasn't altogether sure it would be the truth.

The rain stopped and they went ahead and ran three miles. Ben pushed himself to set a faster pace, and with every step he felt he was leaving behind any pain or rejection he felt at the loss of the two of them at BU together. And as he did, he found himself thinking about the other applications he was going to fill out before it was too late.

Everything seemed to be moving faster and busier than it had before. Every morning there were announcements about getting measured for graduation gowns or buying yearbooks. Even Ilona was busy, now that the greenhouse was getting ready for its big season. Most days she left right after school to get to work and worked long hours on the weekends as well. They still hung out, watched TV, got high, and played board games, but more often than not Ilona nodded off on the big leather couch, exhausted from school and work.

One night he came over and found her sitting on the porch flicking clods of dirt out of the soles of her brown leather boots into the yard. "I applied to UMass," he said before even saying hello. Ever since he'd actually applied to the school, he'd been avoiding the topic with her, afraid that she would ridicule him for having no better or more original plan for himself or his future. He had planned on saying it quickly and early so that he wouldn't shy away from the topic the next time they hung out.

"That's good," Ilona said. "Because it would be really awkward if you just stuck around Easton next year for me."

"Yeah, who wants to be that cliché?"

Ilona smirked and nodded her head.

"On the other hand, it's not so far away that I couldn't still stalk you from time to time," he added.

Applying to UMass seemed to give his parents a lot of relief too. They kept saying things like, "It's just a starting point," or "If it doesn't work out you can always transfer." He got the feeling they were afraid they had pressured him into something he didn't want. So when they suggested visiting the school he agreed easily, eager to show them that he actually was an agent in his own life decisions. On the way back home, they stopped at a small, strange school in Western Mass called Hampshire College. On a whim they took the tour and listened to Tony, their green haired, Samoan-American, activist-dance major explain the system of self-designed majors and independent studies.

"Whoa," Ben said when they finally got in the car after passing on a lunch of garden burgers and lentil salad at the student cooperative-run kitchen. "That was different."

His parents agreed and didn't pester him too much about only applying to one school. But that night when he couldn't sleep, he looked up the essay for Hampshire College online. The essay asked him to write about a relationship that had influenced him in becoming who he was. It was easy. He wrote about Tyler.

When he finished, it was nearly dawn, and after rereading it he thought it was kind of sappy and overdone and probably not at all the kind of thing that Hampshire College was looking for in its students. But he saved it nonetheless in a file on his computer he named "rainy day." He still had a few weeks to decide if he would complete the rest of the application.

It rained hard at the end of the following week. It was a Thursday and as gloomy a Thursday as could be imagined for early spring in New England. The flower buds and new leaves sagged on their thin branches as fat cold drops assaulted them from above.

Ben and Tyler were eating Colucci's steak bombs in Tyler's car. They were parked in the student lot—their favorite red booth had been occupied by a couple of cops. "What do you have last period?" Tyler asked as he licked the grease from his fingers, let out a loud burp, and tossed the wax sandwich paper in the backseat of his car.

"Nasty," Ben said and opened the window to let the after-smell from Tyler's greasy onion-and-cheese burp out of the car. "Uh, Pop Culture, I guess, and a study hall. Why?"

"Let's go somewhere."

"Like where?"

"Like the aquarium." He reached across Ben's lap and pulled the handle on the glove box. Inside was a small plastic bag tightly packed with weed.

"Done," Ben said. Getting high and going to the aquarium was one of the things on their senior list they hadn't crossed off yet.

They drove to the top floor of the parking garage at the New England Aquarium and found a corner twenty spaces away from the next car. Tyler rolled a joint and they passed it back and forth, occasionally looking around to make sure they were alone.

Once they were thoroughly baked, they bought a couple of super-salty pretzels from a guy manning a hot dog cart outside the parking garage. Despite wearing a soft felt hat shaped like a ketchup bottle, the guy had the overly-pinched expression of a school principal, and his obvious annoyance at their fumbling for change and knocking over his condiments gave them both the giggles.

"Oh!" Ben exclaimed when he finally chomped down on the warm, chewy dough. His belly let out a loud echoing groan, which made Tyler laugh even harder.

"This pretzel is so good," Tyler said stupidly. "I just want to eat it forever."

"Forever pretzels," Ben mused. "Those would be incredible."

They kept snickering as they waited in line behind a group of Japanese tourists to buy tickets for the aquarium. Tyler turned to Ben and held up his copy of his father's credit card. "This," he said, turning suddenly serious, "is for emergencies only."

"What is our emergency?" Ben asked.

"Finding Nemo," Tyler said, straight-faced except for the tiny upturned corner of his mouth. "Excuse me, ma'am," Tyler asked the African American woman with the purple fade and silver nose stud working in the ticket booth. "We are looking for Nemo."

"Two students?" the woman said. Her tone was hard and her face impassive.

"No," Tyler said. Ben kicked him and pointed to the student rate on the board above their heads. "I mean yes."

"Twenty-eight fifty, please." Tyler slid his credit card under the Plexiglas partition. "And no outside food," the woman added as she pointed to their pretzels and then slid the credit card through the swiper next to her computer screen.

Matching her seriousness, Tyler began to stuff his entire pretzel in his mouth without chewing. Ben started giggling and several of the Japanese tourists turned to watch. Ben stuck his head down near the opening in the Plexiglas and spoke loudly, his mouth on the metal tray where money was exchanged.

"But these are forever pretzels," he said.

Tyler started to choke-laugh as he tried to chew the mountain of dough that was stuffed between his cheeks. "No outside food," the woman repeated. She passed the credit card slip through for Tyler to sign.

"But they last forever," Ben heard himself say. He was laughing so hard a few tears were even pooling in the corner of his eyes.

Tyler signed the slip and held up the New England Aquarium pen with its white striped fish logo. "I'm going to take this with me," he said seriously.

The woman rolled her eyes and motioned them on with her hand. They staggered out of line over to the large outdoor tank where six or seven seals were swimming past the glass, their speckled bodies undulating underwater. They watched, hypnotized, as the seals made laps in the dark water, their white underbellies almost luminescent in contrast. Their trainer, a woman with a sun-wrinkled face and pink Crocs on her feet, threw fish at the seals when they skittered up to the platform where she stood.

"They were out in the ocean," Tyler said. "And now they're here, in like fifteen feet of water and maybe thirty square feet of space. Do you think they know they've been screwed?"

"The food's good," Ben said as two seals pushed and shoved for the trainer's snacks.

"Yeah, but they're prisoners," Tyler said sadly. Ben wondered about the weed. Was it laced with something? Tyler never got morose when he was high. "Do you think we're like that?" he asked.

"No," Ben said, determined to turn the conversation around. "Those guys trapped in the mine in Chile were like that. People in domestic violence situations are like that. Poor people, like, homeless people without options are like that. We're just in high school."

Tyler cocked his head as one of the seals swam over to where they were standing. "Drama?"

"A bit," Ben said.

"What do you think he's thinking?"

"Probably *who's that douche bag who didn't save me any pretzel?*"

Tyler laughed and started waddling back and forth, waving his arms like flippers and barking like a seal. This sent up a wave of chatter from the Japanese group next to them. They went inside the aquarium.

It was dark and warm, and the whole place smelled like seaweed and pet food and faintly but not offensively like shit. Ben and Tyler leaned over the railing, staring down into a large tank below them, and watched as a biologist in scuba gear held up a small penguin with bright yellow head feathers. Meanwhile, other penguins slid sleekly through the water and disembarked onto the fake rock islands scattered throughout the pool. They wore tiny metal bands around their feet. Behind the biologist, another guy in a wetsuit pushed an underwater vacuum through the tank, sucking up penguin shit with a long accordion hose.

"He probably went to college for that," Tyler said.

"What do you think he majored in? Poop scooping?"

"They probably called it fecal extraction practices."

A group of kids on a field trip came charging up to the tank. Ben and Tyler scooted to the side as the kids threw elbows and shoved to get to the front. One of the very last kids to reach the tank was a chubby kid with a dirty face, crew cut, and a Pokémon backpack. He was accompanied by a tired-looking teacher who kept gently redirecting him to keep up with the group. The kid found a spot at the railing right next to Tyler and Ben. Ben watched as the kid slid his backpack to the floor and, after first checking to see if he was out of sight from the adults, pulled a half-eaten peanut butter and fluff sandwich from his bag. The biologist looked up. Ben saw him eyeing the kid with the sandwich.

The kid was oblivious, and Ben felt butterflies in his own stomach as he anticipated the ridicule the kid was about to subject himself to. As the biologist kept talking, the penguin adjusted its position in the man's hand, bent forward slightly, and crapped all over the guy's arm. The elementary school kids burst into hysterics. The backpack kid laughed so hard he started choking and then shot a chunk of sandwich out of his mouth and into the water below.

It *was* gross, but the biologist guy acted like a bomb had been dropped in the tank. He shoved the tiny bird backwards and, with over-exaggerated arm movements, pushed himself through the water and scooped up the sandwich chunk. The other guy pointed his hose at it, and it was sucked up and gone. The hysteria of the group now doubled. The guilty party tried to play it off. He shrugged and took another small bite of his sandwich before shoving it back into the plastic baggie. A tall, thin man with an Aquarium button pinned onto his sweater and glasses on a silver chain took him by the arm to a bench off to one side, while the tired teacher trotted behind. Meanwhile, Biologist Guy flipped his shaggy hair out of his eyes and proceeded to lecture the group about the dangers of "outside food."

Ben wasn't laughing. He could only feel the inner embarrassment of the kid, clearly an outsider, and felt the whole thing crushing his high quite prematurely and unnecessarily. "Let's get out of here," he said to Tyler with one backwards glance at the kid who was sitting on the bench kicking his backpack while his teacher looked at something on his phone. They walked around the long spiral that stretched around the main feature of the aquarium, a multistory cylindrical tank in which fish, sharks, and giant sea turtles swam in slow circles as though caught in some eternal slow-motion laundry cycle. They found a viewing station that was empty and sat in the little window alcove, one side of their faces pressed against the glass tank wall. They stared straight ahead for a while, captivated by the slow moving but ever changing parade of scaly creatures.

"You know that kid isn't you," Tyler said.

Ben didn't have to ask who he meant.

"I know," he said. He watched as a long thin fish with a yellow stripe wiggled past the window. "It's not you either." He saw Tyler's reflection contort slightly in the green tinted glass of the tank wall. The curved glass gave Tyler's face an even sadder look. Ben had a sudden urge to tell him about the essay he had written—even better would have been to pull out a copy and read it. He wrestled irrationally with the idea of bringing it up on his phone somehow but quickly realized that was impossible—but not because of technology. How could he share the way he truly felt about Tyler if he didn't have the guts to tell him what he knew about Scott? What kind of friend did that make him? That knowledge felt like a gap that was forming and slowly but unstoppably widening between them. He felt it even more clearly because of the fuzz in his brain from the pot. The way you could sit next to someone having the same high, the same experience, and yet the high created a separation all its own, a divide. Would saying something let him reach across it or just widen it even more?

An announcement came over the aquarium PA for a sea otter show starting in five minutes. They made their way back down the winding ramp and outside, where bright patches of blue were visible through the patchwork of mottled gray clouds. They took a seat on the metal bleachers and watched as the aquarium trainers put the wriggling brown animals through their tricks and acrobatics. It was nice to have something that took away the need for conversation for a little bit. But by the end, Ben knew he couldn't put off talking to Tyler any longer.

After the show they walked out in back of the aquarium and sat on a bench facing the ocean. It was warm when the sun blazed through one of the open patches in the clouds, but the wind was blowing fiercely, stirring up whitecaps in the harbor and snapping the flags of the small boats tucked in their slips next to the pier. Ben stared in the direction of Georges Island. It was a former military fort, now a tourist destination, and the site of his eleventh birthday party. Not really a party, more of an excursion with his dad and Tyler. He never really liked birthday parties once he figured out that most of his guests were just the kids of his parents' friends. After he put that one together, he usually just asked to do something with his dad and Tyler.

Ben looked down at his hands. He was mostly straight again—just a little bit of fuzziness from the pot left over. "I don't think you came up with that game," he said softly. The wind created a whistling sound in his ears, and it was hard to tune out the flapping of his jacket sleeves as they filled, like sails, with the cold spring air. Tyler was staring out at the water, but Ben knew he had heard him. "And I'm pretty sure I know who did," he added. He turned his head ever so slightly so he could register Tyler's expression. There were tears tracing a single, orderly line down his cheeks.

Ben took a deep breath. He figured this was his one chance. He wanted to say it all. "It was Sco—"

"It doesn't matter," Tyler interrupted sharply. "I was old enough to know better. I should have known better. What the fuck?"

"Wait," Ben said, "you think this was *your fault?*"

"If I didn't listen to him. You know. If I wasn't so impressed by him and his stupid car. If I didn't let myself think it wasn't that big of a deal. I mean, that's what he told me. This just feels good. It's not a big deal. Guys do this all the time, right?" Tyler stopped the torrent of words. He put his head down on his knees and let out a yell, and in it Ben heard all the frustration and all the pain, all the things Tyler never showed anyone. And then Tyler jumped up and ran to the edge of the pier, and for one horrifying moment Ben thought he might throw himself into the frigid water, but he fell to his knees and began heaving against the wooden beam, hacking and coughing and screaming to bring up whatever was inside him that felt like poison.

Ben walked over and put a cautious hand on his back. He left it there when Tyler didn't flinch or push him away. He

213

knelt down and stared at the green water. The posts of the pier were wrapped in long ropes of seaweed. There were a few light brown chunks floating in the water. "Forever pretzels," he said lightly. Tyler's shoulders started to shake again, but Ben could tell they were the gentle shakes of laughter. Tyler leaned backwards and planted his butt on the pier. Ben sat down next to him. It didn't matter that the boards were damp and cold. Tyler wiped at his face with a sleeve. "I'm a mess," he said.

Ben shrugged. "It's not that bad," he said. But wasn't exactly sure what he was referring to.

"What am I going to do?"

"I don't know," Ben said. "Maybe you should talk to someone. I mean, besides me."

"What, like a guidance counselor? Fuck no. I don't need to talk about it. I need to forget about it, and I certainly don't need Higginbotham talking to me about it. Wouldn't that just light him up?" Ben knew that talking about it was the right thing for Tyler to do, and that Tyler needed someone who would know how to deal with this kind of thing. But Tyler was shaking his head and seemed so certain.

"No, I'm straight with you and that's what matters." Tyler looked at him, his eyes dark and serious. "Don't take this the wrong way, but I don't ever want to talk about this shit again. Not with you, and not with anybody. Definitely not with some shrink."

Ben saw the window closing, the stairs falling out from under him like when the Fellowship was trying to outrun the Balrog in the Mines of Moria, its hot fire-whips threatening to ensnare them and pull them down forever.

"No," he said.

Tyler looked up at him, annoyed.

"That's a really terrible idea. This is all coming up for a reason. I don't know what the reason is, but I don't think it's just about me and making things right with me. You were weird all fall and it's better now but I don't think it's gone. I don't think it will ever be gone until you get rid of it the right way. And—" He paused. "And I'm sorry that I don't know what the right way is, but I'm pretty sure just burying it somewhere is a terrible idea. This is some poisonous shit, Ty, and it's going to find its way back to the surface."

Ben was sweating, like seriously sweating. He wanted to pull off his jacket and maybe even his sweatshirt but it just didn't make sense. It wasn't even warm out. He never told anyone what to do or say. Maybe that was it. *I've never told you what to do!* Ben wanted to shout at him. *So listen to me now, dammit.*

Tyler shrugged. "All right," he said. "But I'm done for now."

CHaPTeR 26

They were quiet on the way home from the aquarium; the buzz had worn off and the words spoken between them felt like an extra passenger squeezed uncomfortably between the two front seats. As soon as Tyler dropped him off and he threw down some dinner, Ben hopped on his bike and rode over to Broadway Gardens. The store was closed, but Ben walked in anyway and pushed past the heavy plastic curtain into the greenhouse. He made his way through the first two buildings without seeing anybody as he followed the faint but ever increasing thumps of music coming from the last of the hoop houses.

In the last building he found Ilona. She was spraying some plants with bright neon flowers while nodding her head to an old Rage Against the Machine song. The beat was throbbing forth from the ancient paint-spattered boom box set up on a plastic chair near the door. Ben snuck up behind her and tapped her lightly on the shoulder. Ilona whipped around.

"Fuck you, I won't do what you tell me!" she shouted along to the lyrics.

"Nice," he said. "Are you almost done?"

Ilona nodded and then gestured at him with the hose. He

hopped backwards before she could do anything about it. She smiled wickedly. The greenhouse was one of the only places that Ilona smiled on a regular basis. There was something else about her that looked different that night, but he wasn't sure what it was and Ilona didn't really tolerate staring. When she turned off the hose, coiled it, and placed it under one of the long wooden benches, she looked up and he realized what it was.

"Hey," he shouted over the music. "Your hair's different." It was pushed back off her face somehow. It made her look younger, not innocent but more open somehow.

Ilona looked at him suspiciously. She walked over to the boom box and shut off the music. Then she pulled the thin elastic headband down around her neck and her hair fell back around her face. "So?" she said. "Where've *you* been anyway?"

"I don't know, around. You've been working."

"Not *that* much."

"Your hair. It looks different. I mean, it looks good."

"Yeah, it matches my corporate polo," she said, pulling at her Broadway Gardens work shirt. She gave him another funny look and then just shook her head. "What's going on?"

Ben took a deep breath. "Uh, a lot, really."

Ilona put the radio on the floor and pulled a second beat-up plastic chair from behind one of the wooden tables. They sat down and Ilona stretched out her legs, propping up her boots on Ben's thigh. "You mind?" she asked. She listened as he recounted the day at the aquarium and the conversation with Tyler.

"Whoa," Ilona said when he was finished. "That Scott guy should be arrested. Did you know him?"

Ben winced at the sound of the name. "Yeah, of course I knew him. He lived at Tyler's house for a year at least." What else did he know? He knew Tyler liked him a lot at first and then hated him. He never asked why. He could have asked why. There was a slow drizzle of watery mud leaking off Ilona's boot and down his pant leg, but he didn't push her away. Instead he let his hands fall on her bare calves, just let them rest there like they might on the arms of a comfy chair. Even without moving his hands, which he didn't dare do in case Ilona accused him of being some kind perv, he felt the smooth skin and the tiny prickles of new hair.

Ilona was staring up at a hanging plant with large purple blooms dripping down out of the basket. Suddenly she reached up and grabbed one, shaking a dusting of dirt down on top of Ben's head.

"Thanks," he said.

"Sorry," she said. "Listen, that is really messed up."

"Yeah, I know."

"I mean, it's one thing—the two of you and whatever. But the babysitter? An older guy in a position of power? That's just wrong."

"I know."

"Did you tell him that?"

Ben paused. "Not in so many words."

Ilona shook her head. "What is it with you two? You can't say shit to each other."

"We're working on it," Ben said, because he hoped it was true.

Ilona shrugged. Then she looked down as if she were just noticing his hands on her legs. Her mouth curled up at the corner. "Want to go get drunk?"

"It's Thursday."

"And in four hours it will be Friday. Come on, we'll go to my house. I can throw your bike in the jeep. If you need to swing by your house and fish your balls out of your mother's purse, it's on the way."

"Ha, ha," Ben said. "My mother doesn't believe in purses."

"Of course she doesn't," Ilona said. But he was already following her out of the greenhouse, thinking about what was going on in his first few classes the next day since he was bound to be more than a bit fuzzy, if he was present at all.

He *was* fuzzy for class the next day, but then after school he found himself back at Ilona's, sipping Captain and Coke on the roof of her house. It wasn't technically her roof, just a small area outside her bedroom window where the living room bumped out into the yard. Tyler was there too, and they were all thoroughly buzzed. It was a freak warm day, and the sun was making them drink more and drink quickly. He wondered if being drunk or high two days in a row was enough to qualify you as having a problem.

Hanging out with Tyler *and* Ilona took some of the pressure off—as though with her there it simply wasn't possible to talk about all the things that they should talk about. Tyler was dating someone again—one of Megan's friends, actually, which was kind of weird. He wondered if Megan knew about it and if she cared. He didn't plan to bring up Scott again or anything else related to what Tyler had confided in him, so he was pretty surprised when Tyler, who was sprawled out with his head in Ilona's lap and his legs overlapping Ben's, blurted out, "How do you know if you're gay?"

Ben coughed hard, sending an ice cube spinning out of his mouth into the boughs of a nearby pine tree. "What do you mean?"

"What do you mean, what do I mean? I mean how do you know? Does everyone just know? Or do you think it could just sneak up on you?"

Ilona leaned back, her elbows pressed into the roof shingles. Ben couldn't tell through her mirrored trucker glasses where she was looking. "Do you want to hump dudes?"

"No," Tyler said.

"Do you want them to hump you?" Tyler shook his head. "Well then, mostly likely you're not gay."

But Tyler looked skeptical. "But what if I'm repressing it? I mean, what if it's like this seed buried in me that's just waiting to grow?" Ben remained silent. He couldn't help but feel like it was only Ilona who should say anything on the topic. Like Tyler wanted him there, but not to speak.

Ilona took a long, slow sip of her drink. "I'm not an expert, but I'm pretty sure most people know if they're gay by the time they're in high school. And if they don't know or they're repressing it or whatever, they definitely wouldn't be having this conversation. I mean, repression is repression. There's not repression-lite." She gestured with her drink, which sloshed up and over the rim onto her thighs. Tyler turned his face to one side and licked the soda and booze mixture off her leg. Ilona knocked his head around with her legs. It was a weird juxtaposition to the topic of conversation.

Suddenly Ben felt like a complete asshole. What was he doing here? It was so obvious what was going on, or what was about to go on. He stood up suddenly, but the booze made his head spin. "Where are you going?" Ilona asked.

"I gotta piss," he mumbled. He stepped back through the window and hoisted himself over Ilona's clothes, which were mounded on the floor. He closed himself in her bathroom and sank down onto the closed toilet lid, holding his spinning head in his hands for a minute. When he stood up he realized he really did have to piss, which he did and then splashed his face with cold water. He stared into the mirror trying to figure out if he was really jealous, and if he was, did he have a reason to be? And if he was, what the hell did that mean anyway? And then Ilona pushed the door open.

"You really don't understand the meaning of a closed door, do you?"

"You said you had to piss, not take a dump. I figured you were probably hiding in here being all weird and overthinking things."

"That's not what I'm doing," he mumbled. Ilona just raised her eyebrows like she knew better. "Shut up," he added.

"For the record, I get it now."

"Get what?"

"What you see in Tyler. I mean, I really thought he was a douche bag. I kind of wanted him to be a douche bag. He's so damn pretty." Ben felt the burning feeling in his gut migrate up into his throat. Ilona pushed her shades back up onto her head, which made her hair fan out like a spiky blue tiara. "He's good, isn't he? Sincere. He loves what he loves."

"I gotta get going," Ben said.

Ilona squinted at him. "Why? Because he licked my leg? Don't be such a sour-pants kid." She pushed gently on his chest. "That's not going to happen with me and Tyler. I don't care how pretty he is."

"Why?" Ben asked, embarrassed that he needed to know, embarrassed that he was so obvious about this thing.

"Because he's all this." She gestured in front of her face like she was showing off a mask. "He might not act like a head case in public, but he is one. And I'm not really into head cases. I get enough of that around here with Judy. We're all freaks, I just prefer it when people fly their flag on the outside instead of pretending so hard to be normal." She exhaled sharply through her nose. "Sound like anyone we know?"

"Shut up," Ben said again.

Ilona just rolled her eyes. "Don't puss out and leave. I've got a plan for us, for later."

"All of us?"

"Not like that, you filthy monkey. I told you, I'm not getting involved with the two of you and your weird sex fantasies." She laughed as the fire rose up in Ben's cheeks and he pushed past her out of the bathroom. He thought about leaving, casually yelling "see ya" and walking out of the house. But he didn't. He didn't want to be anywhere else.

CHAPTER 27

"A gay bar?" Tyler sounded skeptical.

"It's not just a gay bar, it's a club. An all-ages club," Ilona stressed.

"Called the Man Ray?" Ben said. "It sounds like a gay club."

"Well, I'm pretty sure they don't check out your sexuality at the door," Ilona said. "Come on, we can go dancing." She looked at Tyler. "You can test your theory."

"You think he should pretend to be gay?" Ben said.

Ilona sighed. "No, not pretend to be gay. Just, you know, saturate himself in a little bit of the homo-world. Maybe throw on a tight V-neck T-shirt."

"Those are gay?" Ben pulled at the collar of his long-sleeve shirt, peeking in at his undershirt. Crew neck.

Ilona shook her head. "They don't make you gay, dummy, they're just enjoyed by the gays. Tyler can chum the waters a bit and see how he responds. Who knows, maybe I'm wrong. Maybe he's a big closeted Mo in the making." They stared at her. "A ho-mo?" She shook her head again. "You two are so straight, sometimes I think I might die of gender role boredom."

Ben didn't say anything, waiting for Tyler to shoot the idea down. But Tyler sat up suddenly. "I'm in," he said. "Seriously."

"I thought you had plans with Lexi?" Ben asked.

"I'll text her."

"To come with us?"

"No!" Tyler said. "But *you're* coming, right?"

Ilona grinned at him. He scowled back, "I guess so."

The line outside the club stretched halfway down the block. Ilona made them leave their jackets in the car. She said there would be nowhere to put them in the club. Ben was cold but he didn't argue. He didn't really want to admit that he had never been to a club before, much less a gay club. He was pretty sure, at least, that Tyler never had either. They had to walk past the long line of people waiting to get in to take their place at the end of the line. Ben tried not to make eye contact with anybody, but he was aware that they were all being checked out, by guys and girls.

Only Ilona seemed at ease. She jumped up and down to stay warm and chatted with the people in front and in back of them as they waited to get in. At least the line was moving, which gave Ben hope and something to do instead of just standing there admiring the graffiti on the club wall. They had spent a little too much time stuck next to the neon pink cock and balls with the words "Man Ray" spurting out the head of the penis.

Finally they were at the front of the line, where they paid ten dollars for the privilege of wearing a pink plastic bracelet stamped with the words "Under 21." Two older guys with skintight jeans bypassed the line, blowing kisses to the bouncer and eyeing their underage bracelets. "Jailbait," one of them whispered as they went past. When they opened the heavy unmarked black door behind the bouncer, a blast of music and flashing lights surged into the street. Ilona hopped up and down excitedly and pulled them along behind her into the club.

The music was a pulsing techno beat. Ben thought he recognized the sounds of last summer's pop hits threaded through behind the beat. Ilona pulled them into what would turn out to be the first of many dance areas. She pushed them back against the wall and yelled for them to wait there. A few minutes later, she was back with three plastic cups of beer. "How?" Tyler shouted at her.

"It's easy," she shouted back. "You just ask someone to get them for you." Ben looked around nervously. "It's not a high school dance," Ilona shouted. "No one cares!" It seemed she was right. He was glad to have it. This was definitely a situation that could use a little bit of the edge taken off. He sipped slowly from his cup, letting the headache—probably from drinking earlier in the afternoon—drift away. The place was packed, and it wasn't like a high school dance where people formed small groups and sort of half-talked, half-danced until that one song came on that made everyone forget that they felt like a complete asshole and start shaking around in whatever ridiculous way seemed cool and acceptable at that moment. Not that he had ever even ventured as far as one of those half-dancing circles. Usually, if he had even made it to a dance—it meant Tyler had dragged him along—he just hung out with some of the other soccer guys on the sidelines, checking out the freshman and sophomore girls and pretending like they were cooler for being on the sidelines.

No one here was pretending not to dance. He had never seen men dance the way the men on this dance floor were dancing. Their whole bodies moved like they were made of some kind of superheated liquid. And they were touching each other, grinding and folding into one another. He watched one guy who was wearing bright yellow pants and a thin white tank top. He was dancing with one guy and then another, and sometimes he was dancing by himself, totally unself-consciously. Ben wished that for once in his life he could be that unself-conscious and not care what people thought when they looked at him. Suddenly the man looked around and made eye contact directly with him. Ben shot his eyes in some other direction, feeling like he was naked. When he slid his eyes back to check, the yellow pants guy was still looking at him, smiling and dancing all the while. He beckoned at Ben with a hooked finger. Ben smiled nervously but shook his head. "Careful," Ilona said. "Unless you want a dance partner, it's better not to make eye contact in here." She laughed at Ben's obvious discomfort. "You want me to pretend I'm your girlfriend?" She pushed him back into the wall—which was covered with sound absorbing black foam—and began nuzzling at his neck. Holy shit, he was hard in a second. This was Ilona! He pushed her away. She was laughing and tossing her head to the pulsing music.

At least when he looked up the yellow pants guy was dancing with someone else. Ilona used her magic to get them another drink, which Ben drank more quickly than the first. Abstinence could wait for the weekend. Tyler set his drink down between his feet and pulled off the long-sleeved T-shirt he was wearing to reveal a tight black V-neck. Ben felt his jaw drop a little. "What?" Tyler said. "I just want to know. And this is the place to find out." Even Ilona looked a little surprised. Within a few minutes, a guy with a Mohawk and a silver tank top gyrated in their direction and asked Tyler to dance. Ben stood there, mouth agape, as Tyler followed the guy out onto the dance floor.

"Do you think we should go with him?"

"Why?" Ilona said. "The guy's gay, he's not a rabid dog. I'm impressed. I didn't think Tyler would do it." Then it was just the two of them. "So," Ilona said, whispering in his ear so he could hear her. "Are you going to dance with me? Or am I going to have to go find some gay boys to hang all over?"

Normally he followed pretty strict rules about dancing—which meant that he didn't. But nothing about this situation was normal. And the thought of standing here by himself with his beer and warding off potential male suitors was way worse than any way he might embarrass himself on the dance floor. Plus, he could still feel warm spots on his neck where Ilona had pressed her lips. "Okay," he said. She grabbed his hand and pulled him behind her to the center of the dance floor. He pounded what remained of his beer and let the crumpled cup fall on the floor. He shrugged, and Ilona laughed and looked like she might have said something. It was so loud in the middle of the dance floor. He couldn't hear anything. He tried to dance, but the not-hearing feeling was sickening and distracting. He started wondering about ways to get out of the club, an illness he could fake or emergency phone calls he could suddenly receive.

"WHAT'S WRONG?" Ilona was staring at him. She looked confused.

He shrugged and tried to fake it a bit more convincingly. Ilona wasn't buying it. He took a deep breath, rubbed his face with his hand, and tried not to touch his ears. "I can't hear anything," he said, almost hoping the music would hide his words.

Ilona smiled at him. It was a strange smile for her, so sincere. She narrowed her eyes a little and shook her head. Then she mouthed at him, "NO ONE CAN HEAR ANYTHING."

And then before he could stop her, before he could push her hands away or even say anything, she reached up, placing her thumbs gently on his cheeks, and unhooked his hearing aids from behind his ears. He could feel his mouth hanging open just a little. The backs of his ears felt like ice and then suddenly they were burning hot and exposed—completely exposed.

It was a dare; he could see that from the playful but kind look in her eyes. She grabbed him by the belt and pulled him by the front of his pants toward her. He didn't try and stop her as she shoved the hearing aids deep down into his pockets and pulled her hands slowly back out. And then she started to dance.

When Ilona was dancing, her hands were over her head and then down at her sides like she was digging for something and the whole time her torso was undulating, slithering like a snake charmer's snake appearing from a wicker basket. He stood there watching her and barely moving. Her eyes were closed or barely open; it was hard to tell. He was letting the blood cool from his face and trying to decide whether or not to pull the hearing aids out and put them back on, the act of which would have to be performed in whatever passed for a bathroom in a place like this. But the longer he stood there, the more he realized he could hear. Not in a miraculous throw-down-your-crutches-and-walk kind of way. But he could hear the music; if anything, it was a little less painful this way, and he could hear the people around him shouting at each other whatever was shouted on a dance floor.

The last time he'd been without his hearing aids was a family party after his batteries had gone dead. He'd spent the entire time in the car faking a stomachache. It was the last time he'd allowed himself to be caught unaware and unprepared without backup batteries. But this was different. Everyone's hearing in this place was leveled. No one stood out. He wondered for a second if this was what Ilona had been trying to explain to him with all her rants about freaks and the falsehoods of supposed normalcy. Maybe there was no normal—maybe normal was a really loud room and everyone, EVERYONE, was trying to hear and understand each other.

Ilona was dancing with her back to him in a skinny white tank top with a black bra showing through. Around the waist of her black jeans, or maybe they were leggings, was a neon yellow belt with silver studs. She began to back up against him, shaking her hips and her head and then reaching back to wrap her arms around him. So he was dancing with her. Actually trying to dance for the first time that night, maybe ever, and he couldn't believe how freaking good it felt. Everything—her body against him, her hands on his neck where usually he never wanted anyone to touch him. Her back rubbed against his chest and her ass was bumping into his hips until he grabbed the sides of her hips and pulled her against him, grinding into her. The crowd pressed them together, and he could almost say it was the crowd making it happen except that he could feel how much he wanted her, how much more he wanted than just this clothed rubbing on the dance floor. He let his hands drift up and under the bottom of her shirt where he could feel the muscles of her abdomen rippling and crunching with the music, and he still wanted more.

As if Ilona could sense he was about to rip her clothes off, she spun around suddenly and grabbed his hand and pulled him through the crowd into a smaller room where the people were packed even more tightly together—something he hadn't thought was even possible. They squeezed through to the far side of the room where there was a small bar. At the end of the bar was another heavy black door with a sign that said "Don't fucking dance here" in red magic marker. Someone had crossed out the word "dance." There was a tiny bit of space to stand there.

"What?" he mouthed at Ilona. She gave him a critical look and then pushed him back against the door. She wrapped her wrists around the back of his neck and then leaned toward him, her lips parted. Right before he could taste her, when he could feel her breath hot against his mouth, she leaned back and looked at him as if to say, "You want this, right?" He answered her with his mouth, slamming it into hers, but she pushed back—her lips and tongue were warm and tasted faintly of beer—mashing into his mouth, her hands pulling at his neck and the back of his hair. And God did he want to be somewhere with her and nakedly squeeze and chew every part of her. For once he didn't try and censor his thoughts or imagine himself on a nice date with her. Did Ilona even go on such things? He doubted it. He just knew that he wanted her and he didn't care where they were or who was watching.

There was a tap on his shoulder. It was the bartender, a beefy dude with slicked-back hair. He was grimacing and pointing to the dance floor. Ben shrugged his shoulders. He couldn't hear him, but maybe the guy wasn't even talking. The beats were so loud he could feel his toes vibrating inside his shoes. Ilona dragged him back into the crush, and they kept on dancing, flinging their arms around each other, waving them in the air, catching occasional glimpses of the equally ecstatic people around them. Ecstasy. That's what the club should be called. He'd never tried it, but Tyler had. His only experience with the word was in *Hamlet*. He remembered his English teacher, Mr.

DePeter, talking about how in Shakespeare's time, the word meant "pure madness." The song changed to an Icona Pop hit from a few summers ago, and the dancing seemed to intensify, if such a thing was possible. Two women with heavy nose rings piercing that piece of flesh between your nostrils were tonguing each other's faces. Not kissing, licking one another.

Ilona caught him staring and laughed. "Come on," she mouthed and pulled him out of the crowd to an open spot on a long leather bench. She pushed him down and went for more drinks.

"How do you keep doing that?" he shouted when she came back.

"I used to come here a lot last summer." She flopped down on the bench next to him and stuck her legs across his lap.

"Is this going to be weird?" he blurted out.

"It's all weird, dude." She gestured around the room. "Weird and crazy and great. Aren't you paying attention?"

There was a scream from somewhere. And then yelling and yipping, which Ben couldn't identify as positive or negative. They pushed back through the crowd, which was also gravitating in that direction to find the source of the noise.

It was coming from the main room where Tyler was dancing shirtless on the bar.

People were clapping and stomping their feet so loudly that they didn't seem to realize they'd lost the beat entirely. The crowd was mostly guys, and Tyler was strutting his stuff on the bar like he'd been doing it his whole life. His hair was slicked back and on the sides with sweat. He caught sight of Ben and Ilona and started waving his hands wildly. The crowd seemed to think this was part of the act and began cheering louder. Ben threw back his head and laughed. This was the old Tyler—the confident goal scorer with his adoring fans. Except in this case it was a group of gay men twirling their shirts over their heads and gyrating to electronic dance music.

Tyler looked over at Ben and Ilona again. He turned around facing away from the crowd, put his hands up in the air, glanced once behind him, and fell backwards into his adoring crowd. They caught him and surfed him back close enough so Ben could hear him gleefully yell, "I DON'T THINK I'M GAY!"

"Not yet, honey," said the skinny guy with a buzz cut who was holding up one of Tyler's shoulders. They paraded him around the room and finally set him down in a corner.

"This was a great idea!" he said when Ilona and Ben found him.

"Where's your shirt?" Ben asked.

Tyler scanned the crowd. "I think that guy has it." He pointed at the Asian guy with a black T-shirt wrapped around his head like a towel.

"YOU'RE AMAZING!" A man grabbed Tyler by the shoulder as he passed by.

Tyler smiled blithely, like a real celebrity might. "Have you guys been dancing?" he asked.

Ben nodded. He noticed Tyler's pupils were tiny. "Did you take something?"

"I don't know," Tyler said. "Maybe. Yeah, it feels like maybe I did take something. Everyone was just so nice to me. It's really nice in here, isn't it?" He started rubbing the sides of his arms and smiling. "I think we should dance more. Do you think we should dance more?" His words were rapid-fire.

Ben shrugged. He was starting to think maybe they should just get out of there before something even crazier happened. But Ilona grabbed their hands and pulled them both back into the fray. Tyler was wild. Not entirely with the beat of the song, but wild and free. So Ben stared up at the millions of tiny dots on the black foam ceiling, and without looking around at anyone he kept that image of Tyler in his head and he tried to dance like Tyler was dancing. He tried to feel that free.

It worked. There was nothing but his limbs, which seemed to be shaking and rotating on their own planes but somehow still moving with the music. The base was pumping so loudly it felt like the hair on his arms was vibrating in time and that his organs were thumping along as well. He didn't need to open his eyes to feel that Ilona and Tyler were near him. He just knew they were and that knowledge, along with the blasting music and the ecstatic feeling that began in the soles of his feet and seemed to exit through the top of his skull, was lifting something off him, something heavy he'd been carrying for a long time. He felt the urge to scream and then he did. A primal yell escaped his mouth, and for just a second he opened his eyes but no one had heard him, either because the music was just that loud or because they were lost in their own private communications with the gods of loud music and psychedelic drugs. So he shut his eyes again and danced.

And then the lights flickered and went out. There was a buzzing, and within seconds the room went purple and everything white shone brightly with black lights. The crowd screamed their approval at the change. All around him, everyone was transformed into glowing Cheshire cat mouths, their eyes dark pupils with the whites like matching glowing crescent moons. "LAST CALL!" Ilona mouthed at them over the din. She pointed to the lights, which apparently were meant to be the indicator. But Ben didn't want anything else to drink. Whatever he was drunk on, high on, whatever he was, was right here on the dance floor. He shook his head and kept dancing, patting his jeans pocket only once to make sure his hearing aids were still there.

When the overhead lights burst back on, the effect was immediate; the energy fled the dance floor like air from a sputtering party balloon that scoots around the room before settling flaccidly on the floor. Everyone began a slow gravitation toward the door in varying states of inebriation. Ben hung back and pulled his hearing aids from his jeans pocket, placing them behind his ears. His head and his body were still buzzing from the noise and energy of the club, so the difference that he could now officially hear again didn't seem that extreme.

It was quiet in the car on the ride home. Ilona hummed to herself, and Tyler flicked manically through group chats on his phone. Ben pressed his cheek to the car window and tried to take in the cold, immense presence of the stars.

CHAPTER 28

Ilona's house was dark when they finally pulled into the rutted driveway a little before two. Ben started to follow Tyler toward the leather sectional, but Ilona caught him by the arm instead. "You don't mind if I borrow him for the evening, do you?"

"Do what you gotta do," Tyler said, walking toward the kitchen. Ilona's hand was warm on Ben's arm, and he followed her up the dark stairs toward her bedroom. She didn't bother with the lights. He tried to ignore the feline hiss and subsequent thump of four feet hitting the ground when they flopped down onto Ilona's bed. There was a momentary nervous twitch in his stomach. What did she expect him to do exactly? With Ilona he was never sure what the limits were.

He worried for about two more seconds and then she started nuzzling his neck again. Was it her lips or her tongue? He wasn't sure, but something was flicking at his earlobe and the sensation was something he could feel everywhere. Then she was scraping his thighs, up and down on either side of his dick, which was threatening to burst the seams of his pants. God, he wanted out of those pants. And then Ilona, as though she could read his mind, twisted the button on the front and helped him wiggle out of his jeans. As he did so, his hand brushed her thigh. It was smooth and taut and she was not wearing pants either.

"Are you wearing boxers?"

"You want me to take them off?" she asked.

"No!" he said. "I mean . . ."

But Ilona was already laughing at him. She rolled onto her back, and he could see the outline of her with the yellow light from the streetlamp coming in between the two massive pine trees outside her window. He pulled her back toward him, and she rolled so she was on top of him, staring down, her lips now level with his chin. "You really are a head case, you know that, right?"

"I thought you didn't like head cases?"

"Mmm," she said and leaned over so she was nuzzling in his ear again and whispered, "You're my kind of head case."

He didn't know how it happened. One minute they were kissing and her hands were rubbing up and down his body. His hands were under her shirt, mapping the contours of her shoulder blades and venturing around to cup her small breasts. He had one hand on her thigh, stroking where he imagined the tattoo was, when her breathing changed in his ear. There was a small sound, like a dolphin clicking, and then another that was identical and he realized suddenly that her hand, hooked on the waistband of his boxer shorts, wasn't moving any longer. And that her mouth planted on his earlobe, was actually just that— planted there. She was snoring.

He would have laughed out loud. He thought for a second of waking her up just to give her some shit about it. But then he just opened his mouth in a silent laugh for the benefit of the shark-shaped water stain on her ceiling.

Ilona wasn't very heavy, and her breath against his neck was soft and sweet. After a few more minutes she started drooling on his neck, which was neither soft nor sweet, and he pushed her gently to one side. She grumbled something and then pulled part of the comforter up over her legs. He was half in and half out of the blanket, and he shifted around, trying to decide if he was really going to sleep there or not. He settled back into the pillow, trying to ignore the apparent lack of a pillowcase. The pillow was an old one, and his head sank deep until he could feel the mattress against the back of his skull, the two sides of the pillow puffing up around him like horse blinders. He was replaying the events of the night—all of it: the dancing, taking off his hearing aids, seeing Tyler paraded around the dance floor like a roast pig at a luau, and the strange salty-sweet feeling of Ilona's mouth against his. He touched his lips, which were still burning a little from vigorous use. All these thoughts and images cycled round and round in his brain until he entered a trancelike state that was something close to sleep.

Suddenly, though he was unsure of how much time had passed, his eyes flicked open, alert in a way they hadn't been before. The sky was still dark and the streetlights still blazed orange through the huge six-paned glass windows. He went downstairs to find Tyler.

He was awake, the large flat screen showing one of the Die Hard movies, and eating from a family-sized bag of Cheetos. Ben stood behind the couch as though he needed to be asked to sit down.

"They had Cheetos here? In the kitchen?"

"Uh-uh," Tyler said, pausing to lick his cheese-dust fingers clean. "I walked to the Sev."

"Can't sleep?"

"Nah, not like usual. I think it's whatever I took. I'm really hopped up." He smiled as one of the bad guys took a two-by-four in the face from Bruce Willis. "He's kicking ass now," he added and pointed with his chin at the open space on the couch.

Ben stepped over the back of the couch and slid down on the soft leather. Tyler passed him the bag of Cheetos without looking over. As soon as he smelled the fake cheese, his stomach let out a huge rumble.

Tyler snickered. "Work up an appetite?"

"Not really."

"Hmm?" Tyler raised his eyebrows in disbelief.

"We didn't really do much,"

"Ilona's cool," Tyler said.

"Yeah, she's good. I mean, she's a good friend. What if we fuck that up?" His mind started to race, jumping ahead to a future without Ilona. He liked who he was when he was with her.

Tyler shrugged. "What if you make it even better?" His eyes never left the TV as he spoke.

Ben considered this as he pulled out a particularly long and skinny Cheeto with a strange protrusion on the top. It reminded him of Judy for some reason, but he didn't say anything to Tyler. He didn't really know if Tyler would get it, and right now he wanted them to be on the same page.

Tyler waved his hand over, beckoning for the bag of Cheetos. On the screen a gunfight was erupting and people were falling backwards and getting shot in that weird late-nineties style where it looked like they just passed out with holes in their chests. "You know her pretty well, though, right?"

It took Ben a second to realize he was talking about Ilona and not Judy. "I guess so, yeah."

"And she knows you." This wasn't a question. Tyler shook the bag around as though the really good Cheetos were going to surface from the mix of crumbs and dust. "No one knows me like that," he said without looking up from the bag. It seemed like maybe Ben should argue with him, but he wasn't sure what to say. "Except you." He popped a handful of cheese crumbs into his mouth and wiped his hand on his jeans. "I don't think anyone else ever will."

There was silence. How should he respond? It was a compliment but also a sad self-deprecating statement. "You don't know that," he said uneasily.

But Tyler just kept munching on the crumbs. To anyone else, he would have looked unconcerned and easy sitting there on the couch. But there was one line across his forehead that Ben had never noticed before and a twinge of distracted worry in his eyes, even as they seemed focused on the movie.

"Hey!" Tyler said suddenly. "Let's order pizza."

"From where? It's four in the morning."

"Shit."

Ben bounced up from his seat and opened Ilona's freezer and there, hidden behind a bag of ice, stacked up on each other like Holy Bibles, was a neat pile of frozen pizzas. "Oh my God," he said softly. His mouth began to water before he could tear open the cardboard box.

"This summer's going to be epic," Tyler called out from the couch.

Ben nodded even though Tyler couldn't see him. He was trying to figure out which buttons on the perfectly clean oven to press to turn it on. It would be an epic summer. Their last summer before college or whatever came in September. Ben gazed over at Tyler as the oven began to click and hum to life.

How many times had they been up like this after a night of partying? How many more times like this would there be? Would he ever be like Julie Snow—done with high school, ready to move on? If he really looked closely, he could see that maybe the tide, slack for so long, had finally turned and begun to ebb.

An hour later, satiated with warm salty cheese, Ben lay down on the couch and let his eyelids grow heavy. When he woke up again it was too bright in the living room. Tyler was sleeping on the other side of the couch, and Bruce Willis had been replaced by a man with impossibly white teeth demonstrating the sucking power of a handheld vacuum.

Ben fumbled with the remote and turned off the TV. He staggered upstairs, feeling a little guilty that he'd left Ilona and hoping she'd still be asleep and wouldn't notice. He managed to tuck himself back into her bed without jostling her, but when he turned onto his side she said, "Where'd you go?"

"Bathroom."

"Liar. You smell like pizza."

"Tyler and I were—"

"I don't care," Ilona said. "I know you and your boyfriend can't be apart for more than like ten minutes anyway. Just be quiet and let me sleep some more." She flung an arm over him and scooched forward until her hips were pressed against him. It felt good. He felt stupid for thinking she'd be mad. Ilona didn't get mad about shit like that.

When he woke up again the sunlight was warm and full. He checked his phone. It was 10:30. He nudged Ilona, who tried to pull the covers up over her head. "What about Judy?" he whispered.

"Not home 'til later," she said. "Doesn't care anyway."

He tried to fall back to sleep, but the light was too bright. He messed around with a new game on his phone. He looked at Ilona a lot. The parts he could see, anyway. Right where the comforter met the bed, there was a strip of her skin visible. Her tank top was riding up and her stomach was moving with the soft exhalations of her breath. He imagined her in really sexy lace underwear. That was kind of interesting, but her head kept getting replaced by a Victoria's Secret model when he thought about it for too long. Figures. Ilona probably wouldn't tolerate wearing some hot lace underwear anyway. Her boxers were dark red with old-fashioned cars on them. He recognized the pattern and thought he might have the same ones at home somewhere.

Finally he poked her in the side. "Wake up," he said. Ilona made a noise that was somewhere between a whine and a moan. It was clearly an objection. "Let's go get pancakes."

She moaned again, but this time she opened her eyes. She reached across him, pressing her chest against his to push the button on his phone. "It's too early," she declared and flopped back on to the pillow.

"It's 11:30. Come on, get up."

She lifted her head again and smacked her lips together. "Ugh, it tastes like one of Judy's cats crapped in my mouth."

"Do you always say exactly what you're thinking?"

"What else would I say? Some boring social bullshit so other people can feel comfortable? No thanks."

Ben shook his head. "There's a toothbrush for that."

"Oh yeah." Ilona was suddenly animated. "Like washing your mouth out with soap—a social bullshit toothbrush. Guaranteed to scrub the nice-nice from your mouth and leave only the brutal truth."

"Maybe you *should* go back to sleep," he said.

Ilona sat up and clobbered him with her pillow. She leaped with surprising agility across the piles of clothes and into the bathroom. Ben heard the sounds of water running and then her spitting. When she came back, her face was damp and there was a tiny smudge of toothpaste in the corner of her mouth. She sat cross-legged on the bed and stared down at him critically.

"What?"

"Can I try them on?"

"Try what on?" But he already knew and pushed his head back farther into the pillow.

"Your hearing things. Are they hearing aids? That sounds like something for old people."

"That's what they are."

"Don't get sour with me. So can I try them on or what?"

"No, that's gross."

"Why? It's not like they were up your nose or anything. What's gross about your ears?"

"Ear wax," Ben said. "And they get sweaty. I don't know. It's just gross."

"Hmm," Ilona said. She squinted, her eyes glimmering with a plan. "So you need a little convincing, okay." She moved across the bed and straddled him with her butt just above his waistline and pinned his hands down at the wrist. His heart started pounding. If she grabbed them he was going to throw her off onto the floor. He wasn't even thinking about doing it. It was just what was going to happen. But she didn't grab for his ears. Instead she brought her face down so that she was just an inch above him. Her toothpaste had cinnamon in it. He had never noticed her eyelashes before, which were short but fully framed her eyes. She was studying him for something.

Then she leaned forward and kissed him. Softly at first, but his mouth opened up to her and his heart, which had already been pounding, seemed as if it might burst out of the confines of his rib cage.

She left his mouth and loosened the grip on his hands as she kissed her way down his chin and down the side of his neck. She took the neck of his T-shirt in between her teeth and tugged on it a little bit before kissing his chest between his collarbones and holy shit she was still going south. Her legs were over his thighs now and she was nuzzling around at his belly button and he thought he was going to die or explode or both when she licked at his left hip bone with a darting tongue and then did the same thing on the right. But then she stopped. He waited for a second and then lifted his head off the pillow. She was staring at him, a self-satisfied smile on her face.

"I'll keep going," she said smugly. "But first I want to try them on."

Wordlessly, he pulled off his hearing aids and gave them to her. She could do whatever she wanted. He watched as she slipped them on. It was so weird he could hardly look. Then she was lying on his chest again, her chin digging into him. "See," she said. "Not that big a deal." She pulled one off and he made a grab for it. But she pulled her hand back. "Not even that waxy."

"That's disgusting."

Ilona shrugged. "A lot of things are more disgusting. They are bigger and heavier than I thought they'd be, though." She moved her jaw up and down so her ears wiggled. "And I thought I'd be all, like, supersonic with these on. But it's just a lot of loud buzzing."

"Because you can hear fine," he said tersely.

"Wow, you're really freaking out about this, huh?" She stared down at him. "It's not that big a deal!" She said it slowly and with emphasis that, from anyone else, would have pissed him off. But he knew it wasn't about his hearing. This was about being seen by someone—just him by himself, not the goalie or Tyler's best friend or even the deaf kid. This was as naked as he ever got with anyone, and he wasn't dying or falling to pieces. It was safe and completely liberating all at the same time.

"So," she said, "you want pancakes?" He shook his head. "Huh, was there something else then?" She grinned. "French toast?" He shook his head again. "Oh, now I remember. It was this, wasn't it?" She licked his stomach right above the waistband of his boxers and the noise that came out of his mouth was somewhere between a sigh and a moan. She was still kissing him as she tugged his boxers down. He fell back into the bed and kept falling with the warm, incredible sensations that started with Ilona's mouth but seemed to flood into every other part of his body.

"Please don't make any jokes about whipped cream," he whispered daringly.

Ilona snorted, and that was all.

CHAPTER 29

"Talk to Ilona?" Tyler checked the ball to Ben and then took a shot that glanced off the edge of the rim. They were playing a halfhearted game of Horse in Tyler's driveway on Sunday afternoon. Ben had lost track if he was a H-O-R or a H-O-R-S

"Nope."

"Text her?"

"She doesn't have a phone."

"Huh." Tyler contemplated this. "Is she working? Did you go by?"

"Nah, it's kind of busy right now. I don't know if they'd really want her to have people show up there, you know?"

Tyler checked the ball again, but Ben wasn't watching and it bounced hard off his chest. "So you're doing this on purpose?"

"Doing what?"

"Being a dick."

"What? No! I mean, no."

Tyler dribbled the ball in place and then looked up and sank his shot, nothing but net. "She goes down on you. You're telling me that you like her, and then you just let it go?"

"Ilona's not like that," he protested.

Tyler shook his head. "Don't be cold. You're not cold."

Ben dribbled, pretending to consider various angles for his shot. They were both right. Ilona wasn't the kind of girl who wanted him to bring her flowers and hold her hand. But Tyler was right too; he wasn't cold. He didn't want to be cold. He wanted to care about Ilona as much as she would let him. He smiled to himself, adding this to the small but growing file of things he was sure of about himself.

He had told Tyler about the blow job while they were at IHOP. When Ilona came back from the bathroom and they were both grinning, she just rolled her eyes and sat down to her blueberry pancakes. "You two are pathetic. Did he say it was good at least?"

Tyler gave her the same smile that had gotten them real maple syrup for free from Tracy, their waitress, and said, "I think he enjoyed himself."

"Jesus," Ben had said, looking around nervously, as though the nearby table of senior citizens, clearly just back from church, knew exactly what they were talking about.

He checked the ball to Tyler, who bounced it back to him. This time he caught it before it smacked him in the face. "What do you care, anyway?"

"Ilona's cool," Tyler said. "You shouldn't fuck it up."

Ben took a shot and missed. "All right."

"All right, what?"

"I'll call her. I'll go over there or something."

Tyler seemed satisfied with this answer. "Good," he said. "Better."

That afternoon Ben drove by Broadway Gardens, but Ilona's jeep wasn't in the parking lot. He knew he should go by her house, but he kept circling the turnoff for her street, getting farther and farther from his destination until, bizarrely, he ended up at the mall. He pulled into a parking space and wandered into Newberry Comics, deciding he'd browse the CDs and used DVDs for a while before deciding on his next move.

He was holding a copy of *Game of Thrones: Season One* in his hand when two people turned down the row where he was standing. The girl had bleach-blonde streaks in her otherwise black hair, and the guy had his hair dyed a bright atomic green. They were arguing about an animation series, manga or something. The girl was wearing black-and-white checked tights underneath skintight jean shorts. She had her pinkie linked to the guy's pinkie. There was something about that gesture of attachment that tugged at Ben.

He walked to the front of the store where they sold the body jewelry and hair dye. Then he plunked down twenty-seven dollars and forty-three cents for a bottle of fire engine red hair dye and the *Game of Thrones* DVD and felt that somehow he was hedging his bet.

Ben pulled right into the driveway behind Ilona's jeep to avoid chickening out and leaving before she knew he was there. He got out of the car holding the bottle of red hair dye and feeling like he was awkwardly late for a date he didn't know was even happening. Before he could knock on the front door, he heard voices from around the side of the house. He walked around the porch and was greeted by an unusual scene. Ilona was wearing a long green dress slit down the middle nearly to her belly button. She was wearing makeup—loads of it, all dark and glittery around her eyes, and she was perched on this tall older guy's knee. The guy was dressed like a lumberjack in a red-and-black checked shirt. There was another guy who looked a whole lot like the first guy, taking pictures with a giant camera. He was wearing a faded black T-shirt and skinny jeans.

Ilona jumped up. "Hey," she said. There was only that one word for him to try and gauge if she was happy or annoyed or angry by his sudden presence. It wasn't enough to go on.

"Hey," he said back. "I thought you'd be working."

She crossed the porch to where he was standing. "So you stopped by hoping I wouldn't be here?"

"No." He was flustered already and hiding the bottle of hair dye behind his leg. "I went by Broadway and I didn't see your car. I don't know."

Ilona looked amused. "These are the Calvins. That's Harris," she said, pointing to the lumberjack, "and this is Elwyn."

"Oh," said Ben, "the, um, mural guys."

"Yeah, I'm helping them shoot some photos for their new album cover." She put her fingers up for air quotes. "It's not that big a deal. They're putting it out themselves."

"Thanks a lot," said the lumberjack.

Ilona flipped him off. "What they're really doing is sleeping on my couch and eating all my food."

"So they're fighting over the last dented can of tuna," Ben said.

The guy with the camera threw a grin his way.

Ilona narrowed her eyes at him. "Ha, ha," she said. "What are you doing here? If the last of the tuna's gone, I mean." She reached behind his back and grabbed the paper bag with the bottle in it. She looked honestly surprised when she peered inside. "You want this?" she asked.

"Maybe," he said.

She looked pleased and pushed back on his chest with her pointer finger so that he had to walk backwards around the corner of the house. "You want to hang out?" she asked when they were out of sight of the Calvins.

"Yeah," he said. He'd known as soon as he saw her that Tyler was right and he was right to be there.

She pushed him up against the side of the house and leaned into him. "You going to invite me over?"

"Sure," he said. His legs felt warm. He was trying not to look at her mouth and think about where it had been.

"For dinner? With your parents?"

He hesitated. "That's what you want to do?"

"Kind of," she said. "I kind of want to be sure I'm not, like, the freak you're going to keep in the closet or under your bed."

"*Under* my bed?" he said grinning. Ilona scowled. "Okay," he said. "I will invite you to dinner."

"Plus, we need to finish that long-ass book of yours."

"It's almost over anyway."

She stepped back, looking surprised. "So after all that, they're just going to waltz up the side of Mount Doom and toss the thing in?"

"Huh," Ben said, "you're actually paying attention. And no, it doesn't happen exactly like that."

"I never said it was a *bad* book," Ilona said. "So are they going to die? Like, sacrifice themselves in the fire or something? Or, wait, I bet Sam's going to die. Like saving Frodo's unappreciative ass somehow."

"Do you want me to tell you?"

Ilona shrugged. "Sure, whatever."

"They both live."

"Really? Like, happily ever after?"

"I don't know. More or less, I guess. Until the next demon tries to take over Middle-earth."

"Well," she said, "that's not all that bad, really."

CHAPTER 30

Ben was on his way over to pick up Ilona when his phone rang.

"Dude, answer your texts for once," Tyler said when Ben picked up.

"I was in the shower."

"Did you run without me, asshole?"

"No, I have that thing tonight," he paused. "With Ilona . . . and my parents."

"Oh, shit, right! Bro, are you nervous?"

"No, what could possibly go wrong with Ilona and my parents in the same room?" Tyler laughed and Ben pulled over so he could finish the conversation before he got to her house.

"Don't sweat it. Hey, guess what I got today?"

"What?"

"A link to my roommate questionnaire for BU."

Ben was quiet. And so it began—these places they would go without each other.

"Hey, you still there?"

"Uh huh."

"Anyway, I started answering all these questions. There's like a million of them about how messy you are, how much you party and study, and what kind of music you like. And then at the end they ask you a bunch of stuff about other people. You know, like what kind of person you get along with. And you know what? The whole time I was thinking of you. I was basically describing you." Tyler laughed, but it was a stiff version of his usual laugh. "Weird, right?"

Ben was grinning. He knew Tyler couldn't see him, but it felt like the kind of grin that would make itself felt on the other side of a phone call. "Not so weird," he said.

"Weird to think about next year though."

"Yeah." Ben watched a robin on the lawn of the house across the street peck furiously at the ground in search of a worm. Nature had its own laws. They talked about it in Physics: the way that everything in the universe is always becoming more disordered and losing energy. But energy could never really be gained or lost. If it was lost somewhere, it had to be gained somewhere else. "I already kind of promised Ilona I'd come back and stalk her on the weekends though. It would be a stretch, but I could probably fit you in too sometimes."

"Oh, thanks," Tyler said sarcastically. "I knew you first, you know."

"I know."

There was another little pause. "Have fun at dinner," Tyler said. "Text me later so I know if Dan and Allison survived Hurricane Ilona."

"I will." Ben put down the phone. He took a deep breath and drove the rest of the way down the block to Ilona's house. She was sitting on the edge of the porch waiting for him.

"Please try not to swear in front of my parents."

Ilona closed the car door behind her and promptly flipped him off. "Are you fucking serious?" She shook her head. "Do you think I've never been around parents before? I mean real parents, not alien mutant freaks like Judy."

"I don't know. I just, you swear a lot. And I would like, I mean, it would be nice if my parents got to know you a little. I just. I don't want them to think bad things about you." He stopped. "This is coming out wrong."

"Yup," Ilona agreed. "Don't worry," she added. "It will be fine. I've been out of captivity before. I know how to behave."

They pulled up to a stoplight and he glanced at her sideways. She was wearing a pair of dark red pants that weren't exactly jeans and a black shirt that actually had a collar. "You look nice," he told her, wishing there were a word besides nice that meant the same thing but didn't sound quite so boring.

"Thanks. I'm not wearing any underwear."

"Jesus Christ!"

"Yeah, well, I was kind of figuring I might get you alone in your room for a while, so . . ."

Sweat began to bead on his forehead. He flexed his hands around the wheel, trying to ignore the images that were shooting through his brain like a flipbook on crack. "That's probably not going to happen," he said.

"No shit, Ben," Ilona said. "I just haven't done laundry in a while, that's all."

"Oh," he said.

"You sound disappointed."

"Well, I kind of liked the first story better."

"Oh, well then. What time is dinner?"

"Um, six thirtyish."

"Ish?"

"Yeah."

"Are there any dead-end streets between here and there?"

Ben put his foot down on the accelerator. Ilona laughed

as he took a the little dirt road that led to a semi-abandoned development project.

"I guess so," she said as he stopped the car in a houseless driveway.

He stared at her for a second, hoping she would lean forward and take charge like she had before. But she didn't, so he leaned in, and she leaned back. He got flustered. "I'm sorry," he said, thinking maybe he'd misunderstood.

"For what?"

His mind raced. He was always sorry for something. "For what I said about you swearing. You don't have to be anyone different from who you are."

"Really? Or are you just saying that because you think you're going to get some?"

Then she sighed. "It's a decent apology really, kind of unnecessary but decent enough. I don't know if it's going to get you another blow job."

"That's okay," Ben said. He swallowed hard. "I want to do that to you."

Ilona cocked her head. "Huh."

He nodded.

"Well, that's a much better apology." She unbuckled her seat belt and squeezed between the bucket seats into the back. He followed her, hoping this wasn't that complicated since he had no idea what he was doing. He figured Ilona would tell him if he totally sucked at it. He grinned. "What's so funny?"

"I don't mind not knowing things around you," he said.

She pulled at the collar of his shirt, his body squeezing between the two front seats until he was lying on top of her and their faces were too close not to kiss. "Freak," she said softly, her mouth warm, her lips brushing his.

acknowledgments

One of the seeds of this book is the experience of finding friendships that make you feel at home in the world. I am lucky to have so many wonderful friends who make me feel supported, encouraged and loved for exactly who I am. So thank you.

Thank you to my agent; the incomparable Lauren MacLeod. In addition to being incredibly thoughtful and responsive, you also gets credit for suggesting that I write a book about male friendship and then patiently waiting for its creation. Thank you to Alix Reid for your nuanced editorial eye and for drawing Ben out of his shell and onto the page. Thank you to Andrew Karre for your vision and to all the talented people at Lerner Books for helping to usher this book into the world.

Special thanks to Courtney Tomazin and Ethan Lowell for fielding a flurry of strange questions about all things related to life with hearing impairment—any mistakes are my own. And to Coralie Eileen who knows firsthand that truth can be at least as outrageous as fiction.

Thank you to my wonderful teaching colleagues and librarian friends; especially Kris White, Louise Capizzo, Maureen Passarelli and Karen Sandlin Silverman. A special shout out to my students, past and present. Thank you for laughing with and at me and for ever being an inspiration.

Thanks to my parents for raising me in a home where friendship was family and especially to my father who embodies E.M. Forster's words, "Only connect."

Finally, thank you to Lance, Eliana, and Avi. You are my dream off the page.

ABOUT THE AUTHOR

Sashi Kaufman is a middle-school science teacher, author, and amateur trash picker. *Wired Man and Other Freaks of Nature* is her second novel. When she's not writing she is most likely out in nature or eating ice cream. She lives in Maine with her husband, two children, and three feral chickens. Visit her online at www.sashikaufman.com.

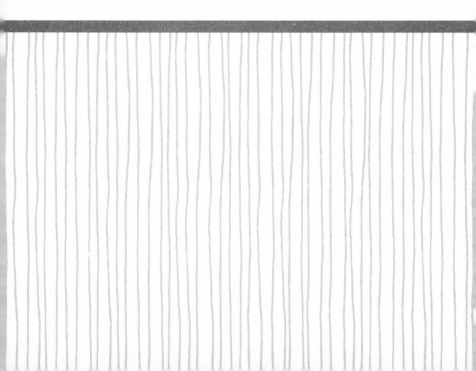